SUMMER DRIFTER

Whisper Ridge, Wyoming - Book 2

RJ SCOTT

Love Lane Books

Dedication

Always for my family.

Summer Drifter - Whisper Ridge Wyoming #2

Cover design by Meredith Russell. Edited by Sue Laybourn.

Published by Love Lane Books Limited

ISBN: 9781785642937

Summer Drifter

RJ SCOTT

Love Lane Books

Chapter One

QUINN

Last Fall

"ALEXANDER."

"Quinn," I corrected my father.

His lips thinned at the deliberate slight. I was named for an entire family tree of Alexanders, each one of them more messed up than the one before. I'd taken to using my middle name as a way of distancing myself from painful memories, and from a family I didn't belong to.

I took a seat on the empty side of the conference table, facing my father, Alexander Dawson Senior, former senator, liar, abuser, and head of Dawson Pharma, plus his lawyer, a conniving asshole called Yan. My mouth was dry, my stomach heaving, my chest tight, but I took a breath and tucked my hair behind my ear. My father's eyes narrowed at the gesture and that simple reaction helped me to center myself. I'd dyed it the brightest purple I could find, my eyes were smoky with liner, and my lips berry-red, this was me—the me my father hated.

Hate might've been a strong word, but it wasn't as though he loathed me in a way that was fixable, where one day we'd magically make up, hold hands, and skip around declaring our rediscovered connection. He detested me for the fact I wasn't his biological son, although he'd never admit it and the fact I was gay.

I'd hated him right back for the longest time, despite years of therapy. But if I was going to survive then I had to shut my heart to my toxic family, and I would be done. We'd buried my brother seven days ago, and as soon as the earth fell on him I was finished with the life that had been carefully planned for me. Maybe it was the way my father stood by the grave and showed no sign of emotion, or it could have been that I'd finally gotten through the fog that surround me, but I'd gone through my life in a daze, manipulated by my parents, expectation laid on me so thick I couldn't breathe.

"You want to tell us what the fuck you want, *Alexander*?" my father asked, lifting a brow in question. He wanted me to be the silent shareholder, supporting his votes, working the fact that the Dawson family still had the majority share in Dawson Pharma.

Well, they did until thirty minutes ago.

"Will your lawyer be joining us?" Yan peered at the door as if he was expecting someone to enter.

"No." I didn't need a lawyer for what I was doing here—hell, the team I'd hired was busy dispersing money right now.

"Is that wise?" the lawyer commented, and then glanced at his boss who rolled his eyes. My father was not a subtle man. "We're not aware of any issues that need addressing."

"Yan, you wouldn't believe the issues I have here, but none of them need a lawyer sitting next to me." My heart pounded as I fronted them. "I think you should leave."

My father snorted a laugh and stared at me. "He's not going anywhere." I knew my father better than most people did. I'd seen him at his worst, and I knew that tone —it was dripping with contempt. My fight-or-flight instincts kicked in, terror lodging in my chest, but I forced myself to breathe through it.

He can't hurt me anymore.

"I've sold every single one of my shares in Dawson Pharma, including the ones I inherited from Max's estate. Twenty-two percent in total. Gone."

A muscle twitched by my father's eye, shock clear as day in his expression, and then his jaw tightened, and he sneered at me.

"The fuck you have," he snapped.

"Antitrust," Yan offered immediately.

"No," I said with calm. "There are no antitrust issues. Williams, Byers, and Green are seeing to that."

Yan paled at the name of the prestigious firm of antitrust lawyers. Even with his own team, plus the million dollar retainer I know my father paid him, he was small fry compared to them. Yan glanced at my father, and his expression was desperate when he faced me again. "We're prepared to pay over the offer you accepted—"

"The fuck we are," my father roared. "Get the hell out of here, Yan."

"As your representation I—"

"I said leave."

Yan looked as if he was going to argue again, but then he left me and my father alone. Alexander Dawson Senior never took his eyes off me as he stood, and I stared right back, aware of how far I was from the exit and that there was security I could call if this went south. He stalked around the table to me, but I held up a hand.

He vibrated with anger, this big bear of a man who was half a foot taller than me and fifty pounds heavier—a ticking time bomb of fury.

"What did you do, boy?"

"Sold every single share."

"You waste of fucking space!" my father snarled, but then his anger gave way to a practised smugness. "You won't have the time to spend any of that money when I take you for every penny you made." Threatening anything with money was his go-to step when his entire world revolved around the almighty dollar. Without the shares that myself and Max held, he wouldn't own the board anymore, and the way he stared at me, I know he was fully aware of that fact. He was trying to regain control, thinking he could work his way around the law and get back the shares. I'd seen him do things like that before, which is why Williams, Byers, and Green were in my corner.

I feigned a calm. "That threat only works when I actually want the money I made, but every single cent is currently being dispersed to charities."

"Why would you do that to your family?"

"Is that the same family that sent me to a camp? Or the

father who hit me so hard I lost consciousness, who broke my arm, tried to kill me when I was eight—"

The time bomb exploded, and he grabbed me by the throat and pushed me up against the wall, my feet leaving the floor. Blackness consumed me, and I saw stars when my head hit the paneling. Now *this* was the father I knew, the horrific demon inside the urbane businessman who could trick everyone else. This was the man one who abused my brother and I with hands and words since I was old enough to understand pain.

"I will fucking destroy you," he roared. He tightened his grip and I saw spots in my vision, but my words were nothing more than a whisper. He released me so fast I hit the floor hard and my hands went to my throat, pressing the pain he'd caused, just to ground myself.

"You don't scare me!" I choked for a breath as tears of pain filled my eyes. "I can… prison… fuck you."

Maybe prison was enough of a trigger word to break through his hatred and he went straight for verbal abuse as a defense.

"Fucking waste of space. Look at you crying," he sneered, as I tried to breathe. "You're as weak as Max was."

"He was a better person than you will *ever* be." I wasn't going to let this monster know my pain at hearing my brother's name spat with such venom.

"Fucking queer," he yelled in my face, but there was fear in him; I could almost smell it.

I stood my ground. Name-calling was the last resort, and I'd heard way worse in my years under his roof. I wasn't going to lie down and take his shit anymore because it was poison and I'd been slowly dying.

"I have enough on you to put you inside for a very long time. Names, dates, pictures of what you did to me, evidence of the shit you've pulled. You come near me, and I will release every single fucked up secret behind Dawson Pharma doors." I straightened my back.

"You little shit, you can't—"

"We're done." I backed out of the door and stalked past my dad's bewildered PA, then headed to the rear exit and stepped out into the cool Boston fall. Even though my emotions crashed and burned the tears still didn't fall.

I caught a flash in my peripheral vision, and winced, thinking the paparazzi had realised I would leave through the back entrance, but it was just the sun glinting off the huge monstrosity that was the head office of Dawson Pharma. My fear of getting photographed, or hurt, was real, and I took random sidewalks to reach my car in the underground parking lot three blocks from the office, before locking myself inside. Too many times the media had tracked me for something that my father had done, and I was finished with it all.

I couldn't do it anymore.

And the tears fell.

From icy control I couldn't stop crying, gripping the wheel for support and letting years of pain and grief well up and roll down my face in burning tears. I wanted Max back with every beat of my desperately miserable heart, and I'd held hope for so long, thinking Max would come home, but he hadn't. My brother was dead and the hope was gone. *Everything was gone.*

A loud thump hit the window, and a man peered in. He wouldn't be able to see me through the tinted glass but I hated that he was even near me.

"Fuck you," I shouted. I didn't recognize him, and fear knifed through me. I didn't know all the media vultures by sight, and I was alone in a dimly lit parking area and this could be anyone out to hurt me, because of my name or money.

"I'm here to help you," the man called, then knocked again. "My name is Connor."

"Leave me the fuck alone!" I started the engine and checked the mirrors to reverse, hoping to hell he moved out of the way so I didn't run him over.

He slammed a photo on my windshield, then moved it just as quick. "This is about Max."

I reacted blindly to the photo and my brother's name, and with 911 ready on speed dial, I lowered the window a crack. I don't care what this asshole wanted to say about me, but if he planned on dragging my brother's name through the mud then I was ready for a fight. Hell, if this stranger wanted an interview then I'd give them one before running them the fuck over.

Connor peered through the crack. Was he armed? He didn't seem to have a gun pointing at me, or a camera. At this point I didn't know which was worse. "Alexander, please, I have something I need to show you."

"Then show me."

I heard Connor muttering, saw him frown, before he slid the photo through the small gap. It slithered to the floor, and I leaned over to pick it up, seeing writing on the back but ignoring it to check the photo. Part of me expected a blackmail image, but instead it was a simple photo of my big brother, Max. He was maybe six or seven here, standing next to a horse, but I didn't recognize the shot, and turned it over to see information.

Laurence Lennox, Lennox Ranch, Wyoming. It was dated only two years ago, which didn't make sense.

"What do you want?" I asked, confusion making me frown.

"Can we please just talk?" Connor asked from outside. He had his forehead against the window and he looked destroyed. "My cousin Natalie was at the commune where your brother died. Please, let me in." He didn't seem to be threatening me, in fact I thought he seemed close to tears, and I did the singularly most stupid thing I'd ever done. If he killed me then whatever, it wasn't as if I cared about anything today. I released the locks, and the dark-haired man slipped inside then shut the door. I locked us in again because I could handle one man, but if he had accomplices...

"Connor Mason, PI," he introduced himself, and we shook hands. "I don't know where to start," he murmured.

I tucked my hair behind my ear, my hands shaky with adrenaline. "How about you give me an executive overview?"

"Your dad hired me to find Max."

Shock gripped me? This was another one of my dad's lackeys. I unlocked the car and shoved at him. "Get the fuck out."

"No—"

I connected to 911, but he reached over and pressed end call. For a second we tussled, and then he slumped back in the seat. "Actually, you know what? Call the cops because I've got nothing to hide. But you have."

"What?" This wasn't making sense, but I hesitated to pull in the cops when he said I had something to hide. What did he mean?

"There are things I never told your dad. I don't work for him anymore. I want you to trust me… you *have* to trust me."

"I don't *have* to trust anyone. What do you want to say?"

He was relieved, but there was some hesitation in him, as if he was going to tell me the absolute worst of news and he didn't want to. After a pause he exhaled noisily.

"I never told your dad what I found, even though he'd been the one to hire me. I had a bad feeling about him. He said he didn't want Max to come home, that I had to track Max down and tell him so." Why didn't that surprise me? Our father didn't want Max or me. "I was told in no uncertain terms that he wanted me to make sure Max stayed away. That there was a bonus if no one saw him again." There was so much innuendo in that simple sentence. "So, what I'm telling you now… I'm trusting you with this because I've been watching you. I saw you at the funeral."

"You were at the funeral?" I hadn't seen him, but grief had blinded me to everything that day. He ignored me.

"I know what you've done today with your holdings in Dawson Pharma. You sold everything today, didn't you? Removed yourself from the family."

"How do you even know that?"

Connor shrugged. "I have sources. But I'm trusting

you by even showing you the photo. See, that photo isn't of Max, it's of a boy called Laurence Lennox."

"The name on the back."

"I think he's your brother's son."

I blinked at Connor, struck dumb. "Huh?" was the only coherent response I could muster as anguish fought with a flicker of hope in my chest.

"I have reason to believe Max had a son when he was at the Brothers of Chiron compound, and I think Laurence is that son."

"Max had a son?" I repeated, and my chest tightened so much that my vision blurred.

"Yes." Connor nodded.

"I'm an uncle?" Wonder pushed aside distrust and anger. I'd lost hope so long ago when Max had vanished; ten years he'd been gone, and then they'd found his remains, and told us he'd been dead for much of that time. For so long I'd imagined him out there living his life, and all that time he'd been dead. A sob caught in my throat, but the emotion forced to the surface was optimism, and then the tears fell again, and Connor gripped my hand.

I could be an uncle.

Chapter Two

LEVI

Spring

"I'M SORRY TO SEE YOU GO." JAMES KINGSTON PUSHED HIS hands against his desk, then sat back in his chair and sighed dramatically the way he did when things weren't going his way. He had one of the biggest horse-training facilities in Nebraska, unlimited funds, and a reputation that I'd helped to add to over the past year. "You're almost like part of the family."

Nope.

My family was my horse, Blake's Billy, Blake for short, and my dog, Sky. I wasn't part of anyone else's family.

"I'm not good at sitting in one place, sir." I kept to my standard answer, which implied I was a man with itchy feet who wandered from state to state, season to season, planting my trailer, my dog, and my horse, on new land where the wind took me. James didn't have to know I wasn't being entirely truthful, and that I was plain bored with everything being so damn easy here. I'd run out of challenges and I needed more.

He huffed again. "I can't make you stay, but you're fully aware that the bonus payout if you stayed another year could be substantial."

I gave James a wry smile, shook my head, then watched the last hope slip from his old eyes. I mostly liked my time on the Kingston Ranch—it had investment that made other ranches look like amateurs, and anything I needed to do my job was available. The guys were cool, there was a vibe that kept me even-headed, and once or twice when I'd first arrived, I'd considered maybe the JK was a ranch where I *might* stay. The thoughts didn't last long, chased away by monotony, and the shiny lure of whatever place was going to be my next destination. I wasn't running from anything— I just didn't need roots. I craved new spaces and challenges of my own without the chokehold of expectations. JK had gotten the best they could from me, and there was nothing more for me to give.

"Thanks for your faith in me, sir, but I have plans."

He sighed with the greatest of drama, then appeared to relax when it occurred to him that he couldn't change my mind. "Where are you heading next?"

Home was my trailer, heart was the horses I worked with, and I had a list as long as my arm of places I could move on to, but I had no specific idea. It was the most amazing problem to have. I could go anywhere, do anything, be whoever I wanted to be, all on my own dime, with no worries, and I could face a whole raft of new challenges, and win.

"North," I murmured without a specific town or ranch in mind.

He muttered, then pushed an envelope toward me. "Receipt of the final payment into your account." I took the envelope then stood with him and shook his hand. "We'll always have you back," he said with hope, and I smiled.

"Nice to know," I lied, then headed to my trailer, where Blake was all ready to go into his stall, Sky in the passenger seat panting—her odd-colored doggy gaze was right on me. "Ready to leave?" As if they both knew we were leaving for good, Sky barked, and Blake stomped in the back. Sky had never quite settled at the JK, not being allowed the freedom to roam other ranches had given her, and Blake had been aloof among the other horses stabled there, as if he were vastly superior, which of course, he was.

Blake was a special kind of horse, and Sky wasn't made for being locked up or tethered to a post. The three of us needed our freedom, and in a few short minutes the JK was in my rearview mirror as I headed to the gates along the ranch road. A truck was coming onto the property, and as it drew nearer to the drive, crossed into the middle of the road, and blocked my way. I braked, pulled the rig to a stop, and turned off the engine. The fuck? A cowboy jumped out of the cab, and wait… was that Micah *freaking* Lennox? He should've been in the ass end of Wyoming, so what was he doing here?

"Mikey?"

"Micah, asshole," he corrected me, "fuck, it's good to see you, Levi—"

"You're blocking the damn road!" I hooked my thumbs into my belt loops and fixed an angry glare at my old rival.

In clean jeans, polished boots, and a white shirt, Micah was every inch the tidy horseman, and not the isolated cowboy I'd once hooked up with. He'd even tamed his hair, and the beard I'd grown used to was gone. Last time I'd seen Micah Lennox I'd been on my knees for him in a decrepit hay barn that stank of horse shit and damp, hearing him call me by another man's name. Fucker.

He'd vanished from the training circuit a few years back, rumors had him going home to his ranch in Wyoming, which had started gossip and nonsense about why he'd stayed away from his birthright in the first place. Not that I was interested, because even if I'd owned a cell phone, Micah wasn't top of my list of people I wanted to reconnect with. He might've been good with horses, maybe even as good as me, but he'd always been closed-off and miserable as fuck, and I didn't handle wretched, angsty cowboys very well. When we'd first met, which must've been four years ago now, I'd tried for a whole day to get him talking, but in the end, it had been me gabbing about nothing, and him staring at me with a stony expression.

"Good to see you, Levi," he repeated and leaned on the hood of his truck, resting his heel on the grill before tipping his aged hat back to stare at me.

I returned the look, wondering which one of us was going to back down first. I couldn't help checking for the misery and darkness Micah had carried around like a protective cloak, but all I saw was brightness in his eyes. He was less… shadow. Almost as if he was present in this life and not just a bystander.

Never let it be said I wasn't dramatic.

So less shadowy was the only way I could describe him as I waited for him to say something. But, if there was one thing I hated, it was empty silences, and I kicked myself even as I pushed for more.

"So exactly why are you blocking me leaving?" Suspicion hit me. "Are you coming to work here?"

"No, I'm not here for that," he said and frowned.

"So, what the hell *are* you doing here?" I gestured at his truck blocking the road.

"Heard you were here working for James Kingston and I needed to talk to you. Called him, and he said you were leaving. Thought I'd catch you on the ranch."

I quickly worked out the general distance between Wyoming and here, then shrugged. "You know they have phones here, right?"

"I wanted to talk to you face-to-face."

I was immediately suspicious. Face-to-face implied that whatever Micah wanted to say was something important, but other than working with each other a few years back for the total of four angsty months, there was no connection between us.

"The fuck, Mikey?"

"You know if I called then it would've been easy for you to ignore me."

"I can just as easily ignore you standing here. Move

your damn truck." I turned to leave because it was easier just to go than look at Micah's idiot face.

"No, wait, Levi—I tracked you down because I've got a proposition for you."

"I don't give free blowjobs anymore, cowboy," I drawled as I turned back to him, and caught him rolling his eyes.

Sky whined, knowing she couldn't get out until I gave her permission. I whistled low, and the gray and white collie jumped through the open window and was at my side in an instant, vibrating with excitement. Sky loved messing with Micah, curling her lip and baring her teeth at him whenever he got near me. She *really* didn't like sharing me with anyone.

"Your blowjobs weren't good enough for me to hire you for that," Micah deadpanned.

"Wait," I clutched my chest in fake horror, "did the great Micah Lennox crack a joke?"

"Whatever, Levi. I'm here to book you for a contract, working for me at my ranch."

I rested my ass on the hood of my Ford, mimicking his stance with my boot on the grill, leaning back on my elbows and covering my shock as best I could.

"You've got to be shitting me."

Micah shrugged, and then stared down at my dog with suspicion. He'd decided to go the carefree conversation route to counter my shock, because then he started talking nonsense. "Sky's looking uh… good," Micah needed to search for the word, and I snorted a laugh.

"Yep," I countered, and waited.

"I told you I've been looking for you."

"Yep, you said."

This was going to be one of those conversations I hated having, full of unsaid words, and pauses loaded with meaning.

His smile slipped, "Look, Levi, I'm sorry for… all the shit."

"Uh huh?" I wasn't ready to let him mutter those words and think that all the tension between us was done.

"It was just a name," he mumbled again.

"Just a name'? You called me Daniel on two separate occasions, the last time when I was on my knees with your cock in my mouth."

"You and me? We weren't serious." He winced as soon as he spoke. "Would it help if I said sorry for being an asshole?"

"I need an apology from you like I need a horse standing on my head."

He sighed again, and by this time Sky had edged closer to him, letting out a soft growl that had him checking his feet.

"What if I told you I'm marrying Daniel in two weeks?"

Now *that* was a shock. Micah was like me—as isolated as a mountain lion. I didn't let on that he'd said the very last thing I expected him to, and I eyed him with suspicion. "Congratulations," I offered because it was the polite thing to do. Sky stood and turned a couple of times before settling again with her muzzle on Micah's boot. "So, if I'm reading this right, you tracked me down to tell me you were up and marrying? It was just a few blow-jobs, Micah, so if this is some twelve-step program to make things right, you really don't owe me shit."

"I'm not here about… that." He full-on blushed, and that was a new side to a man who'd gone through an entire summer of low-key getting off with me. "I have this new client, he's bringing a couple of four-year-olds to the L, and I want… need… look, can we get a beer and talk?"

"Fuck no. Spit it out, *Mikey*." I tipped my head to the early sun, loving when spring chased the winter out with green and yellow, and the warmth on my face was real.

"I'm offering you a summer contract."

"I'm sorry?"

"To work with the horses at the Lennox Ranch, I mean."

"Well, I guessed it wasn't for daily blowjobs." I snorted a laugh at the obvious joke, but the laughter subsided when I noticed his stare hadn't wavered and that he was dead serious. "For real?"

"I mean it, Levi."

"What? You want me to work with you after you spent an entire summer telling me I was only the second-best horse trainer in the continental US, and I didn't know my rope from my hat?"

"Jesus, Levi, you gotta know I was messing with you." We both knew he hadn't been messing at all. "I want the best, and that's you, and you know it for the truth. I'm already up to my neck in commitments, and if you came back up to Wyoming then together we could have a real chance to make a difference. Low salary to start, but shares in profit for the season, land to pitch your trailer, a proper contract, no more no less because I know you hate that shit. Space for Blake, a temporary home for you and Sky."

At the sound of her name, Sky stood, then glanced back at me before squatting and pissing awkwardly up the front left tire of Micah's truck. I wanted to laugh, but instead I enjoyed the horror on Micah's face.

"I have offers," I said. Three in Montana that I could list off the top of my head, and as many way down in Texas. "And none of them include seeing any part of you again." I deliberately stared right at his crotch, because sure as eggs were eggs, I could get Micah to react. Only he didn't go redder, or get furious, or push me to my knees. Instead, he winced, and then stepped toward me, shoulders back.

"Listen, Levi, I had my reasons for being an asshole, I don't expect you to think I'm different now." He took his hat off and raked a hand through his hair until it stuck up. "I reconnected with Daniel, and even though the reasons will never leave me, I'm working my way through everything that happened. If I promise to stay out of your way, does that make you feel any better inclined to working at the L?"

I stared at him for the longest time, searching for the lie in his eyes, but there was nothing I could see, and I sighed. It wouldn't hurt to hear him out.

"What have you got?"

"I'm already working at capacity, and I'm scratching around and building this business from the ground up, and now two new horses out of the Ebben-Loner stables that I hadn't planned for, with acres to manage, and I want the best cowboy in the continental US to help me with the training side. I'll pay well," he added, and then winced again. "Eventually, when it all works out end-of-season." He reached over and handed me a card.

I glanced at it to see the sapphire-blue wording of Lennox Ranch, and the names under it, *Micah and Rachel Lennox*. "Rachel?" I commented as I pocketed it.

"My sister."

Micah has a sister? I was stuck on the fact that the horses were coming to Micah's ranch from the Ebben-Loner stables, which had turned out some fine horses.

"What line?" I asked.

"Glimmer, Poco Bueno, Sunny, Blossom Berry. Good horses."

"I guess." I tried to hide my excitement. The lines were exceptional, and the chance to get my hands on two high-caliber horses would be worth working with Micah.

"So, we probably also need to talk about us." Micah's tone was eighty percent defiant and twenty stressed.

"What about us?"

"I told Daniel, my fiancé, you know, about everything we did. I don't have secrets from him."

"Okay, describe him so that if he tracks me down with a shotgun, I know not to kill him first."

"Ha freaking ha, wise guy. I'm not looking to hook up with you again." He looked uncomfortable. "You have to know that Daniel and I both have our pasts and we're together despite our mistakes."

That short sentence was weighed down with emotion.

"You're calling me a 'mistake.' Ouch." I clutched my chest in pretend shock, then smirked because I couldn't help teasing Micah as I'd done when he was grumpy and miserable twenty-four-seven.

Micah ignored me. "FYI, Daniel has soft brown hair that sometimes looks like there's red in it, hazel eyes, he's a doctor, we're going to be married, and he's mine."

Wait, this was a warning? Was I seriously being warned away from Micah's new husband? Then it hit me just how much love dripped from the description and yet more family shit. My smile remained, but inside I felt a hundred kinds of weirded out.

"I'll let you know." I whistled for Sky, and we were back in the Ford in an instant, waiting for Micah to move his truck. I kind of hated that I was so intrigued by the change in Micah, and that I wanted to find out more. But Wyoming *had* been on my shortlist of places to see the sun this season, so what would it hurt?

I'd made up my mind to take the offer even before I passed him, but I waited until three hundred miles later at a stopover to call him from a beaten-up payphone to tell him I'd be with him in a month.

I could have gone up right then, but I didn't fancy getting embroiled in a wedding, so yeah, a month seemed like a good delaying tactic.

After all, I was very good at blowjobs, and he'd said another man's name when he was shooting down my throat.

Asshole deserved to wait.

Not that he was an asshole right now, apparently. All because he'd fallen in love with this Daniel guy and somehow that was the miracle to mellowing him? What must it have been like to fall in love with someone who changed you so fundamentally?

And why would anyone ever want to create a family only to leave themselves vulnerable to being hurt?

Not me. Ever.

Chapter Three

QUINN

SUMMER

THE CALL CAME THROUGH JUST after I passed the twenty-mile sign to town, and Molly's name flashed across the space-age video screen that I doubted was standard in this car, even if I was sitting in a brand-new Lexus SUV. It could only be one of two people, my best friend Molly, or SEAL-turned-PI-turned friend, Connor.

"Team Quinn, this is Quinn Rhodes speaking," I joked brightly, because if either of them thought for one minute I was losing my shit then they'd be out to Wyoming in a flash. It felt weird to be using the last name of Rhodes after so many years as a Dawson, but taking my grandmother's maiden name was a final fuck-you to the family I'd cut myself off from. My granny Rhodes had a wild time, widowed young, and with a girlfriend at her side when she'd passed.

It was her who'd set up trust funds for me and Max,

and it was her I aspired to match in spirit. The money she'd left for the two of us was the single thing I had left now, but it wasn't a few thousand, it wasn't even a few million, it was more money than I'd need in a lifetime.

More money than I wanted. Impossible greed-inspiring millions that dragged me down at every move.

"Hey Q."

Hearing my best friend's voice lifted the anxiety that had tracked me from Massachusetts to Wyoming and made me smile. The closer I got to Whisper Ridge, the more fear piled on top of stress and grief, and the pain was so sharp that I held tight to every smile I could muster. I'd spent years with hope only to have it viciously ripped away, why would coming here to find my brother's son be any different?

Breathe.

"Get this, according to several media outlets, you carry the curse of the insanely rich and spoiled," Molly cut straight to the chase.

"Tell me something I don't know," I muttered, and searched for somewhere to pull off the monotonously long road leading off the I91 and into Whisper Ridge. Molly and I had missed each other at my last stop which had been over three hours ago, and I needed to take some time to breathe before I got into town. Now was as good a time as any, and it gave me a chance to concentrate on whatever she was saying, and I peered at the road ahead. Were there really no places to pull off that didn't involve me scrabbling in the dirt?

"Quinn? You still there?"

Her voice held so much concern, and I smiled so she

would hear it in my voice—if that was even a thing. "Yeah, sorry, I saw a rabbit or something," I lied.

"Jesus, they have mountain lions out there, are you sure it wasn't a lion?"

"I'm sure it wasn't—"

"You said 'or something.'"

Yeah, because I was making it up. "Oh look!" I exclaimed with fake excitement, "the bunny is running right by my car."

"For real?"

"Totally for real."

I imagined her narrowing her eyes at me, and I smiled at the thought of her judging me for my inability to lie. I'd sold all my shares in Dawson Pharma, then spent the time since then planning and plotting, and hoping that what Connor had told me was true and that I could be an uncle. All through the winter I'd laid the foundation for disappearing from the media spotlight, not even dying my hair, not going to events, winding down social media, and most of all taking on Connor and Molly as part of what we jokingly called Team!Quinn. My dad had long since cut me out of his life, he didn't scare me, and it wasn't as if he would hurt me now, after all he had what he wanted with me out of the family picture.

Well, apart from me handing the huge stake in Dawson Pharma to rivals, but he'd worked through that with gritted teeth. He didn't care about me, but he would care about a possible grandson.

So I set about making sure he wouldn't find out about my going to Wyoming, and that had led to the crazy idea of me faking illness and pretending I needed to spend time in a clinic. Connor thought it was an insane idea, even more so when I told him that I was coming to Wyoming alone. I wasn't in physical danger, so why would I need his brand of jujitsu-taekwondo whatever? This visit to Wyoming was on the down-low, and that was the way it would stay.

Arrive, meet Rachel and Laurie, set up a couple of college funds, leave without telling them who I am.

Simple.

Molly continued her assessment of my ruse, and I tuned back into her words. "So, in summary, they're saying *gay Dawson son loses his gay-ass rainbow shit and ends up throwing everything away to be full time gay waste of space and get his gay head checked out at a celebrity clinic with a lot of other gays*."

I rolled my eyes even though she couldn't see me. "It doesn't say that."

"Okay, not word for word, but mostly that." She cleared her throat. "It's more an op-ed than actual news, so plenty of fodder for socials. You need to promise me you won't look at any of the posts or the comments."

I finally lost the will to find the right place to stop and instead pulled to the side of the road, bumping into a huge pothole, and abandoning the SUV to sit diagonally, back half still on the road. Then I paid closer attention to what Molly was saying, or as much as I could with exhaustion chasing me.

"Pinky swear I won't Google my name." I sighed and rested my head, the headache that had chased me through Nebraska having caught up with me when I'd passed the sign welcoming me to Wyoming. I pressed fingers to my temples wondering if the med kit in the car contained Advil. Knowing Connor, it probably had a complete surgical kit with defibrillator—he worried about every detail. The SEAL turned PI was both my friend and security expert, and spent his entire waking life determined to keep me safe by any means possible.

"At least the media think I've left Boston." The rest of my anonymity would be bought by Connor who did all the technical side, which ensured I remained off-grid. Growing up as a Dawson, with all the money and the privilege, made Max and I fodder for gossip, and I was used to them tracking our every move. They started when Max had gotten his first DUI, and when he vanished, I'd become just as much of a target. Even now that Max's body had been found, then buried, they still wanted a piece of me, waiting for me to break down in public—just for the headlines. Fucking Dawson name.

Fucking Dawson money.

"Yep, as far as anyone knows you're taking an extended stay at the Mitchell-Everyman Clinic, who incidentally have thanked me for the enormously generous payment to build an art therapy studio and confirm that should anyone enquire you're *officially* a guest for the next two months, working on your mental health."

"So that's me completely off-grid now."

"Yep, Secret Squirrel, fully-fledged gone."

Now I could track down my dead brother's partner, find Max's potential son, spend time with them whilst not revealing who I was and keeping the entire family away from journalists and the threats that followed my money. I'd set up a college fund, make sure they were okay, and then I'd move on and make a new life for myself away from the Dawson name I'd been cursed with.

Easy, right?

"Are you okay, Q?" Molly's tone had changed, and I knew she was going to be asking me a shit ton of questions about my feelings, and I really wasn't ready to do that right now.

"I'm good, stop worrying. In other news, I finally changed the color of my hair."

"For real? What color?"

"Flamingo Pink."

She snorted a laugh and it made me smile. "Photos or it didn't happen."

"Hang on." I took out my Connor-approved cellphone and descended the vast distance between my seat and the ground, then checked out the best angle for a selfie with the mountains in the background for Molly. She was past worried I'd decided to do this disappearing act, but it wasn't an angry-worried, and she was always there for me when I fucked up and had been since we were kids. The same as I was for her.

I posed in front of my phone, tilting it, pouting, and with a cheesy thumbs up, but I could see I looked like shit, so I wiped away the smudges of last night's eyeliner and rooted around for the lip-gloss I kept permanently attached to my side. I needed to appear halfway normal to persuade Molly I was okay. After that small touch-up, I took five or six shots, then contemplated which one to send showing the mountains in their best light. Or me.

Whatever. Finally, I chose one that had the right contrast between my hair and the mauve mountains and sent it.

"Jesus, that's seriously pink," she snorted a laugh. "I love it."

"Thank you." I kicked a stone and watched it disappear into the grass.

"Babe, you look exhausted," she added, and my small moment of confidence dwindled to nothing.

"I drove all night, only stopped twice, so I'm tired is all," I reassured her.

"You need to look after yourself."

"I promise."

"Okay then, that's all I need to tell you for now. We're about ten miles out from Dad's place, Connor's meeting us there, and I've already seeded Instagram that I'm taking time to find myself after my best friend ended up in a clinic, anything to support the story, but really it's an excuse for a vacation."

I couldn't help laughing at her cover story. Molly was the most put-together person I'd ever met, the stability to my chaos, her husband Greg was a rock, her family close-knit, and their sprawling farm in New Hampshire held a lot of good memories for me.

"Have fun, Molls." I sighed and rolled my neck. "I'm sorry that being part of my cover story is chasing you out of Boston."

"It's not, I promise. You need time to visit your potential nephew, I need time at Dad's place with my big sexy husband looking out for me." I heard a man's voice, and imagined Greg driving, with Molls in the passenger seat.

"Say hi to Greg for me."

"Quinn says hi."

"Say hi back and tell him to enjoy having his pretend breakdown," I heard Greg joke, and it made me smile. He'd married Molly, and by virtue of that he'd been dragged into the mess, and I owed him one. He was wrong though when he used the word *pretend,* because I felt as if my whole life was in a spiral and that was the definition of breakdown for me.

"How close are you to Whisper Ridge?" Molly asked.

"I just passed a sign for twenty miles out, so really close."

"How are you feeling?"

"Excited, scared, hopeful." I huffed a laugh. "Hungry," I added.

"Make sure to eat, yeah?"

"Always."

When the call ended, I felt entirely alone in the vast wilderness with the mountains rising either side of the road, and the sky so blue it hurt my eyes. I hoped the Ridge Hotel had a bed comfortable enough that I could get some sleep. At last, I was on Wyoming soil, stretching and then leaning over and touching my toes, feeling my spine pop as I unwound all the knots from driving. Then I stared at the SUV that Connor had gotten for me and eyed the climb to get up to the seat.

"You need a Lexus, he said, take the RXL, he said. It's safe and it suits you, he said." I muttered the words with little anger. There was nothing wrong with the Lexus, it was luxury on wheels, but it was also this colossus that made me feel like a little kid when I was driving it. Five-eight of me didn't sit so well in a SUV built for giants, and I eyed the height of it ruefully, knowing I'd have to clamber back in, and that there was no sexy way of getting up there. Connor had said this model was the best thing for an extended stay in the wilds of Wyoming, and I'd let him talk me into it. He'd been adamant he wanted me to be secure, and I bet if I'd known what I was looking for there would be gadgets incorporated into the vehicle that made me safer, or trackable by him. It probably came with enough added tech that it could launch itself into space.

"I'll climb up there in a bit," I explained to the SUV and huffed a laugh at my stupidity before turning to face the view, taking a breather before heading into town.

I heard the rumble of a vehicle long before I saw it but thought nothing of it as a great silver horse trailer lumbered past, the kind with a truck and a big rear that formed stalls to hold horses. I waited for it to pass, curious as to what kind of horse was in the trailer. I loved horses, about the only *normal* thing I enjoyed according to my parents, also I now owned two of them, a detail I'd neglected to tell Molly. She was going to lose her mind when I mentioned that detail, but I wanted to make sure I was well entrenched at the Lennox Ranch before I told her anything that might make her drive right out there to save me. The rig slowed, then stopped farther up the road from me.

"Everything okay?" A man jumped down from the cab. Not just a man—a fully-fledged cowboy.

"Yeah, I'm good," I shouted back.

"Did you have a flat?"

"No, I'm all good. Thank you for stopping." I thought he'd leave then, but he didn't. Instead, he sauntered over to me, glancing at my Lexus and no doubt laughing at little me next to the big SUV. He was broad, slim-hipped, jeans, Stetson, and stubble, all in one sexy package, and I forgot my headache. I had a thing for the rough and tough worker, the alpha type who spent all day in a demanding physical job, but who was happy to bend over for me when I—

"If you need me to get someone to help you, I don't have a phone but I can surely send someone back for you." He pulled me from the image of him bent over the back of *anything* and me…

I loved the way he spoke, his voice like crunchy honey, all gruff and smooth at the same time. *Wait, is crunchy honey even a thing?*

I held up my cell. "I have a phone, and it even has reception, go figure." I huffed a laugh, but when he didn't smile, I realized I might have sounded rude. "I wasn't being sarcastic…" *Shit, stop talking.* He was hot, he was sexy, and I was a mess of nerves whenever I was faced with my greedy lust made manifest. He frowned, and I clutched my phone, because where had my self-preservation gone? He was a stranger, I was alone, we were in on the side of an isolated road. I should at least have had 911 ready to go.

"Town's that way," he thumbed behind him, the frown deepening. "I think."

"You think?" *Not a local cowboy then? Shame.*

He shrugged. "Sign said so. So, as long as you're okay here."

"Yes, thank you."

He eyed me with curiosity, but I guess it wasn't often you got to see some guy on the side of the road with pink hair, eyeliner, and gloss. I waited for the comments, for the homophobia, for the sneer, but instead he checked me out from head to toe—I imagine it was to make sure I was okay, but boy, the heat pooled in my groin.

Down boy.

He tipped his hat, and then with a casual gesture that I guessed was a wave, he ambled back to his cab and pulled away, I heard a snort from the horse trailer as he moved off slowly. He was a cowboy, and he had a horse—that meant his sexy-level was immediately through the roof. I began a set of stretches, using the trunk as a barre, and ran thought from first to fifth position.

And then I headed into town.

Chapter Four

LEVI

Ending up with my trailer hooked ass ways around a bend on the corner of Fremantle Street and Black Bear Drive was not how I thought I'd start today. There'd been no signs indicating it was a bend that just kept on going, but what did I expect? Whisper Ridge, Wyoming was about as remote as it got, and I was lucky people lived there at all. It took three of us to get my rig straightened out, me, a woman who told me her name was Mrs. Windham and who seemed to know an awful lot about everything, plus a sullen teenager who kept rolling his eyes. I wasn't sure he was rolling them at me or the woman, but at least he was good enough to explain that the Lennox Ranch was over five miles in the opposite direction.

Blake was one miserable horse in the trailer and was happy to let me know all about his dissatisfaction by stomping and snorting. Not to mention Sky who panted in the passenger seat and was no help at all. She was sulking because I'd made her stay in the cab, but the way my day was going I was worried she'd end up pinned between the trailer and the Whisper Ridge Mini-mart.

I should never have stopped to see if that guy was okay. I couldn't in all conscience have left him, but I wished I hadn't stopped because he was…

Gorgeous. Short. Cute. With wide, silver eyes, and layers of vibrant pink hair, and I swear he was wearing liner smudged under his eyes, and his lips were plump, kissable, and glossy. I typically didn't do cute and pretty, but I couldn't deny he'd made me pause and contemplate things I didn't know I wanted. I bet *he* didn't hide who he was, with the hair, the skinny jeans, and the T-shirt with the rainbow on the front. I bet he was out there living his authentic life, not like me all closed-up and keeping my secrets close to my chest.

I blamed *him* for the fact I was stuck, because I'd been wondering if his hair was soft, instead of concentrating on the map in my hand with directions to the Lennox Ranch. I really needed sex. Stat.

Cowboy switch seeks top or switch for current sex life drought. Cowboy seeks connection he doesn't really want. Cowboy wants orgasm that isn't by his own hand.

"If you're walking, it's through the graveyard and over the hill," the teenager finished, which wasn't overly helpful given the trailer behind me, and how we'd never make it up any kind of steep hill with the weight of my trailer, along with Blake in the back.

I tipped my hat at the woman, and gave the judgmental teenager a nod of thanks, and then headed, way more cautiously, through the town. *No more thoughts of men with anime eyes, and more focus on Whisper Ridge.*

I knew it wasn't big, nestled at the foot of the mountain, and way off the I91, but back on the right road, I took note of the highlights of the place for reference. A cowboy should know his surroundings, and against my better judgment this place was home for the summer. Diner with signs proclaiming they had the best breakfast in town, check. A hair salon, pet shop, grocery store, gas station with another mini-mart, check. School, check. Small comfortable-yet-shabby hotel, yep. There was a store for clothes, and I needed more jeans, so I added that to my mental list, and a coffee shop that I wished I could stop at right then, but I was aware I'd block the entire road. There were no big outlets of any sort, but I guessed all of that would be over in Collier Springs, not in this end-of-the-road town.

I kept straight on through town and then the road opened out and I climbed the hill to finally reach the gate to the ranch, passing through to a parking area in front of a ranch house. It wasn't the fanciest I'd seen, not the sprawling estate of my last contract, or the McMansion of the one before that. This place had a brutal honesty about it, from the white weathered boarding to the tidy yard, everything had an air of age with a ton of shit that needed fixing. Gutters were uneven, and there was a crack in a window on the top floor. I was used to turning up at places where there was money to burn—the Lennox Ranch was not that place.

I killed the engine, and Sky stuck her head out of the window, sniffing the air, and curious about what new adventure we were trying out.

"What have we gotten ourselves into, eh?" I asked her,

and she glanced at me with her all-knowing doggy grin. "I tell you, sweetheart, what we've got is a shit ton of underpaid trouble." I was there to train horses, but that wouldn't take up one hundred percent of my time, and assisting in fixing this place up was the unspoken extra. Hard work didn't scare me, but there was a lot of fixing that needed to happen here.

"Well, there we go then." I scratched Sky's ears and she wagged her tail furiously, desperate to get out. "Stay here, okay?"

She stopped panting, handed me her paw, looked up at me with the cutest expression she could muster, but the last thing I wanted was her out there doing fuck-knows-what where I couldn't watch her.

"Stay."

I swear she huffed as she leaned against the passenger door and deliberately pointed her snout to the roof. Drama queen.

Climbing from the cab, I straightened my shirt, settled my hat back on my head, and then gave the seat of my pants a cursory brush. Blake, Sky, and I had been traveling on and off for three days now, and I was tired of the road, ready to get my little family settled, then a shower and a good night's sleep. I checked around for signs of life, guessing I'd need to knock on the door, when it flew open, and two kids darted out with a laugh and a yell. They slid in a scramble in front of me, with wide-eyed expressions, one with engine-red hair, and another pale blond, both boys covered in flour. I didn't get a chance to say hi, because a woman came running out after them, a toddler in her arms, laughing like a loon. She stopped in the same dramatic fashion, skidding, then stepping between me and the boys.

"Can I help you?" Her tone was cautious, as if she expected me to grab the kids and run, or maybe steal something else important. I could see Micah in her eyes and the way she lifted her chin—this had to be Micah's sister, Rebecca? Rita? No, Rachel.

"I'm looking for Micah Lennox, ma'am," I drawled, removed my hat, and ruffled my hair before giving her what Micah had once called my disarming, flirty, fake-as-shit smile. It wasn't fake, and it had been enough to get me into his pants on several occasions, so I knew it worked. "He didn't tell you I was coming?" I teased in my best aw-shucks tone.

"He might have." She remained cautious and was giving nothing away.

"Levi Brennan, ma'am, here for the summer." I held out a hand and saw the moment the tension eased in her and she took it.

"Oh, you're early, we weren't expecting you for another week. I'm so sorry..." Her smile dimmed, and I couldn't have that happening to such a pretty face and a sweet woman.

"I made good time; thought I could get an early start."

"Oh yes, of course, never mind me... I'm Rachel Lennox, Micah's sister."

"Pleased to meet you, Ms. Lennox."

"Please. Call me Rachel. These tearaways are Laurie and Archie, and this is Oliver."

Laurie darted around her at the mention of his name, a cute kid with all that long blond hair, and intriguing gray-green eyes. There wasn't much of Uncle Micah in the kid, but what Laurie did have was the biggest and widest smile and an expression full of mischief.

"I'm Laurie, and I'm eight-and-three-quarters, my brother is only two and he doesn't do much."

"I'm nine, and I'm Archie," the redheaded kid added. "What are you doing here?"

I was always cautious around kids, knowing they were breakable, but in the same way I'd be cautious about a rattlesnake. They were all smiles and cute one minute, and then demanding and worrying the horses the next. I couldn't have children messing around my horses when I was training them, and I didn't want any reason to get irrational or out of sorts, but as long as they stayed out of the way they were okay.

I'd never get angry with a kid, I couldn't, I hadn't inherited that nasty streak from my bastard of a father, or lack of patience from Momma, who didn't give a shit about the kid she'd birthed and dumped on her sister. I didn't know about my siblings, maybe the temper had passed to them, but it wouldn't come anywhere near me. Still, I had it inside me I was sure, and one day it might come out if I didn't keep myself in check. So yeah, caution.

"Hey there." I placed a smile on my face, and met them cute for cute. "I'm Levi, I'm twenty-nine-and-three-quarters, and I'm here to work with the horses."

We all nodded at each other after the brief exchange, then shared grins.

"Levi!" Micah hurried over to us, his hand extended, and after a deliberate pause I shook his hand.

"Mikey," I muttered.

"Micah, and don't start that sh—stuff again." He glanced at the kids who weren't paying us any attention, and instead had their heads together, pointing at Sky. "Anyway, you're early."

"Had nothing better to do."

He rolled his eyes. "Whatever."

"Snappy comeback."

I didn't really want to work for Micah Lennox, and I was going to make sure he knew how that went while I was there. We'd worked alongside each other in the past, and I'd had to put up with his shit, but at least he'd never been the actual boss of me. Still, I wasn't going to turn down the chance of working with horses as storied as the ones he'd said he had coming in from the Ebben-Loner stables. Maybe a small part of me was fascinated by how Micah, a closed-off asshole in a former life, had changed since we'd worked together. I didn't dislike Micah as such, but couldn't be bothered with his secrets and him needing to dissect every little thing we'd had going between us. I'd wanted to get off, and move on, he was all about wanting to discuss how we weren't in a relationship, angst, pain. *Whatever.*

Who even wanted a relationship? Fuck-then-leave was my mantra and it had served me well so far. All I'd wanted with Micah was a summer of orgasms, all he'd wanted was to wallow in angst. I hadn't had time for his crap.

Well, fuck, he had me here, reeled me in, and got me thinking that I could maybe spend a summer doing some good, banking more cash before I hightailed it to Texas for the winter.

"Well, I'm here, *Mikey,* now what?"

He exchanged a glance with Rachel that was probably in sibling code and read, *yeah this is Levi, he's the asshole who doesn't give a shit about much except horses.*

"Can I pet your dog?" Laurie interrupted, and pointed at Sky who was hanging out of the window panting a doggy grin and waiting for me to call her down.

"Be careful, she bites," Micah instantly warned.

I bit my lip to stop my snarky response. Sky had only ever bitten two people; the vet last time I'd taken her when he'd tried to inject her, and Micah who was top of her shit list. How he'd managed that I didn't know, but he wasn't a dog person, and I got that she sensed it and just wanted to fuck with him.

"She's a soft thing," I defended, then whistled, and Sky was at my side in an instant. Laurie went to a crouch and petted her, Archie squatting next to him with a grin. "She's called Sky."

Micah hovered with his hand extended, ready to leap in to save his nephew any minute, as if he was expecting my sweetheart of a dog to turn on the cute kid any second.

"Why are her eyes different colors?" Archie asked.

Laurie joined in, "Yeah. Look, Uncle Micah, she has one blue and one brown."

I held back the smile that *Uncle Micah* would've been interested in anything to do with Sky. "She's a merle, it's genetic," I explained. "Like, she was born that way."

"I want a dog like this," Laurie announced, and Micah winced. It never failed to amuse me that big bad Micah was unsure around an itty-bitty dog.

"Me too, I want ten of them," Archie announced.

"Leave them be now," Rachel murmured, and guided the boys away. They grumbled under their breath about things not being fair.

Micah focused back on me, taking a deliberate step back from Sky, and raising an eyebrow when she crawled a little closer on her belly. I would've laughed, but I was still in serious mode about arriving there.

"Wanna show me where I'm parking the trailer and turning Blake out?"

"Yeah, good call. Follow the road round and take it slow. We've had some subsidence that needs work."

I guessed fixing that would be part and parcel of me being there, training, cowboy work, maintenance, I'd done it all in my time, working for a place to sleep and food in my belly. Micah sidestepped Sky and walked past the house and farther uphill, and I whistled for her to get back in the truck cab.

"Welcome to summer in Wyoming," I said to her and got a hand lick for my efforts.

Micah guided me into a space in the corner of a fenced pasture, and I noticed there was a hook-up for power and water—the earth freshly dug over and still not settled.

In silent partnership, we hooked the trailer up to the utilities, then he went back to the house, saying he'd give me time to settle Blake in, and showing me the space that was all mine for the summer.

I opened the stall door and met a very disgruntled Blake, who snorted his displeasure right in my face. I made a show of wiping myself off, then led him out of the stall and onto the pasture behind my truck. After a moment of posturing, during which time I ignored him, he laid his head on my shoulder and nuzzled me. He hated to travel, but he loved me, and I loved him, and this was going to be okay. There were views of the mountain, a glimpse of town beyond, and other than that it was wide open nothing.

"Just our kind of thing, eh Blake?" He bumped my arm and I petted him for a longer time, just communing with my horse, the sun beating down, and me feeling absolute peace. When I was sure Blake was good, watching him sniff the air for horses, danger, and the rest, I headed back to the trailer and checked all the hookups. Then, with all that done I sat in the single chair in my living area with a coffee, which was the first thing I did whenever I reached a new place.

The short wall living quarters in the trailer were nothing more than a shower toilet, the tiniest kitchen known to man, one comfy chair, and a bed in the space above the truck. It was a convenient home and it suited me fine, a place to eat if I needed, sleep when I wanted, and to sit and contemplate life when I had the time. I poured another coffee, craving the bitterness of the black stuff, then stepped out into the sunshine, tilting my face to the sky, and drinking in all of the rays. This was my happy place, not just the trailer, but my horse, my dog, and the heat of a summer's day.

"Everything okay?" Micah was back.

"Yep."

"We need to talk." He was hovering by my truck, and he seemed a hundred kinds of uncomfortable.

"I didn't do anything yet, Mikey," I teased.

He didn't correct me and instead he was dead-eyed thoughtful. "I want to..." he took off his hat, and I knew things had to be serious. "I know we haven't always seen eye to eye—"

"Or mouth to cock—"

"Jesus, Levi, will you stop?"

I made a show of zipping my lips.

"We're pushed to the limit here, in terms of man hours and income." He frowned as if the official terms were things he'd never have to say.

I wanted to joke and say that with a great ranch came great responsibility, but I didn't recall him enjoying superhero movies the same as I did, and there was no way he'd get the bastardized reference.

"Hence why you're paying me on completion, I get that." Then something occurred to me. "You are still paying me, right?" Not that it mattered in the grand scheme of things, after all I'd started out by working for board and meals when I'd been booted from home and had had nowhere to go and not much in the way of real-life experience.

"Hell, yeah. I'd go without myself to pay you first."

"Well that's kind of dramatic," I teased, but he wasn't smiling.

"These extra horses—they will be make-or-break for me and Rachel, and by extension her kids. You met Laurie and then there's Oliver, plus Archie is kind of a permanent fixture. I just wanted you to know, that whatever we had in the past—"

"Snarking, shouting, and blowjobs?" I said in all innocence.

He checked around him. "Less of that with the kids here," he warned, and then sighed.

We'd already covered the fact he was married, and that his husband knew all about what me and Micah had gotten up to over a summer a few years back. Apparently, they had an honest marriage after years of secrets. What that meant I had no idea, but I was all about honesty. Micah seemed fierce, and then he sighed again.

"Spit it out, Mikey."

"Micah, fuck's sake, my name is Micah." Then he shook his head. "Whatever. Call me whatever you want, because it means one hell of a lot that you're doing this."

"Holy shit, Mikey, it almost sounds as if you're being sincere."

Micah forced his hat back on his head. "You're an annoying asshole, Levi, but you're the best, and I need the best to make this work. So I owe you one."

That last part was added grudgingly, but it seemed to come from his heart, and this was a changed man standing in front of me. Someone who cared.

"Okay, I get you."

"Also I wanted to tell you about Archie."

"Archie? The red-headed kid?"

"Yeah, his mom… doesn't do so well, and he spends a ton of time at the ranch. Good kid, but he wants to work hard all the time as if he must prove to us why he can stay around here. If you see him…" Micah frowned. "Just don't let him overdo it, okay? He's a kid, and he should be having fun with Laurie."

"On it, boss."

"Okay then." Micah laid a bag on the step. "Uniform."

"Huh?"

Micah's expression was serious. "We're doing this right, cowboy." He pointed at his chest and quite apart from the fact he was dressed almost identical to me in jeans, boots, and Stetson, his tee was pale blue and had *Lennox Ranch* in capitals on one side, along with the silhouette of a horse. I opened the bag and there were four T-shirts all the same color.

"You've got to be fucking with me."

"Nope."

"I should leave right now," I muttered.

Micah winced before pointing at them. "One on, one to go, one in the wash, one spare. You can use the laundry in the house, ask Rachel to fix it for you," Micah forged ahead and ignored my griping. He might've been all mellow now and married to his Doctor Daniel, hell he might not have been the grumpy fucker I'd hooked up with anymore, but he was still bossy as fuck and I wasn't sure there'd ever be a day he wasn't the bane of my life. Of course my refusal to wear the T-shirt at first wasn't legit, given he paid my salary, and I'd signed a summer contract that meant I should at least try to stay in line. Although I didn't recall notice of having to wear a uniform.

"We don't have much going for us here, Levi." Micah's tone had changed again, filled with worry and fear, and that was the tone he'd used when he'd come to find me and offered me a contract. I was a sucker for hard luck stories, and Micah's had to be a doozy to push that much angst into his expression. "The ranch needs fixing, we need money, and what you're doing for us, along with me, it could make this place work. Whatever you think about me, or how I work, and whatever I think about you, I need us to be a united front for the time you're here."

I stared at him, trying to make sense of this new Micah, the one with the desperate expression. What the hell was going on at the Lennox Ranch, and why did I feel as if I'd landed in the middle of some great mess.

It's just for the summer. Not my monkeys, not my circus. Train the horses, get paid, leave. Done.

"I'll wear the damn shirt," I muttered, and then tugged my road-worn shirt over my head and pulled on one of the ranch ones.

I didn't have to be happy about it though.

Chapter Five

QUINN

The Ridge Hotel, proudly jutting out at the corner of Main and Abernathy Street, was a remnant of an older time. It needed new paint, but the inside was clean, and the owners, Marjorie and Emmet Lowe, were kind and attentive. Well, they were after Emmet, not a day under seventy, stared at my hair with wide eyes and Marjorie slapped him upside the head.

My pink hair was just *me*; the makeup was *me*. But I got that in a small Wyoming town I stuck out like a sore thumb, and I did have fleeting regrets that I should have thought things through before I'd decided to reclaim my identity in such a dramatic fashion. Emmet apologized, Marjorie flustered, and I swear the cookies in my room, a whole jar of them, were her way of apologizing for her husband. Of course, the actual apology from Emmet was kind of sweet when he said I was brighter than a peacock, and it helped I was munching on the best cookies I'd ever tasted at the time.

The room was at the front of the hotel, and what I'd

been given was more like a large suite, with a sofa, a table, a bedroom with a large solid wood bed, and an old but shiny bathroom. The view took in part of the town and past that to the same mountains I'd taken a selfie in front of. I'd slept fitfully in the huge bed last night, only managing a few hours' sleep, not used to the quiet when I'd lived in a city most of my entire life, but I'd woken up with a smile, and stretched with a feeling of peace that sunk into my bones.

I was there, I was going to find out if I was an uncle, and I was going to meet my horses for the first time since selecting them.

Yeah. Horses. My horses. The ones I'd bought on a whim because it gave me an excuse to be up at the ranch to carry out whatever investigations I needed to do. I had an appointment at Lennox Ranch on Friday, to meet the trainer hired especially to work with my horses, a cowboy called Levi Brennan who was well-respected. At least that was what Molly's dad, Owen, had explained after he'd done his research. He'd tried for Micah as a last-minute scramble to create my cover story, but Micah was booked out—seemed like my offer, through Owen, to pay more worked though, because this new trainer appeared on the horizon, and suddenly my harebrained plan to observe the Lennox family up close went from zero to sixty.

I couldn't just go and buy horses and head up there, it'd been a long and complicated story to get to this point, and one I'd not even shared with Molly, who would kill me as soon as she got to her dad's place and found out what I'd done. Particularly when she found out it was Owen who'd facilitated said purchase and was an integral part of my visiting-Lennox-Ranch cover story. She'd thought I was staying in the hotel for a week or so, visiting the ranch, meeting Rachel, checking on Laurie, and then coming home. She was wrong; because if Rachel's son *was* my nephew, then I might not be able to let them know who I was, but I wanted to *know* him, so that meant staying longer, maybe even the full two months, or at least spending as much time as I could at the ranch. Was Laurie my nephew? Did he love the same things as Max had done?

I pulled out the map of the town that Marjorie had handed me as part of my welcome pack, dislodging a voucher for discounted breakfasts at the diner, and then traced the road up to Lennox Ranch. I couldn't believe after all this time I was finally this close.

My brother had left home on his eighteenth birthday, ten years ago, and I'd been fourteen. I thought Max would come back, that this was just another dramatic moment in his larger-than-life meltdowns, but I never saw him again. Connor, searching for his cousin had tracked him to a cult, Brothers of Chiron, run by the enigmatic Callum Prince, but by then it was too late. Max had disappeared again, vanished from the commune as easily as he'd disappeared from my life, but it was okay because I imagined him out there living his best life free from our father, free from pain.

Hope had turned to anguish when a hunter had found his body last fall, in a shallow grave outside commune land, his body riddled with bullets, his features burned away. They'd had to identify him through dental records, and the coroner suggested he'd died a minimum of five years before. All the time I'd held hope that I would see him again, promised him every night as I fell asleep that together we could make things righty and he'd been dead the entire time. Desolation took hope's place when we buried my awesome, big-hearted brother on a beautiful fall morning.

Only Connor had watched me at the funeral, he'd waited, and he'd watched, and had finally trusted me with the biggest secret of all.

There was a slim chance that Max had been a dad, that somewhere in the middle of Wyoming there was a boy who could be my nephew.

A boy who lived maybe three miles from where I was standing at a place called Lennox Ranch.

The ranch itself, where Rachel Lennox and her sons lived, was outside of town, and there were two obvious ways to walk to it from here; the first was through a graveyard that went straight onto ranch land, the second, more obvious choice was through town, passing the diner where breakfast, with or without a voucher, sounded good. I had things to do today, stop at the bank, check the opening times, work things through, but first I had a shower and then dressed in the same suit I'd worn the last day in the city, before standing in front of the mirror. My pink hair had lightened a little, but not much, and I added some kohl to my eyes then slicked my lips with my favorite raspberry gloss. I stopped as I stared at my reflection and then bent at the waist as grief and anxiety gripped me.

"I've got this," I told my reflection. "The hair will fade; I don't have to..." I picked up a wipe to clean my face but stopped. "This is me." This was a mantra I used every time I caught sight of myself. "I am me. I am small and I am fierce, I am Quinn *freaking* Rhodes, and I am me."

I dropped the wipe and then smiled at myself.

I've known hate, I've seen hurt, I've had hope, I lost hope. I am *me.*

I headed out to the diner and ate the fluffiest of pancakes and a ton of crispy bacon without spilling any syrup on my suit. Then it was straight to the bank because I had an account to open and a safety deposit box to rent. The assistant manager, Rose, never blinked once at the amounts or the instructions, and with a printed note in my pocket with details of the accounts, I felt as if I'd achieved the first step. Leaving the bank, I had a bounce in my step, glancing around the old bank building and creating stories of robberies long past because my overactive imagination would not stop.

I walked straight into a wall.

A wall with arms as solid as anything and that caught me and then pushed me away. Files went this way and that, and I inhaled the most amazing scent—fresh air, cinnamon, hay, man… it was all way too much to catalogue in one go.

"You found town then?" the wall drawled and bent to pick up files.

I went to a crouch to help him, but as usual I just made matters worse because we banged heads, and I was mortified and incapable of controlling my grip.

"Sorry," I murmured, as I picked up and promptly dropped a file, knowing I was scarlet with embarrassment. I peered up into amber eyes that belonged to the same sexy cowboy who'd pulled over in his truck. He was all stubble and hat and irritation, and I'd walked into him like an idiot.

"Maybe watch where you're going?" Amber-eyes said with a smirk.

"Yeah, sorry, my bad," I muttered, and bypassed him as close to the wall as I could get and left the bank without looking back. It was already warm, and conventional wisdom meant I should have gone back to my room to change. But burning with the embarrassment of smacking into the sexy cowboy, plus the fact I was hot under the collar, I marched down the main street with purpose, imagining he was watching me walk away.

I found myself on the road leading up the mountain and refused to think about how I'd walked straight into someone. Particularly someone whose scent refused to leave my nose, and whose irritation was as sexy as a smile. *Stay focused.*

I was a freaking fish out of water, cowboy-hassling, idiot, who was now walking up a hill, wearing a suit, and regretting every moment of it.

A mile out of town I came across the remnants of a construction site, a fenced-off area with a trailer inside, and then found a new-build house which turned out to be the first of a row of houses. At least under the trees there was shade, and I scurried from shady spot to another, checking out the houses. They were all rustic, solid, brand new, and had enough land around them that each one felt secluded. I took a break on a bench under a tree, enjoying the beautiful views, pulling a couple of much-handled photos out of my pocket, and examining them as I took a break.

In the first one, big brother Max was nine, laughing, eyes sparkling, hair all over the place, me at his side, holding his hand, even then a small-for-my-age five. The other photo was of a small boy, older than Max, one I could've easily mistaken as being Max himself, if not for the recent date on the back. This was not Max in the second picture, but a young boy called Laurie, who'd been born in the same cult that Max had died in.

They looked alike, I knew that from the photo, but Laurie might not have been Max's—only Rachel would be able to answer that question, and that was why I was there. I couldn't tell Rachel why I was there, or who I was, but I wanted to meet Rachel, and Laurie at the least. Not to mention she'd had another baby, although there was no chance the baby was Max's, given the coroner's findings.

I shouldn't really have been up there this close to her and the children yet; it wasn't part of the plan that Team!Quinn had created. Connor would've been so pissed with me wandering up here without thinking, but he was always telling me he wanted me to hold back, to get surveillance, but I wasn't comfortable authorizing spying on a conventional ranch near a perfectly ordinary town. The lure of what might be at the ranch, though? That was intoxicating.

I pocketed the photos and carried on walking, heading uphill, and spotted a man outside the second to last house. He was hammering a realtor sign onto the front lawn, and he smiled at me as I drew nearer.

"Morning," he called.

I stopped walking to peer at the house beyond. It was very much a cabin aesthetic, the same as the rest, with a wide wraparound porch, and it sat very well in the scattered collection of sprawling houses hidden away behind trees.

"Morning." I noticed that the smiling face on the board was the same man as the one wielding the hammer. He jumped down the small wall and extended a hand, shaking it with enthusiasm. "Scott Sheridan." He didn't have the oily self-assurance of the realtors I'd dealt with in Boston, and I couldn't help but smile back.

"Quinn Rhodes."

"Were you here for a viewing? I didn't get a call, but as I'm here…"

"Oh no, I was just walking this way, heading up the mountain."

He frowned and tracked the direction I was waving at, glancing back at me, and scanning my suit. "The mountain? You mean the ranch?"

"Yep."

"Not far to go," he added, and then waited for me to explain why I was heading up there, but I knew who Scott Sheridan was, because he was in the very brief notes Connor had sent me with a family tree of sorts. Scott was brother to Daniel, who'd recently married Micah, who was Rachel's brother, and Rachel had the potential to be the mother of my brother's child. I needed to be careful.

"Just walking," I repeated, and then with a nod I sauntered away as if I wasn't feeling overwhelmed that I'd had my first encounter with Laurie's extended family. I passed the final house—one with an entire front yard of whirling rainbow windmills. That house was smaller than the others, but out of all of them it was the most welcoming, and for a while I peered at the place until I realized this wasn't the city and things weren't there for people to gape at.

Stranger with pink hair tackled by Scott-the-realtor for gawking.

Laughing at my idiocy, and shocking myself at the sound, I turned and stared a while at the peak of the mountain, and then decided I could kill time and at least find my way up as close to the ranch as I could get and have a look at it from a distance. The final hurdle, it seemed, was a blocked stone bridge crossing a slow trickling stream, and my attention was caught by a small, polished plaque.

Isaac, December 2009, RIP. I traced the name and wondered how Isaac had died, and why there was a plaque on the bridge that went nowhere. There was a track leading up the mountainside from here, but it had been truncated by the new builds. Maybe there had been a road, and he'd died on that road somehow. Had he died an old man? Or was he young like Max had been? I was moved by the plaque and the sunshine and the mountain, until all I could feel was pure emotion building inside me. I bet a hundred people came to this place and knew who Isaac was, and it hit me that no one except me and Molly would visit Max's grave and think the same thing.

My mood plummeted as it always did when I imagined Max all alone in the ground. I missed him so much, but my emotions weren't raw with pain, it was grinding me away inside, stealing my positivity, and one day I worried my smile just wouldn't come back. Then the other worries hit me. What would it be like when I eventually got to meet everyone at the ranch? It was all well and good organizing horses, and cover stories, but face-to-face with one of the last people to see Max alive—how would I react?

Fancifully, I imagined Laurie running over to me and recognizing that I was his dad's brother or some wild thing, and as I considered this story that would never happen, I found my way from the bridge and onto an open road which narrowed to a track as it headed upward. The grief loosened as I lifted my face to the sun, then shrugged off my suit jacket before tossing it over my shoulder by hooking my finger into the collar. I was so close to connecting with Max somehow, that I couldn't keep my excitement at bay, and as I imagined all kinds of other fanciful scenarios I was lost in a world of my own. I stretched tall and then danced a few steps.

Thud.

Whatever hit me I didn't know, a plane maybe, an entire house. Whatever it was, I was on my back like a turtle staring at crystal-blue skies and feeling as if my whole world had been turned upside down.

"Jesus! Are you okay?" Someone close by cursed, rough hands poking at me.

"Get off me!"

"Fuck! You again? How did you not hear me?"

I blinked up as the sky disappeared and there was a dark-haired man with amber eyes right up in my face, the man from the road, and the bank, my nemesis, and he was pressing on my chest, and it hurt like a mother.

"Leave me alone!" I flapped at his hands, shoving at him, finally getting purchase like I'd learned in self-defense classes, getting my attacker into a hold, and flipping him before sitting on his chest. He flailed the same as me, and then he flopped back into the dirt.

"The fuck?" he snapped, but all I saw was my cowboy wannabee rescuer, his lips parted, and a hazy glow around him, almost as if stage lights were surrounding him as he got ready to rip his clothes off.

"Sexy Cowboy," I murmured as adrenalin coursed through me, then clamped my mouth shut. This wasn't a bedroom. Or a club. And as the stars cleared, I could see flashing temper in his eyes. I wriggled down and ended up on his groin, cradled between his muscled thighs.

Uh oh. Cue him thumping me, which led me to going into full defensive mode to keep him on his toes.

"Why did you hit me?" I demanded, my hands on his belly.

"Get the fuck off me—"

"You hurt me."

"What the…? You were the one who danced into the middle of the road, I was *right there,* following you." He tried to buck me off, but I was like a rodeo star the way I held on.

"You were *clearly* too close."

"I wasn't *too* close; you danced backward asshole."

"Says you."

"Jesus, what in the name of all that's holy…" He scrambled to stand, but I sat a little longer than was necessary, just to show him that even if I was only five-eight and slight with it, I could hold my own. Finally, I let him up, although to be honest he was built like my type of man, all spirit and broad chest, with flat stomach, legs that went on for miles, and I didn't want to move at all... Fuck, I really needed to get the hell off this man before I did something embarrassing.

Eyes on the prize, Quinn.

I stood as fast as he did, brushed off my suit, and winced at the twinge of pain in my right leg and my shoulder.

"Are you okay?" he asked, but he wasn't showing concern when his eyes filled with anger and frustration.

"I'm fine," I lied, and smoothed my hair out of my face, tucking it behind my ears and hoping I didn't look like a complete idiot. *Of course I look like an idiot, I shuffled-danced my way out in front of his freaking truck. I'm lucky I didn't die before I even started this new life.*

Die. Oh shit, now I felt as though I was going to pass out.

"Get in the truck," Mr. Cowboy ordered, and yanked the door open, shooing a beautiful grey and white dog into the back.

"I'm okay," I tried to explain. There was no way I was getting into a truck with a stranger—even one as sexy as the cowboy who was yanking his Stetson down on his head and scowling at me. "I don't need to go to the hospital even if you did hit me."

"I'm not taking you to the hospital, and the truck hardly brushed your ass. It was you that did a dramatic swan dive onto the ground." He opened the door wider. "Get in."

"I don't know who you are." Okay so this wasn't

Boston, but I had stranger danger down to a tee, and it had kept me safe so far. If he wasn't taking me to the hospital, then where was he taking me?

"I'm... fuck my life." He pointed up the hill. "Start walking, it's just around the corner."

"What is?"

"The house." Implied was the entire added *what are you, stupid?* Jeez, was I that close? How did checking out the area get to me being on the ranch doorstep? "You won't get in the truck, then you walk the rest of the way and I'll be right behind you making sure you don't fall over and freaking die on the property."

"I'm not going to the ranch yet," I said, and picked up my suit jacket to shrug it on before crossing my arms over my chest. I was *so* not ready to go the ranch, particularly all confused like I was right now.

"Yes. You are." He copied my stance and we stood in the face-off long enough for me to get a good look at his growly-frown, and his generous lips, and his hard chin, and the way sunlight reddened his dark hair. I didn't have to read minds to guess what he was thinking, and I stood even more upright, pulling myself tall, and waited for the inevitable battle.

"I'm fine. I'm not going to the ranch." I wasn't ready to see Rachel or Laurie yet.

"You'll get me fired." The man's demeanor changed, and he slumped as if this was the end of the world. Shit. For real? He pointed up at a security camera on a corner post, and fuck, had that entire mess been caught on camera? What if it seemed like it was his fault, when it had been *me* who'd walked in front of his car. What if the angle made it appear as if he'd mowed me down? I didn't want to be responsible for a cowboy losing his job.

Fuck. "Okay."

As soon as I agreed the whole losing-his-job act vanished, and I suspected I'd been played. I could've easily walked away, so how was he going to stop me. Yes, his truck was half-blocking the road, but I could run, but what if the return of his confidence was a way to hide the fact he *would* lose his job if I didn't get checked out. What if under the rough tough exterior, he was a poor cowboy who would lose everything. I hated my head sometimes, when I thought round and round in circles until I couldn't decide on anything.

I eyed his truck with suspicion, then knowing he probably deserved me to deliver an explanation to *someone* about why the incident had happened, I turned my back on him and with as much pride as I could muster, I headed the way he'd pointed, making sure to stay at the side of the road. I could hear the rumble of the truck behind me, and he was right, I should have heard him, and I couldn't believe I hadn't. I'd been too lost in my own head, too excited about a wonderful possibly non existent future to be paying attention to having something big up my ass, and not in a good way. Now, I needed to calm down from the high-tension mix of embarrassment and fucking-ouch.

I couldn't believe I'd sat on his chest, then slid down to his lap, or that it had felt very nice and solid, and the kind of body I'd like to crawl over.

Stop it now. Big manly, amber-eyed cowboys aren't gay. Or bi. Or even remotely interested. I bet it was like *Brokeback*

Mountain up here, all furtive rustling in a tent, tortured love, and stoic masculine sadness. I wasn't sure how a creative like me would ever survive, but to see Laurie and maybe end up playing a part in his life? That was worth every irate cowboy I messed with.

Just no more calling him sexy. Okay?

Head high, the June sun way too warm on my back in the damn suit, I turned the corner and came face-to-face with the house. Lennox Ranch sprawled this way and that, lots of action going on, a horse tethered to a rail, the sounds of people talking but no one in sight, a horse whinnying from afar, two kids on bikes cycling down a field in the distance. Was one of them Laurie? My heart stopped and I weighed up biding my time and playing it cool against running down the field to check.

A breeze ruffled my hair, and in a flash of my wild imagination I imagined Max was there with me, his spirit following me from the city, tethered to me by memories.

So close.

Chapter Six

LEVI

One minute I'd been following someone up the road assuming the hair meant it was the cute guy from the bank and road, the next they leaped in front of me, arms flailing, right into the path of my truck. Thank fuck I'd been idling my way up and even though I had to brake it wasn't hard enough for Sky to even slide off her seat. The idiot couldn't have been hit hard but he'd done this whole dramatic, flailing swan dive, disappearing, and for a second, I'd thought I'd really hurt him. I'd never exited my truck so fast in my life, sliding to a stop next to the man on the ground with his bubblegum-colored hair splayed out, eyes shut, sprawled on his back in his fancy-ass suit looking like a model, cheekbones and all. Was he breathing? What had I done? Had I been going too fast? Was this all my fault?

"What the hell!"

I'd gone to a crouch, trying to find a pulse when he opened his eyes, staring the sky, blinking and then he'd groaned so I moved where he could see me, and his eyes had widened. Up this close they weren't silver, but a light gray, darker near the iris, and framed with the longest lashes I'd seen on a man. He had an elfin face, high cheekbones, and along with his bangs of vibrant pink he was red in the face. Oh yeah, and he'd been glaring up at me.

Then, I didn't know how, but he'd caught me in a chokehold and managed to flip me upside down before I'd even blinked. I was a head taller than him, and he looked as if a stiff wind would have blown him away, and yet somehow, he'd gotten the upper hand, sprawled all over my chest and then my groin. He smelled of strawberry, and he was delicate-boned and cute, yet he'd pinned *me*.

My cock was hard, but fuck, my pride dented, and now in my truck I ran through my entire catalog of curse words, which meant my anger wasn't abating. Sky stared at me as if I'd lost my mind, and I probably had. I'd accused him of jumping out in front of me and all he'd done is accuse me right back, telling me I'd run him down. I wanted to grab him and shake him for making me feel as if I'd killed him and if we kept sniping then that was exactly what I would do. I pulled the truck to a stop in the yard in front of the house and hoped to hell Micah was around somewhere.

Sky was out of the truck first. I adjusted my hat, and watched my dog, as easy as you please, jumping out of the truck then sauntering over to Pink-guy before offering him a paw. *Since when does Sky make friends with people?*

Pink-guy went to a crouch, never mind his expensive but dusty suit, and petted Sky.

"Aren't you beautiful, oh you are, and you know it, pretty girl." Sky rolled onto her back, demanding belly rubs, and I whistled to get her back to my side, which she did with reluctance and one longing glance back at her new friend. Somehow, in the space of a few moments, Sky had judged the man and found him to be worthy of giving belly rubs, and I had no idea how that had happened.

"I was just walking," he said as he stood and brushed himself down. There wasn't a point to any of that, given his pants had a rip, and they were covered in dirt.

"Looked more like you were dancing," I pointed out. "In the middle of the damn road."

"Actually, I *was* dancing." He reached tall with his arms and then did this whole shimmy thing, which—holy shit—he was all sinuous and sexy and…

He's an idiot who walks in front of trucks. Head in the game, Levi.

Then he blinked at me innocently and tucked his hair behind his ears.

"Don't do that—dance I mean—in a road—ever." Jeez, he had me tripping over my words.

"What am I thinking?" he exclaimed in a voice that dripped money and polite upbringing. "Quinn Rhodes." He stepped closer and extended his hand which I took because I was a cowboy with manners, thank you very much.

"Watch out for freaking trucks on your way back down," I warned him.

He frowned as we released hands. "Nice to meet you Mr. Watch-out-for-freaking-trucks-on-your-way-back-down," he deadpanned.

"Huh?"

Quinn crossed his arms over his chest, then put his hands on his hips, as if he couldn't decide what to do with them. "Well, see. This is how it normally works. We shake hands, I tell you my name, and then you give me your name in return."

I *really* wanted to shove him back into the dirt, but no doubt I'd end up flipped over the truck or some shit. Quinn Rhodes might've been small, and I may well have nearly knocked him on his ass as he left the bank, but he packed a punch, as my left shoulder would attest to. "Levi," I offered, despite our epic face-off in which I looked into his intriguing eyes and waited for him to react.

He smiled at me, and fuck my life, he had dimples, little creases of sexy sassy goodness that I could—*Stop*.

"Hello, Levi, it's nice to meet you again. Sorry for the bank, and apologies if I hurt you when I y'know..." He used a finger to draw a pattern in the air, which I assume approximated the wrestling hold that had had me ending up with a wriggling bunch of sexy man in my lap.

"You didn't hurt me." I huffed and ignored the instinct to roll my shoulder anywhere near him. I'd been thrown from horses many times and ending up flat on my back in the dirt wasn't a new experience. "I'm going to get the boss to check you out." It still rankled that I had to call Micah boss, but in this instance if I could hand all of this over to him then I'd take the benefit of not being the one in charge.

"I don't need to see anyone, I'm fine." There was a fearful edge to his voice, and he wouldn't quite meet my gaze, making my Spidey-senses tingle. Something wasn't right here—a man in a perfect-fitting suit, with his Boston vowels, pink hair, and I was right—there was a smudge of dark around his eyes, and I swore his lips were shiny enough to have gloss on them. Why was *this* man walking to the ranch? Did he live in one of the houses down the road? No one just casually walked this far out of town without a reason.

"Everything okay here?" Micah asked from my left, coming to join the stand-off, and I was never more pleased to see Micah come over to take charge and extend his hand in courtesy to Quinn. "Micah Lennox."

Quinn shook Micah's hand. "You've been expecting me," he said. "Not until Friday actually, but I was just getting the lay of the land. Quinn Rhodes." He dimpled again. Asshole.

Micah was surprised, I could tell, but the way he relaxed meant that somehow, he knew this guy. "Mr. Rhodes. Hello."

"Call me Quinn, please."

"Quinn, okay. You'll be pleased to hear that the Ebben-Loner Stables confirm the horses will be here on time."

"Wonderful news."

Wait. What was happening here? Micah and Quinn were talking as if they knew each other, and what was that about horses? *Oh, this* cannot *be happening.* This couldn't be the representative of the owner from Ebben-Loner with the horses that needed training? Quinn was an idiot and shouldn't have been allowed anywhere near horses.

"I nearly killed him," I blurted, and both Quinn and

Micah stared at me. Quinn was smirking, Micah looked as if I'd pulled the pin out of a grenade and thrown it at him to catch. "Let *Mr. Rhodes* tell you," I added, and then with Sky at my heels I headed to the barns, away from the stranger who'd nearly killed himself in front of me, and then had threatened my equilibrium one pink strand of hair and dimple at a time.

"He didn't nearly kill me."

I heard Quinn explain with an added huff of a laugh. I couldn't help one last glance back at him as it hit me that if he really was our new client then he'd be up here stepping out in front of trucks a hell of lot of times in my future.

Someone save me from idiot men in suits.

As soon as I stepped into the cool interior of the stables, I felt all the mess in my head begin to untangle. It helped when I headed straight for Blake's stall, Sky slipping past me before I shut the stable door and then settling herself in a corner with her nose on her paws to sleep. It turned out that running a man down hadn't affected Sky's day at all. I stole all the affection I could get from Blake as he stood placidly and let me scratch between his eyes before I buried my face in his neck.

I could have hurt Quinn, and that didn't sit right, neither did me being rude nor potentially messing up Micah's business relationship with a new client. Lennox Ranch needed Quinn Rhodes and his money. I was a hired hand for the summer, and I had never fucked up so bad in one single day as I had now.

My head was messed up, I was still hard from all that

gyration in my lap, and I was angry, confused, and felt guilty.

Fuck.

Chapter Seven

QUINN

TALL AND SEXY MICAH SCOWLED AFTER EQUALLY TALL AND sexy Levi's retreat, and the very last thing I wanted to do was get Levi in trouble on my account. Micah was wide-eyed as he stared at me, and I knew what he saw, someone who couldn't be anything to do with horses—that was for certain. I cursed getting knocked down, I was frustrated that I'd been put on the spot like this, and my well-crafted backstory was a jumble in my head. Still, at least talking about getting knocked down put the ranch on the defensive, I guess.

"It was nothing." I couldn't believe I was talking to Micah. If Connor's research was right, which of course it was, then Micah was Laurie's uncle, which made us kind of, I don't know, potential uncles-in-law or something. Was that even a thing? I glanced over to watch Levi disappear around the house, or rather I checked him out while he wouldn't notice, and it was only when Cowboy-Uncle-Micah cleared his throat that I recalled I had an audience.

"Sorry, you were saying?" I tucked my hair behind my ears and smoothed my suit again, wanting to make a good impression on this possible relative who might be the keyholder I needed to talk to so I could meet Laurie. I had to get my head straight and concentrate on talking to Micah, finding Rachel, meeting Laurie, then leave once I knew everything was settled.

"Are you okay?" Micah asked in all seriousness.

"Huh?"

"You look a bit frowny." He motioned to his face. "Pale."

"Oh no, pale is my default setting," I joked. From my first appraisal, Micah was steady as anything, his gaze penetrating and thoughtful, but he seemed friendly enough, although I was a client, so I guess he had to be. I knew his financials, was aware that the ranch was on a knife-edge, which had given me the idea of stabling my two horses for training, knowing it would be a welcome injection of cash and the best way to infiltrate the ranch without anyone knowing who I really was.

"What did Levi mean that he nearly killed you?"

I sent Micah my best innocent smile. "He's exaggerating. It was completely my fault. I walked in front of his truck."

Micah blanched and placed his hat back on his head. "And you're okay? Do we need to get the paramedics out? I should call my husband, he's a doctor—"

"No, I'm totally okay, nothing but hurt pride, and ripped pants." I poked a finger into the rip, which was little more than where the seam had split. Nothing that someone clever couldn't fix—not that I ever planned to wear this suit again. Part one of grabbing life with two hands was to box up all this city shit that was a result of me having to impress people. The suit had been my armor when I visited the bank to set up accounts, a way of balancing the pink hair and lip gloss. I might not have always appeared like a sensible adult capable of much, but a suit plus a bottomless pit of money helped me sell it.

Wearing a suit and projecting confidence was a sacrifice I'd been willing to make for a bit longer.

I hadn't thought this through at all. I'd packed designer-type things, but what I needed was jeans that didn't have a label—unless it was Wranglers. And boots. And maybe some of those fancy cowboy shirts with tassels. Or maybe I should go straight for plaid. Maybe I could find red, or orange, or pink. I liked pink, but orange would clash with my hair. I needed to fit in more, blend with my surroundings, not make a nuisance of myself.

Of course, I'd already jumped in front of a truck, so it was Ranch 1, Quinn 0.

"We should put this in the accident book..." Micah waved around him, but I had no idea what he meant by the random gesture.

"You have one of those?" I didn't mean to sound judgmental on this dusty ranch, standing opposite a tired-looking cowboy, but my Boston vowels inevitably made me sound like a superior asshole.

Micah straightened and frowned. "I assume Ebben-Loner did their due diligence, and you know we're a professional ranch—we don't cut corners in animal care or health and safety."

Shit. Way to fly under the radar. "I apologize, I didn't mean anything in what I was asking."

He huffed, but it was a quiet thing, a small comment on my question, then he appraised me from toe to nose and back, and not in a sexy way. "Mr. Rhodes—"

"Quinn."

"—I still think we should get you to a doctor. Because if a ranch truck hit you—"

"Actually, it was more like I hit the truck."

Micah was confused and he half-jogged to the house and opened the door, "Rachel, can I get you out here?"

My heart raced. Rachel was the single reason I was there, but I wasn't prepared to see her. I'd planned our chance meeting down to the last detail and it didn't include me being covered in dirt, in a torn suit, and lightheaded from hitting the ground hard.

The door opened and I held my breath. The woman who stepped out had blonde hair tied up in a smooth ponytail, and she looked good, happy as she smiled at Micah and me. Brother and sister exchanged a few words, and as if they'd come to some agreement, she walked over to me.

"Rachel Lennox. Good to meet you, Mr. Rhodes." She extended a hand, and I shook it firmly. This was the woman who'd caught my brother's eye, and it would've been so easy to break down there and then and petition for a DNA test. But a test meant regulations, and filings, and then the can of worms would well and truly fall open.

Making any of this official would put Rachel and her children on the media's radar, not to mention my father's attention. There was no way in hell I would subject a child to the torture of being a Dawson, not for all the memories in the world of my brother.

Familiar grief gripped me, and I couldn't form words as I met Rachel's steady gaze.

"Is everything okay?" she asked with a frown.

I snapped back to what I was thinking. "I'm sorry, I had the... thing..." I waved down the path.

She frowned at me. "Mr. Rhodes—"

"Quinn, please," I interrupted and smiled at her.

She released my hand and stepped back, and there was no obvious sign she recognized Max in me at all, although her eyes were a little glassy, as if they held emotion that couldn't be contained. I didn't know her, so for all I knew she could have been peeling onions, because I wasn't anything like Max, so it wasn't as if she was facing his doppelganger. We'd shared a mom, but he'd been tall like our dad, broad, the silent type, not a bright bird like me with dubious paternal heritage; he'd been six feet, I was a head shorter, he'd been unhappy and had shown it, I'd learned to fake happy daily.

"Do you think we need to call Daniel to check him out?" Micah asked.

"I'm fine. I promise."

"We should document the accident as it was on Lennox land," Rachel suggested.

"We can do that." I would have agreed to anything right then so I could get away before I did anything stupid and blurted out a ton of questions.

"I'll get the book, then leave you in Micah's capable hands," Rachel left to go to the house, reappearing almost instantly with a leather-bound journal. Micah dutifully filled everything in, and I signed where I was told, but I was scattered, and wanted to follow Rachel and stare at her some more. Was Laurie here somewhere? Was it him in the field?

Is he Max's son?

"I'll come back at the time we agreed, Friday, three p.m., then we can talk officially, owner representative to uhm… cowboy." I stepped back a little when he wrinkled his nose.

Micah blinked at me and then nodded. "Sure." If he thought I was a scattered idiot, then he was kind enough not to mention it.

"Okay then."

I had nothing else to say, unless I started a discussion about his hat, or a cow, or something equally inane.

"Where did you leave your car?"

"I walked."

"From town?"

"Yep." I glanced up at the sky. "Perfect day for it."

I shook his hand again before he asked any more questions. "Nice to meet you, Mr. Lennox." Then, with as much dignity as I could muster in my scuffed and torn suit, I headed down the hill, back toward the hotel. The walk seemed to go fast as I lost myself in thinking about how beautiful Rachel was, and how she was exactly who Max would've loved, and in the fantasies, I imagined the moment I would meet Laurie.

And thought about how amazing it could be if he *was* Max's son.

Not that he'd ever call me uncle, I couldn't tell him

who I was, but at least I'd know Max wasn't entirely gone from the world if he'd been a dad.

That had to be enough.

Chapter Eight

LEVI

"WHATCHA DOING?" A SMALL VOICE ASKED, AND I STEPPED back from Blake.

Laurie was visiting, and no doubt Archie would be at his side. The two boys were thick as thieves, and according to Rachel, they often had their heads together, planning whatever the next great adventure was. Laurie was Micah's nephew and a permanent ray of sunshine in his world—all questions and love for the ranch and his uncle. This was only my first morning at Lennox Ranch, but just seeing Laurie and Micah together had me rethinking some of what I knew of Micah from the old days. There was no sign of repressed agony in him now, and I laid the reason for that at his family's feet—Rachel, Laurie, and of course his husband, Daniel, who I was due to meet tonight.

I felt as if the entire world owed the good doctor a beer.

"Hey, Levi, whatcha doing?" Archie popped up as well.

"Talking to Blake," I murmured, and stepped back and

away from my horse, to face the boys leaning over the stable door.

"What did he say back to you?" Laurie asked with all the curiosity that'd had him questioning me earlier about why the sky was blue. I mumbled something about atmosphere, which I thought I might have picked up from *NatGeo*, but who knew.

"Blake's a horse. He can't talk," Archie said with an exaggerated eyeroll.

"He so does, Uncle Micah said so."

"He neighs, like all horses," Archie added.

"They so *do* speak."

"You're stupid." Archie elbowed Laurie, who grinned at him.

"No, *you're* stupid."

I cleared my throat and they both stared at me with sudden rapt attention as if I held all the answers to the universe. I didn't know why, but this morning they'd taken to shadowing my every move, even wanting to come to the bank with me. I'd drawn the line at that, much to their disgust.

"Horses *do* talk," I began, and leaned against the wall next to the door.

"How so?" Archie sounded incredulous, but about this I knew I had all the answers.

"Blake always knows what I'm feeling, even what I'm thinking. Then he goes right ahead and shows me affection at just the right times."

"Yeah but he can't talk," Archie insisted. "Not for real."

"He leans into me, or twitches his ears, or maybe he'll push my arm. He's there when I need quiet, fast when I need speed, and slow when I need to calm down." Archie frowned, but Laurie was enthralled and glanced from me to Blake and back again. "When we smile, means we're happy right? You don't have to say you're happy, you can just smile and as long as it gets into your eyes, then everyone knows you're doing okay."

"Like dirt gets in your eyes?" Laurie asked.

"No, like when your eyes get all sparkly with happiness."

Laurie and Archie exchanged glances, and I was convinced I was making no sense.

"So what next?" Archie climbed another rung and leaned even farther, peering at Blake.

"Well, when you're sad you might cry, right? And you want hugs?"

"Uh huh." Now Archie was intrigued by wherever this was going.

"Watch Blake's ears, look at the way his lower lip is loose, the way he holds himself, he's happy and chill. But, if he saw I was sad, he'd change, and come over to me and press his muzzle to my face. He's telling me without speaking that he's there for me. Always."

Archie opened his mouth to ask more but there were footsteps and the sound of voices, and Rachel appeared next to the two boys.

"Thought I told you to wash up for lunch," she admonished the kids, and Laurie was the first to climb down. "Go around the back way, don't mess with your uncle and our client out front."

I guess Quinn was still out there, which is why I was staying exactly here.

"Yes, Mom," Laurie said and sprinted around to the back of the house as if the hounds of Hell were on his tail.

"Yes, ma'am." Archie hopped down before sauntering away at a more sedate pace. He had a way about him that boy, all sass and confidence.

"Were they bothering you?" she asked, all serious.

"Not at all, ma'am."

"Rachel," she reminded me.

I tipped my hat. I was always respectful, and with only a single day under my belt I wasn't ready to go calling people by their first names.

She crossed to another stable to her horse, a soft-hearted bay called Beans, and buried her face in his mane, murmuring to him in a low voice I couldn't hear. I'd done the same thing, seeking comfort with my horse, and I hated to think that Quinn had upset her, after all that was the direction she'd come from. Quinn hadn't struck me as one of the bad guys, but who ever *really* knew a person? After all, he was an entitled idiot who liked to throw himself at people. He *looked* rich, so horse management or whatever his title was must've paid well, but he was a gorgeous in-my-face idiot. I thought long and hard about asking Rachel if everything was okay, because a cowboy never comes between a horse and their friend, but there was something about the way she gripped Beans' mane and buried her face so hard, as if she was hiding tears, or letting out a silent scream.

"Are you okay, ma—Rachel?"

She pulled herself together as if she'd recalled where she was. "Of course, just ghosts is all," she said a little too brightly and scratched Beans' muzzle, then pressed a kiss to his coat.

Did she mean a literal ghost? I couldn't say as I'd ever seen one, but I never discounted things I didn't understand. Take my instant attraction to Quinn—that was a non-understandable type thing.

"Ignore me, lunch is ready in ten if you want to wash up."

"Thank you, ma'am, I'll be right in."

She shook her head, clearly deciding not to push the call-me-Rachel thing, and then glanced at her watch. "Ten minutes or there'll be nothing left if the boys get to it first."

I followed soon after up to the house. "I swear if Quinn is going to be there as well..." I muttered to the dirt, and washed my hands at the outside tap with the soap and cloth left there for hot and dirty cowboys, stomping the dust from my boots. I wasn't sure what I'd do if Quinn had been invited in, because there was something about him that messed with my equilibrium. My sex drive sparked, my brain told me to get the hell away, and stuck in the middle was an uncomfortable space. Still, I took extra care to smooth down my new blue T-shirt just in case.

When I glanced through the kitchen window, there was no sign of pink hair so maybe he hadn't made it to being invited in. I opened the door into the kitchen and there were new people I hadn't met in the kitchen, but *thankfully* not Quinn. One of them had Laurie on his knee, making the boy laugh as he tickled him.

"Hi, you must be Levi? I'm Daniel, Micah's husband,"

he called over to me. I hadn't been expecting to meet him until tonight, and I was intrigued.

I extended a hand over Laurie's head. "Howdy," I drawled as we shook hands, sizing Daniel up in the blink of an eye. Handsome, smiling, calm. The doctor who had changed Micah from surly and secretive to open and vulnerable. Interesting. "Levi."

"And I'm Chris." I glanced back at a guy laden with bowls that he deposited none too careful on the table and shook his hand as well. "Daniel's younger and much better-looking brother."

"Nope, that would be me," Scott said, carrying cutlery. "For my sins, and clearly the best-looking one in the room." Scott, I knew, because he'd been there last night and I'd met him along with Rachel, I'd never realized he was Micah's husband's brother.

Micah huffed and placed a sloppy kiss on Daniel's mouth. "Don't listen to either of them, your brothers are both ass—"

"Micah!" Rachel warned.

Micah was chagrined. "My bad." Still, it didn't stop him kissing Daniel again before straightening then ruffling Laurie's hair. He did the same to Archie, and I couldn't help but see the way Archie preened and then stared up at Micah as if he hung the moon and the stars. This was a whole new side to Micah, a softer more settled side, and it appeared from this brief meeting, that his marriage with Daniel was strong and there was clearly love there.

Hell, Micah had been as discreet about his hookups as I was, but I don't think he'd ever suffered for who he fucked. Still, the fact that he was happy, connected, and in love wasn't the ending I'd expected for him.

Or for me.

"I happen to like this one best," Rachel murmured and caught Scott in a sideways hug, which soon turned into a mini smooch.

There was so much romance going on at this table it was ridiculous.

"Was hoping to get some help with riding," Chris interrupted the smooching with an eyeroll, and I realized he was talking to me. He caught me glancing over to see what Micah was thinking and snorted a laugh. "I'm not letting Micah anywhere near bossing me around," he said and then fist-bumped Rachel.

"Sure, I can… yeah."

He lifted his pants leg, exposing a prosthetic, "Even with this?"

Nothing about that fazed me, I'd done work with veterans in a place in Tennessee and worked with ASD kids at a spread in Texas—I was a great believer in the abilities of everyone and the benefits of horse therapy, and I could help Chris no problem.

"Sure." I felt someone's stare, realizing it was Micah, and his expression was tight. I didn't know why he was judging me for my simple acceptance, but when Chris thumped Micah in the arm, hard enough to get him stumbling back, the tightness evaporated.

This family was happy, and connected, and there were probably a million experiences that made up that thump. I wasn't interested in the history or machinations of any of them.

Still the intrigue of which men were brothers at least took my mind off Quinn.

I'd gotten myself all het up about Quinn being in there, and I typically didn't give two shits about who I broke bread with, if they kept to themselves and didn't ask me awkward questions. For some reason Quinn had gotten inside my head, and I put it down to the fact I'd run him over and I felt guilt… just a little… not that it was my fault at all.

It's just adrenaline.

I'm not disappointed he's not here with his sexy sass, his bright eyes, and hair a man could hold on to.

I'm not.

Chapter Nine

QUINN

I WOKE THE NEXT MORNING, AND THE ACHE IN MY shoulder that had plagued me last night had eased, helped by a couple of painkillers and positive thinking—or at least positive ignoring. I had a colorful bruise where I'd hit the ground, but years of dancing and gym meant I'd tumbled rather than collapsed, so it wasn't all bad.

It had taken a long time to get to sleep, mostly because I couldn't get comfortable, but also because I think I'd been overwhelmed by new experiences and thoughts about Rachel and the way she'd stared at me, worrying at her lower lip.

Had I been too intense? How had I reacted when I'd seen her? Had I stared too hard? Had I winced? Had it seemed as if I'd wanted to throw myself into her arms and beg her to tell me about Max?

But it wasn't only Rachel and Micah and the ranch that filled my thoughts, because I kept replaying my three closeup meetings with Levi. The cowboy stole my breath, and that was a new sensation, all swoopy and weird.

Maybe it was him mixed up with every other emotion I'd felt today, and objectively I knew I was capable of lust, I'd had sex, but never had attraction smacked me in the face quite so hard. It didn't help that the lust part was wrapped up in embarrassment, but there it was, together with everything I needed to do in Whisper Ridge. Every time I closed my eyes it was a crap shoot whether I would worry about what Rachel had seen in me, fantasize about meeting Laurie, or get hot with embarrassment over Levi. When it was Rachel and Laurie, I felt grief, pain, loss, but also optimism.

Whenever it was Levi's turn in the kaleidoscope of sensations, I vividly recalled the incident in the bank when I'd walked into him, the scent of him surrounding me, and the ranch road where I'd walked into his truck. I was hot with mortification, then turned on, then embarrassed again, so between that and planning my entire fantasy future as Uncle Quinn, sleep was impossible. What I needed was coffee, and while I could've stayed in the hotel for breakfast, I decided to skip that and saunter around town. I needed to get some clothes today, along with other sundries, plus another visit to the bank to do final signatures on paperwork, so I might as well get a head start.

As soon as my watch showed it was seven, I headed out and grabbed a quick breakfast and copious coffee in the small Whisper Ridge Diner that served the crispiest bacon I'd ever eaten. Then, with a to-go cup in hand, I found the nearest store that sold western clothing. The *only* store. Although it wasn't advertised as a western store as it might have been had it been on Fifth Avenue, the windows were full of practical jeans and shirts, and boots, and I needed one of everything, or a pair at least, if not more.

And a hat. I needed a Stetson.

When I'd left Boston, I'd left with whatever I could fit in a duffle and a suit bag. I needed clothes, and I needed to not stick out like a sore thumb. I had jeans, but they were designer, ripped and skinny, and I knew enough about ranch life to know that skinny jeans didn't work. I wanted to look like Levi, even if I was a head shorter, and probably thirty pounds lighter. I didn't have his ass, or his muscled legs, I was a dancer-slash-artist, so I was toned but edging toward too slim if I forgot to eat. Jeans, shirts, boots, I needed it all.

The store didn't open until nine, so I spent half an hour sitting on a bench in front of a small coffee shop, people-watching and feeling guilty that I'd gotten my coffee at the diner. I received a few second glances; knew I must've been a weird sight to find in the center of Whisper Ridge with the rose-colored hair I had going on. No one who walked past wore designer jeans, or custom shirts, and I tried not to meet anyone's eyes or start any conversations.

I could hear Max in my head. *Own that hair, little brother!*

"Morning." A man sat next to me. Not an *ordinary* man, but someone in uniform, a sheriff.

"Morning," I murmured back, that itch of feeling as though I'd done something wrong just a reminder that I might have run away from trouble, but trouble could still find me in the middle of nowhere, Wyoming. The times my parents had had me followed as a teenager, or arrested, or assisted home on one pretense or another, meant I had a healthy respect and an irrational fear of all that was the establishment.

"Sheriff Windham." He extended a hand.

I shook it. "Quinn Rhodes."

"Mr. Rhodes."

"Quinn," I corrected.

He sipped at hot coffee. "Noticed the Mass plates on your car. You're a long way from home."

"I am …" I bristled because why would the sheriff be checking plates?

"Not that I meant to check," he reassured me, "but I was checking out the SUV, it's an LX 570, right."

I glanced at him. "Yeah."

Sheriff Windham let out a low whistle. "Nice."

"Thank you, it's way too big for me," I blurted, and I swear I was so close to turning scarlet.

"Anyway, I wanted a quick chat, just to give you a heads-up on something you need to think on."

I waited for him to send me a message from my father who didn't even know I was here, because I was *that* paranoid.

Instead, he quirked a smile, and sat back on the bench, arm extended away from me. "Turns out you are kind of a big thing," he started, and that got my attention completely. Had the media found out where I was? How could they know? I'd only left a few days ago, and my clinic stay cover story was well-documented. I knew my car wasn't being tracked—Connor had seen to that—and my satellite phone was brand new and in Connor's name.

Team!Quinn had covered my tracks well, to give me time just to be me, but that didn't mean I wasn't assuming the worst.

The sheriff chuckled, but it wasn't in an evil way, more amused was all. "You seem shocked, but see, I got the information from my mom who knows everything there is to know in this town. She works at the doctor's office, and heard from Doreen, whose sister Miriam works late shifts in the diner, who is best friends with Lester at the store, who got it from overhearing you at the bank explaining your entire business to Rose, the assistant manager."

Now I blushed; I know I did because I felt hot. I recalled explaining to Rose that I would be expecting a deposit to open a local account and that it was vital there was discretion. Hell, we'd been in an office, with a closed door, but I'd not noticed whoever this Lester guy was. Had he been listening through a damn vent? The fuck?

"Old bank, but new thin walls, and added small town mentality," the sheriff answered all my questions in one, and then he smiled. "You might want to err on the side of caution if you want to keep anything in the way of secrets."

He was right. I needed to be careful about everything, I had to protect myself.

"I'm not a big thing," I muttered.

"Is there anything I should know?"

Oh yeah, nothing at all. Liar. No one in Whisper Ridge would have cause to recognise me, I was media-infamous in a very small Boston bubble and had no currency in the middle of Wyoming.

"No. I'm here on business at Lennox Ranch, but thank you for the heads up, officer."

He saluted me with his coffee. "Any time. Welcome to Whisper Ridge." He strode away as quietly as he'd arrived.

I finished my coffee, then tossed the container into the recycling bin situated next to the trash before reading the message on the front: *Whisper Ridge Thanks You.*

"Whisper Ridge knows my business," I muttered, and then headed over to the store the moment that the sign flipped from closed to open. I think I startled the guy behind the door, an old man with salt and pepper hair and a handlebar moustache, who looked at me, and then away just as fast. The way he'd stared at my hair, then down past the lip-gloss to my denim cutoffs and bright orange T-shirt, was enough to have me imagining that he was about to drawl that he didn't have "men like me in these here parts." I held back the immediate hysterical chuckle and with a quiet "*morning,*" I took a left and pretended I was browsing when I didn't know what I was searching for.

"Can I help you with anything, son?"

"Just looking," I called over, and then hid behind a display of generic saddle wax that was stacked up in a fancy pattern that defied gravity.

The door opened and I groaned to myself that someone else would be in the store and resolved to hide for a bit until the new customer had gone. The last thing I needed was another person watching me demonstrate that I had no idea of what I was doing. I had to have a cowboy hat to start, and I sidled to the hat display, wondering what tone of brown would suit my pink hair the best. Creamy-beige maybe. There was one with a shiny buckle on the side, but as I picked it up, I knew it wasn't what I needed. I chose a darker shade of hat at random and put it on, but the damn thing fell over my eyes, which made me think that it was one way to hide.

"That hat is way too big." A familiar voice made me want to stay hidden under my hat—Stetson—whatever.

I poked the brim with a finger, staring up and under it at Levi who was standing *right there.*

"You don't say," I snarked, and removed the hat. I stepped toward the display to return it, as he moved closer, and somehow I ended up on the floor in a pile of saddle wax. "You pushed me," I gasped because it sure felt like he'd shoved me.

He rolled his eyes then held out a hand. "You walked into the display."

"You walked into me," I huffed, and then ignoring his hand, I turned on all fours and scrambled to stand, hindered by a mannequin that decided to fall on top of me. I lost my cool with the mannequin and shoved it away, which would have been funny had it a) happened to someone else, b) not happened in front of an amused Levi, and c) not caused the head to fall off and roll into the destroyed saddle wax display. *Fuck my life.*

"Are you okay?" Levi asked as if he was being helpful, but I could see the ghost of a smirk that I suspected was about to morph into laughter. I was almost done with him judging me as an idiot. I straightened my shoulders and pulled myself to my full height, which was unfortunately still a good six inches shorter than him. I loathed being laughed at—I'd had enough of that from my own fucked-up family, let alone complete strangers.

"I'm fine," I lied, feeling the heat in my face.

"Come here," Levi murmured.

I glanced up at him. "Why?" I couldn't help but be suspicious and glanced around to see what else might fall on me.

"I need to measure your head." Levi unhooked a cloth measure from the display and snapped it in his hands.

"I'm okay thanks." I could imagine it ending up around my neck and me dying right there next to the headless mannequin, saddle wax tins, and teetering display of Stetsons.

"You can't do it on your own," he muttered, and before I knew it, he'd crowded me, and had the tape wrapped around my head. "Two fingers above the brow, four from the base of the skull, over the ears, that puts you at twenty-one inches, that's six and five-eighths." He was away from me in a few seconds, but that small amount of time was enough for me to catalogue a ton of things.

He was taller than I remembered. I don't know how I managed to take him down to the ground yesterday, because he wasn't only tall and muscled, but he was solid and filled out his worn jeans as if they'd been painted on. He smelled of fresh air and horses, plus a hint of lemon, and something that was perfectly gorgeous sexy male. I was hard in an instant, at the scent of a man who was in my space, and my traitorous cock was demanding that I fall to my knees and offer my mouth. Holy fucking shit.

And for him? Mr. I-know-it-all knock-me-down cowboy with his clear amber eyes, and his cheekbones, and his kissable freaking lips. What was it about him that little-Quinn was getting all excited about?

"How about tryin' this one?" Levi selected a plain brown Stetson and checked the inside rim briefly. "So, you hold it at the base of the crown, then over the head and on, two fingers from eyebrow, four from base. You might need to try on more than one, because different styles have different fits." He was back in my space, and I inhaled his lemony scent as though he was oxygen and I needed air, and nothing about that was right. He raised an eyebrow and I realized he must have asked me a question.

"Huh?" Coherent much?

"How does it feel? There's a tiny bit of room on the temples, but it needs to be reasonably snug so that a light wind can't blow it off your head, but not be so tight as to cause discomfort or distraction."

"You mean like when a cow is running at you, and you have to do the thing with the rope?"

What I'd meant to say was something clever about riding a horse on the range against an orange sunset, with the lowing of cattle in the distance, with added drama and lots of big words, and… nope… I messed it up. Because he was too freaking close to me.

"Yeah," he deadpanned. "Just like that."

I couldn't meet his gaze, and instead I pulled the front of the hat down so I could hide again, but he used a finger and tipped it back up.

"Don't pull it down," he murmured, and then in a moment of fuck-knew-what he slipped a finger under my long bangs and tucked one side behind my ear. "There you go."

I lifted my chin to catch his eye, and for a long, shining moment we stared at each other. I could feel an emotion that I didn't know what to do with. He wasn't laughing at me; he was messing with my hair and staring at me as if I was a bug pinned to a display. Almost as if he couldn't rationalize the horse-owning, short-ass, pink-haired dude in a cowboy hat. No straight guy tucked another man's hair behind their ears with such a soft touch and with so much intensity in their gaze, and Levi went from improbable to yes-please in a hot second.

Would it be such a bad thing to flirt a little with the sexy cowboy? I dipped my gaze, very deliberately raking him from head to foot, and then back again. This was the true test, and he didn't waver at all.

"So why does a suit like you need a hat?" he asked.

I winced. I needed a hat, and all the rest, so I could spend time at the ranch and not stand out like a sore thumb. He had no idea I was going to be dogging his every step to give me the excuse to be up at the house, or near the house at least.

"Souvenir," I lied.

"Expensive souvenir." He wasn't letting this go.

"I have expensive tastes," I deadpanned, and wished I hadn't said a thing because now I sounded like an entitled prick. Which I guess I was, but that was something else altogether.

"Delivery will be here around eleven." Handlebar-moustache guy appeared like a ghost. "You want to come back?"

Levi appeared to consider his options. "I have things to

do in town, I'll check in later." He tipped his hat, all kinds of sexy cowboy, and then nodded at me.

"Thank you," I murmured while wondering what had happened.

"Jim here will get what you need."

And then my sexy smelling, gorgeous, cautious, hair-tucking cowboy left. He moseyed with style, his legs that little bit bowed, his ass snug in the form-fitting jeans, and his thighs just… there.

I wished I could've come up with a better word for him, but I didn't even have control of my cock at that moment, let alone the English language.

"What can I help you with, sir?" Jim asked, and this time he didn't stare at my hair or curl his lip in silent comment.

"Quinn, please call me Quinn."

He didn't immediately tell me I could call him Jim, but hey, little steps. I glanced around in confusion, trying to channel my inner clothes shopper, but I wasn't even the right kind of guy when it came to western-style clothes. I was more the designer pants and trend-setting ties kind of person. But this was day one of a new me, a freer, happier me, and that meant blending in. I didn't want to scare Rachel off, nor Laurie, or shock the baby… in case I was supposed to be channeling the serious uncle type.

"I guess I need one of everything, and then spares of some, and I don't really know what I need. Boots, jeans, uh… jackets? I genuinely have no idea. Should I be getting something with those leather tassel things? Do you even have anything with tassels? I'm not normally this stupid, but I'm like a fish out of water here and I don't want to stand out." Had I *really* just admitted that?

Jim's gaze flicked to my hair, but he said nothing for a moment and then after the longest pause, he held out a hand for the hat which I passed to him.

"I'll put this at the counter and then we'll take it from the top."

Well over a thousand dollars later, weighed down with bags, I stumble-walked toward to my hotel. New boots were heavy and unyielding on my feet, but worse, the jeans seemed maybe a little snug in the crotch, and I wondered how my cock would handle the lack of room next time I was too close to Levi.

I just won't get close to Levi.

Simple.

Chapter Ten

LEVI

THE FIRST THING I FIND WHEN COMING TO A NEW TOWN IS the best place to get coffee. The Coffee Bean was that place and I was currently sitting in a window seat, inhaling a bagel and sipping a strong Brazilian blend on par with heaven. I could people-watch, and after wasting two hours in town at least people-watching allowed me to justify sitting on my ass. The bank had taken ten minutes, the post office five, the rest of the time waiting to go back to the store was me sitting here. I blamed Quinn, because I was blatantly keeping an eye on the store and waiting for him to appear all dressed up in his cowboy gear, and as soon as I saw the familiar pink hair, I was up out of my chair as if I was on springs, and then across the street to get to him.

I was looking out for a client of the ranch.

Liar.

I needed to keep an eye on him with his clumsy ass falling over all the time.

Liar.

I wanted to stare into his gray eyes and lose myself in him for a while.

Closer to the truth.

He was weighed down with a ton of bags, and there was no way he was going to make it back to his hotel without dropping at least one. I paused about ten feet from him unsure what I was doing or why I was so tempted by him. I knew I was disappointed that he was wearing new jeans that were loose in the ass but not worn enough to mold to him, but I also noticed that he was stumbling in new boots and heading for the curb that dropped opposite the hotel. I saw him trip, and even though he attempted to balance, and was damned sexy doing it, he was windmilling toward the ground, but I caught him before he face-planted.

Again.

"Phhnumplle," he exclaimed, and relaxed into my hold as two tins of saddle wax fell out of one of the bags and rolled into the gutter.

I steadied him with one hand and relieved him of half the bags he had, and after making sure he was upright and steady, I picked up the saddle wax. Jim had seen him coming, and jeez, I swear I could see something in that bag with sequins and tassels.

It seemed as if Quinn had bought a heap of tourist shit, and I hope to hell he'd managed to get decent jeans, a jacket, and that his boots fit. Maybe I shouldn't have left him alone in there, but after tucking his damn hair back I knew I had to avoid being near him because proximity to him led to an erection and that was hella embarrassing. Still, he was a stranger in a new town, who clearly didn't know his plaid from his tassels, and something about all of this struck me as funny, and I couldn't help but smile.

"You wanted a lot of souvenirs then?" I laughed when I peeked inside one to see sequins. He was so pissed at me, attempting to grab bags, which I held out of his reach just because I could.

"Stop laughing at me," he snapped with anger in each word, and it was reflected in the fury in his pale eyes.

My laughter died, and abruptly I felt like an ass. A man was entitled to buy souvenirs, and I shouldn't have laughed even if it was funny. "I wasn't laughing at *you*."

"I didn't hear anyone tell a joke." He pulled his shoulders back, but that caused one of the bags to slip, and he had to act fast to catch it.

"Sequins are funny," I said, but that was the wrong thing to say.

"I like sequins."

I should've said something about how sequins were cool, and not funny, and that every person was entitled to have as much shiny as they wanted, but I didn't have the words and instead I found myself caught up in the fact he was so pissed, while at the same time being sexy. With me in the road, and him still on the sidewalk, the gap between us narrowed a couple of inches, but he was still shorter, cuter, sexier, and I had to concentrate before I did something about this inappropriate and useless attraction.

Maybe I could be what he wanted for a night so I could get a taste of him, be the kind of cowboy who was all toppy and in-charge. I could pretend to enjoy it, because at the end of the day getting off was getting off, and my recent lack of shared orgasms was starting to make me think I would do anything to get sex. Then I had a blinding image of me picking him up, with his legs wrapped around my waist, pushing him against a wall, and that was it, game over. I moved back to hide my erection, wishing I could get my hand in my pants and free my cock, given it was being strangled by worn cotton.

"Give me my bags." He held out a hand, and then shrugged as if the shirt he was wearing didn't fit as he wanted. Pale rose and peach plaid, it was shorter than my shirts, but I had to admit that he looked very nice, all pinked-up like that, with his hair caressing the collar. I could've pushed his hair aside and kissed his neck, and he would've smelled of—*stop*.

He was past flushed and straight onto scarlet with temper, or embarrassment or something violent that stopped my thoughts in their tracks. I wanted to hug him and tell him everything was okay and that I wasn't laughing, but I fought the stupid instinct. Instead, I checked both ways and then crossed to the hotel, aware he followed me after a few moments, because he was clomping in his boots. We reached the door and I opened it for him as he muttered under his breath and then stopped just inside.

"I need my bags back."

"I'll help you to your room."

"That's not necessary. Just leave them here and I'll come back down for them."

"You can't leave them here. Someone might steal them."

He glared up at me and then narrowed his eyes in

suspicion. "You're telling me that sleepy old Whisper Ridge has a bag-robber problem?"

"Out-of-towners bringing crime across town lines, yeah." I kept a very straight face, but his suspicion didn't give one iota.

He shifted some of the bags he carried then shook his head. "Pass them to me, I'll be fine."

"Yeah, not doing that."

"I won't fall over if you don't trip me."

"I was nowhere near you when you nearly fell off the sidewalk."

He raised an eyebrow and shook the bags he was holding to indicate he wanted the others.

I switched tactics. "You ever play that game with the donkey, and you put bags on its back until it bucks?"

"Huh?"

"That game, you ever played it? The prospector with the buckets and things."

He was so confused. "You mean Buckaroo?"

"Yep. That donkey is you."

His eyes widened, and I thought for a moment he might smile, but he bit down on that real hard, and instead he glared up at me, blowing an errant layer of hair that had settled over his eye before tossing his head to dislodge it.

Do not tuck his hair behind his ear. Do. Not. Do it.

"Fine," he snapped ungraciously, and then flounced to the stairs, and stomped up them with all the attitude of a teenager being sent to his room. At least I got a look at his ass as it was at my level, and I had to admit I waited long enough so that would be possible, given I was a couple of steps taller than him.

He walked with so much attitude, as if he was daring me to fuck with him, and a small part of my irritation that he'd be up in my face at the ranch, slid away. He was mostly harmless, and I could handle that just fine. He dropped the bags at the door and fumbled for the key, not quite able to get it into the old-fashioned lock and muttering again.

I placed the bags on the floor, took the key, and turned it easy enough, opening the door into a suite. There wasn't a bed in this part, but there was a tiny kitchen area, a sofa, and a table with two chairs, plus a huge television, and two closed doors that I assumed were to the bathroom and a bedroom. This was Whisper Ridge luxury, but then nothing but the best for Quinn Rhodes with his expensive-looking car and his city vowels.

He gathered the discarded bags and then stalked into the room, dropping them onto the sofa then turning back to get the ones I held. Only I was right there behind him and placed them next to his. Then I took off my hat, and straightened my hair, because this was me in polite mode.

"Anything else I can do for you, Mr. Rhodes?"

"Stop making me fall over." He was all fiery eyes and irrational beauty, with his arms crossed over his chest and standing at full height, which with the boots, he was maybe an inch taller than yesterday. *An inch closer for kissing.* My gaze tracked down, from silver eyes to full lips, and then back up, and I could see the emotion in his troubled scrutiny of me. It wasn't so much anger now as defensiveness, and his posture screamed that he was wary of me. He wet his lips, his gaze dropped to my lips and then back up to me, and the heat in there surely wasn't just anger. We had that golden moment where he assessed me, and I stared right back at him.

"I didn't make you fall over," I defended as gently as I could.

He sighed with attitude. "Then why is it whenever I see you, I end up with my ass on the ground?"

I couldn't help the snort of laughter. "Pretty men are always falling at my feet," I flirted, and he went scarlet. I regretted the words as soon as I said them. Flirting meant interest, and he might get the wrong idea.

What if I want him to get the wrong idea? What if he turned to me and said that he wanted quick and dirty sex and was I up for it? He might not have been a long-term proposition but going to my knees for him and then him returning the favor… where was the harm in mutual blowjobs? *Because he's a client, and I can't mix business with pleasure.*

"Pretty men are stupid then," he muttered, but there was no heat in his words.

I had to push because I was an idiot, and his lips were so shiny to kiss. I didn't go around kissing everyone, but I sure as hell was happy to steal a taste of someone who looked as sweet and was plainly out and proud as Quinn. I leaned over, pretending to shift a bag, which left me super close to his pouty mouth, and I could just move that little bit closer. I watched for signs I was freaking him out, ready to retreat, but if anything, he leaned into me, and we were *this close* to a kiss when his expression changed. Connection became denial, something I was acutely familiar with, and the fragile link of attraction that had whispered between us vanished in an instant.

"Out," he ordered.

I put my hat back on and then tipped it before strolling out of the door. "You're welcome."

"Thank you," he muttered. He sure did a lot of grumbling around me, and I could hear his added curse through the closed door.

Boy, his feistiness was making my blood flow south as fast as I could think. He was confusing, irritating, sexy, cute, and everything I craved.

He's the client.

Fuck that. It's not my ranch, I'm just the hired help, I could take sex where I got it—even with the man paying us to train his boss's horses.

Only, that way lies madness.

Chapter Eleven

QUINN

"Fuck!" I said to the empty room, and slumped to the sofa, causing three of the packed bags to tumble down and the contents to slide out. "I'm an idiot." I was miserable. I didn't need or want any kind of attraction that took my eyes off the project in hand, but there was something about Levi that had me daring to think I could hook up in this small town, and not get burned. I wasn't there to have sex, and even if I was, some big tough cowboy who was out searching for a new twink to carry around was not on my to-do list, especially one who tied my stomach in knots, and made me harder than steel just by looking at him.

I needed to reset my emo level and return to worrying about what I was going to find at the ranch, and whether I was an uncle or not. All I could think about was amber eyes, and the puff of Levi's breath on my face when we'd been so close that I thought we were going to kiss.

I glanced at the bags and bags of what Jim had said were cowboy essentials, and I knew I didn't need half of it. Only, as we'd gone around the store, I'd realized the shelves were tatty, the till old and barely working, and I'd felt compassion for Jim, and his curly moustache, and what I assumed were narrow profit margins. Also, he was genuine and attentive, not fake like in the high-end boutiques, tailors, and fashion stores where I'd get my clothes back in Boston. He measured and poked, and made suggestions, and warned me about the stiff boots, and gave me some cream to use on the leather. By the end of the buying session, I picked up cute sequined shirts, one with tassels, and the shirt I was wearing that he'd explained was designed for a girl to wear. Never let it be said that I can't wear peach, lemon, or mauve. It came in those three colors, and I bought one of each, along with one of everything else and a ton of extras. Apart from saddle waxes—I got two of those because I couldn't have enough of that.

I think.

I could ride, I'd had lessons as a child, and had spent every summer at Molly's family's farm. I knew cowboys, I knew horses, but I'd never let myself care about a horse since Daisy. The cowboys fixed my nameless horses, I rode, I sat around and watched the cowboys at the farm, but I hadn't put my heart into it. Safer that way.

"I've never used saddle wax." I startled myself and realized I was talking to an empty room and slid even farther down the sofa. Because I was losing my shit and to top off the spending spree, Levi had appeared—the sexy-as-fuck cowboy with his watchful gaze and the way he stood, loose and sexy and so in control. I wanted to climb him like a tree. Of course, he was also stubborn, irritating, and laughed at me, but I got the sense he wasn't out to hurt me, just that I was a fish out of water, and he found it funny. Or cute maybe.

Levi was a distraction I didn't need, and I knew that my irritability with him was half my fault and half because he was insanely sexy and hot and what I *really* wanted to do was steal a kiss. *Then bend him over the nearest surface and—*

My cell vibrated, as it had been doing since Jim had started showing me around the emporium of all things cowboy. I had a suspicion it was Molly because whoever was trying to get hold of me was insistent, and she would have spoken to her dad by now and found out what I'd done. Also, apart from Connor, I didn't have many other people left in my life after I'd cut myself off from the family name and, more importantly to others, the family money. I'd soon found out who my friends were after the public sale of my stake in Dawson Pharma, not to mention my then donating the entire amount to charity.

Not that it left me penniless, after all, I had my trust fund, but it wasn't as shiny as the influence I could have welded inside Dawson Pharma. With only my trust to my name I was seen as just another spoiled rich kid without any influence.

Checking my phone I saw I was right to think it was Molly. I'd received four voicemails, ten texts, and a long rambling WhatsApp message with added emojis and a gif of a dude giving the finger, asking me what the hell was going on with her dad and what the hell did he mean about me buying horses. Her words were flowery with a lot of expletives, and guilt poked in my chest.

If I'd told her about going behind her back to talk to her dad, and about the investment in the horses then she would have stopped me somehow, citing that she was worried about me and my inability to think small. I'd rather ask for forgiveness than permission when it came to Molly, but when I read the final message that called me a shitty friend who hadn't told her what was going on, I knew she was right. Given the amount of cursing in the messages I suspect wine was involved, because the shitty friend became a love message about how she missed me and when was I coming home? I knew that what I needed to tell her would leave her worried, but I didn't want people worrying about me anymore, because I was a grown-ass man who controlled his own destiny.

She picked up the instant I called. "About time, Q," she snapped. "I get here and the first thing, *the very first* thing, my dad says is that he's had horses sent to the Lennox Ranch for training and that it was you who asked him to do it, and not only that but Connor knows all about it as well? What in hell's name is going on with my dad and you buying horses, and why did I only hear about it now? And why did you tell Connor who has only been on Team!Quinn for six months when you didn't tell me, and I've been your friend for twenty freaking years!"

That was a lot to unpick. "I told Connor because he had to do security stuff, and I told your dad not to tell you until I was here at Whisper Ridge because—"

"You're a shitty friend—"

"Please listen," I pleaded so she'd stop berating me for being an idiot and then, on speakerphone I let everything

I wanted to say tumble out like rocks over water, all chaos and noise.

I cleared my throat. "Before I left Boston, I went up to see your dad and he bought me two horses, one is this beautiful feisty sorrel colt called Sunny, and the other is a roan mare and her name is Glimmer, and they were so hard to get and cost me a shit ton of money that I paid your dad back through something Connor set up. I got them so I could leave them at the ranch as a gift, an investment to make sure that Rachel had something of Max, whether Laurie is his son or not." This wasn't how I'd intended to explain it, and my tension headache was back.

"She has access to money if she needed it. I'm saying this one last time, give her Max's money and stay away."

"No, I can't. Money destroyed my brother, bought him the drugs he needed, killed him. I won't do that to them. We've discussed this over and over—"

"Then you should stay away."

"I can't. I have to know."

"You bought two horses—"

"Look, I figured with what the horses could be worth, and trained they're worth even more, I could leave them here, but it also gives me a chance to see Laurie better without anyone being suspicious."

"Quinn—"

"It's easy because the Lennox Ranch thinks I'm there representing your dad, I'm not even using my real name, I'm Quinn Rhodes here, and I'm staying incognito until I meet up with Rachel and see Laurie for myself. The horses are being delivered to the ranch today, and I didn't tell you because I know you'll think I'm doing this all wrong." Everything spilled out of me in a rush, but she didn't immediately reply and for a moment I wondered if the call had disconnected. I even checked the screen to make sure.

"You're an idiot," she summed up.

"Micah Lennox is one of the best trainers and your dad arranged for the horses in his name to get sent over to the Lennox Ranch, and then he got this other trainer referred to him, Levi his name is, and I've met him and he's…" *gorgeous, dangerous, sexy.*

"He's what?"

"Good with horses." *I assume.* "It's all good, because as your dad's official representative I get to hang around the ranch, because who would believe that I owned horses myself. I mean, have you seen me?"

"Quinn—"

"I love that your dad helped me; I wish he was my dad."

"Oh, babe," she murmured, and I heard and felt the softening in her tone. "You know he loves you."

"Don't be angry with him, it's my fault." I changed the subject before she could agree or disagree. "So did I say the horses get there today?"

"You did, and I refuse to be interested."

"But you *are* interested."

"You're an idiot."

"You already said that."

She sighed so hard I bet she'd gone blue in the face, but then she let out another sigh and it was less angry and way sadder. "Oh, Quinn," she said. "I love you but…

you're going to get attached, and then what happens when the two-month cover story is up? You said you wouldn't stay, you said money corrupted absolutely. You said—"

"I know what I said."

"So, what changed?"

I refused to think about a time when I wasn't incognito, because the freedom of being Quinn Rhodes was intoxicating. "I know enough about horses to work up there with them if I can. I can be there, and observe Levi, the trainer Micah hired, and just *happen* to meet Rachel and Laurie. They wouldn't have to know who I was; I could check everything was okay for Laurie. Then I promise I will leave, because that is what's right and no one would even know I'd been here, and she and the kids would be safe from the media." Everything spilled out as I summarized my thought process, and as I heard myself, I knew it was a mess, but I needed Molly to tell me it was all going to be okay. Because I'd met Rachel too soon, and I hadn't been prepared to see her. My chest was tightening, and I doubled over to breathe, suddenly hit by how much had gone wrong so far.

She sighed. "Only you, Q, only you."

"It's all gone wrong though." I hated to admit this because that meant I wasn't in control. "I had this idea just to check out the ranch from a distance, but this truck hit me and so I've actually met Rachel and I was wearing a suit. And my hair is still bright pink and—"

"What?"

My words died in an instant, because Molly had a way about her that stopped me when I was in full steam.

"What do you mean you got run over by a truck?" Molly asked.

"Just a soft bump is all," I dismissed it casually as if I didn't ache like I'd done five rounds in a boxing ring. "It's fine. Anyway, you should see my horses." I hugged myself because whatever I was doing, they were the most beautiful horses I'd ever seen and the fact that I'd invested in something so utterly perfect filled me with happiness. "I'll send photos, but I have two of them. Just two. It's a great cover story and a win for the Lennox family when I leave them."

"Oh yeah, that will go down well, they'll be asking why you were leaving the horses, and of course it goes back to my dad, who I bet knows nothing about that final part of the plan."

I swallowed my nerves. "No, not exactly *all* of the plan."

"Well, fuck, Quinn. You, Connor, and I talked about this, and you explicitly said you were going to stay in a hotel *for a few days* and *visit* the ranch."

"Hmm, well I'm in the hotel, so that's one thing." I checked out my perfectly wonderful, if worn room, and hugged myself that I was in a place where no one knew where I was. "We don't even know if Laurie is Max's son, and I didn't see him yesterday, so it might take a while to connect," I reminded her, even though saying the words was a physical pain. I hoped… I wished he was Max's son, so much that it hurt, and I was desperate to meet him.

"Couldn't you have just stayed in the hotel and asked for riding lessons or something if you needed a reason to hang around? I thought you were just going to see Laurie, then leave. *That* was the plan."

"That wasn't enough to let me be up there as much as I wanted to."

"I get it, I just don't like it," then she cursed softly. "I love you completely, but this could go badly wrong."

"You don't have to tell me that. I know." I went to the window as we talked, staring down at the town. It wasn't the best view of the mountains from there, but I had a birds-eye view of a quiet main street and watched as a group of people stopped to talk when they crossed paths. Whether Laurie was my nephew or not, whatever the outcome of my place in Rachel's life, or that of her kids, I felt good in a town that wasn't the city. I could've lived somewhere like this, particularly if it came with stoic and enticingly muscled cowboys like Levi. If I didn't stay there, then I was determined to find somewhere like it, and had fantasies of log cabins and beautiful isolation.

For now, I was focusing on Lennox Ranch. I'd learned as much as I could about the place—or at least everything that was public knowledge, and some extra information from Connor. He was specific about the Ranch having three thousand acres, no cattle now, run-down and needed a lot more investment, had new horse-training facilities, and that it was owned by Micah, horse trainer extraordinaire, and his sister Rachel.

I couldn't help it if the cold, hard facts jumbled in my head, and that I'd created this fantasy where it turned out that I was an uncle, and that Rachel knew who I was, and then I could be part of a real family. Living in a house with a large lawn and a wraparound porch, making them breakfast, taking Laurie and his little brother fishing.

Not that I knew how to fish, but I could learn, because it seemed to be a thing kids might like? I could be fun Uncle Quinn, go to all their school plays, help them with homework, support their college teams, sit in the front row at their weddings, hold their children and be Great-Uncle Quinn. I would sacrifice everything I had, and everything I was going to be, just for a small taste of that kind of family.

That fantasy was crystal-clear, and sometimes it hurt so hard to think of it that the grief that it wouldn't happen left me breathless. Molly and Connor didn't know what I had created in my head, because that perfect family was my happy place for moments when the heartache of knowing Max was dead was too much to bear, and I was holding it close.

"Promise me you'll be careful?" she finished, but I was sure that wasn't what she'd meant to say at all. She never held back on telling anyone what she thought, including me, but I hated that she thought she had to be cautious with me. "Don't let this spiral, and if you need me, I can be there in… I don't know, but I'll be there as soon as I can. Greg will drive me."

"To Wyoming?"

Greg snorted a laugh in the background.

"Yep, you know you love me," Molly deadpanned, and there were kissing noises, and it made me smile, until the enormity of the conversation swallowed the smile when she started up again. "I worry about you, Quinn."

"It's just some horses," I offered lamely, and she sighed.

I couldn't focus on the negatives, because I was utterly convinced everything was going to go right.

Or at least I'd fooled myself into thinking nothing could go wrong.

"Just tell me if you have your smile back for real yet now that you're away from Boston."

I glanced over at the mirror but couldn't see myself from this angle. My real smile, and all the tears trapped inside me, had been lost for so many months. At least I'd forced my approximation of a smile out for the world to see—Molly was the only one to see through the mask.

"The horses make me glad, the sky here is so big, and the mountain? You should see the mountain." *And I'm so excited to meet Rachel again, and hopefully to get to meet Laurie.*

"That wasn't what I asked."

"I know, and I promise you just from getting out of the city I already feel easier, and I'll be okay." I didn't confirm the smile part because she didn't mean the smile I gave the world. She meant the smiles that started in the heart—and they'd been few and far between for so long.

"Keep your head down," she cautioned, and I knew what she was saying, that I needed to focus, then she softened her warning. "Love you, Q," she murmured, and affection flooded me when she used the nickname she had for me. I was always Q to her, even when my parents refused to call me anything other than Alexander.

"Love you, too, Molls," I said easily.

"Everything will be okay," she added, and I felt marginally better.

Talking helped, but jeez, I still needed a hug.

Chapter Twelve

LEVI

I COULDN'T GET QUINN OUT OF MY HEAD. I TRIED TO ignore it, but when he'd tripped off that sidewalk and I'd caught him, he'd felt so perfect in my arms, and he'd smelled of new leather and citrus, and I wanted to hold him there just to inhale his scent.

His scent for fuck's sake.

I tended to have a type on those few and far between nights when I got to a bar, or I worked alongside a cowboy, and we killed time with blow jobs after dark. Taller than me for one, stronger maybe, the kind who might boss me around and take me out of myself. Dark hair and moody was also a thing, in fact the person I was describing to myself was the definition of Micah. I'd always been drawn to grumpy-ass cowboys with dark eyes and shitty attitudes, who were passing through. Take it or leave it kind of men who were as free-spirited as me, and not searching for anything past a tumble in the barn, or the back room, or bathroom at a bar.

So yeah, happy smiley smaller dudes with bubble

butts, pink hair, and a smart line in sass were stereotypical needy guys with attitude I didn't have time for, and that was the line I was drawing in the sand. Even if Quinn danced like a sexy ballerina across the road, made wearing a Stetson sweet, or wore his new boots like a boss.

Sweet. *Fuck's sake Levi, get a grip.*

I tried and then gave up because he was taking up too much real estate in my head when I should have been focusing on the new horses and on Micah explaining this, that, and everything else. I drifted away again. Quinn was a study in opposites, real cute even when he was all flustered and irritable, long hair in his face and pale eyes sparking with temper. Boy, he'd hated that mannequin and the way it had attacked him, and I shouldn't have laughed, because that had gotten him even more riled up. Then I'd done the most incredibly stupid thing of my entire damn life, I'd pushed some of that soft loose hair behind his ear. I mean, who even does that shit? Not me. If hair gets in the way, then you grip it hard, so it doesn't get tangled around your cock. Simple. Then when I'd seen him with the bags I didn't need to go over and talk to him. I could have left him to it, but I was drawn to him like a moth to a flame.

A pink, glowing, dancing flame.

"You done?" Micah shoved me.

"Huh?"

He waved a hand in front of my face. "That whole staring-into-space show you have going on?"

I ignored Micah's tone, a mix of sarcasm and exasperation, and blinked at him steadily, daring him to suggest I wasn't paying attention. He lifted an eyebrow in the most sarcastic huffy expression he could, and I ignored him, then opened the gate to the first corral, waiting for the guys to unfasten the right door to the trailer. The first horse out—a sorrel with a temper wasn't at all cautious—he was fire, brimstone, and fuck-you, but he was beautiful. Closing the gate pissed him right off and he snorted his displeasure and pawed the ground as if he was on his way to digging out.

"Have you considered you're just boring, Mikey?" I snarked, and he rolled his eyes which seemed to be his default setting where I was concerned.

He ignored me then and consulted the paperwork. "Sundance Invitation, Sunny, nice bloodline, good buy," he murmured and then gazed at the newest arrival with a frown. "He's a long way past ornery and straight through to being a bastard," was his conclusion.

"Yep," was my summary. Sunny was going to be a handful and no doubt about it.

The guys moved the trailer a short distance, aligning the door up to the next space, a little farther up toward the house, quite separate from where Sunny was currently letting the world know he was pissed.

The second horse, a gorgeous roan, was more cautious getting out and down into the fenced-off area, immediately she hit the ground she headed for the farthest point from the truck, and us, then stayed there. It was as if she was letting Sunny have all the angst with his tantrum and was choosing to fret quietly.

"Glimmer Lena, aka Glimmer, again, good blood. We're lucky to have these trained at the L." Micah sounded proud of himself and given that he was looking to expand Lennox Ranch I would've said he deserved to take that pride and wear it however he wanted. With Glimmer and Sunny, there were now four horses for training, and we were going to have our hands full.

"The owner's rep will be here in ten," Micah said, giving the tail end of an unspoken thought.

"Yep," I popped the p with emphasis.

"Quinn Rhodes, I mean."

"I know who you mean."

"The one you ran over." I side-eyed Micah and could see he was messing with me, because his lips were twitching with a need to laugh. "I finally got him to sign an accident report, although he's adamant it was his fault."

"It kinda was."

"You gonna be polite when he gets here?"

I glance at Micah again and raised an eyebrow. Of course I was going to be polite, after all Quinn was the rep for the owner and as such we should respect him.

Laughing at him in a pile of saddle wax tins probably wasn't a good start.

"Yes, Mikey, I'll be good."

"He's a strange one." Again, he wanted to talk.

Normally I'd have had something to say. Maybe about how Quinn was nothing like I'd have expected of someone representing a serious horse owner. He wasn't a cowboy, he wore suits, his hair was all over the place and soft as down, he was a flighty, light on his feet, dancing fae, that was all I'd come up with. I had my money on him being a former pop star because he looked like one of those flicky-haired guys from a gay comic. Not that I'd seen a lot of those, but enough videos on YouTube that the pink hair and the emotion in his eyes made it seem as if he wasn't of this world.

Also, I was getting hard at the thought of him being in my damned lap.

"What do you think?" Micah nodded at the two arrivals, both in their individual spaces acting like I expected. They'd been used to freedom in their pastures, and abruptly their worlds had narrowed to what we had.

Glimmer was an edgy mare, eyes wide, ears twitching. I'd seen a ton of issue like her, all out of the Poco Lena line, but she was throwing glances that spoke of desiring connection, only panicking with fear. The default setting for any horse was terror, that was half the battle—they were prey animals and expected danger at every turn. Some confronted it like Sunny, and some needed to be shown they could trust, like Glimmer. She'd be okay, Micah and I could handle scared, and we'd seen worse. Horses like Glimmer were a joy to work with once a cowboy had their trust.

On the other hand, Sunny had this suspicious but calculating gaze—nothing coy about him—likely hatching his first escape from the pen. He had a defiant stare, and I tilted my chin at him. Respect where it was due, he'd be the one that would hold stubbornly onto independence, and when gentled he would still hold that life. I liked his spirit, it reminded me of Blake when I'd found him at a sale. Blake had been mistreated, and I'd handed over every cent of a summer's work on making him mine because I couldn't resist the pain and passion in his expression. We'd butted heads like I couldn't believe, his haughtiness remained even now, but Blake had generously allowed himself to be gentled enough to partner me, and I would have put money down that Sunny would be the same.

"I might turn Blake out in the field next to Sunny," I murmured.

"You seeing a connection between them?"

"A shit ton of defiance." I rested a foot on the fence.

"I've decided you'll focus on them," Micah said, as he read from the notes. "I'm already tied up with the two from—"

"I don't think that's a good idea," I interrupted. What I wouldn't have given to get my hands on both newbies, learn their strengths, partner with them, but that meant I'd be talking to Quinn, and he was dangerous in more ways than one. What was the eleventh commandment according to cowboys?

Thou shalt not want to fuck the damn client… however pretty he is.

I wasn't a dedicated top who liked all that coy, flicky hair cute shit. Although he wasn't the quietly cute sort, not when he'd taken me to the ground in a flurry of motion and then sat on my cock. I was a switch, wanted to lose myself in a body as much as I wanted to be taken, and I wasn't seeing that working with pretty-boy.

"I'm not offering a choice." Micah side-eyed me.

I bristled. I was used to working alongside him, not *for* him, but it wasn't just that. I didn't want to be getting myself involved in any way with Quinn. I knew Micah was waiting for me to explain, because he was my peer, he respected me, and he *would* listen if I had serious reasons for not working with the new arrivals. What was I even doing? I was there to work, I had two stunning horses to gentle, and I was living the perfect life. The sun was shining, I had my horse, my dog, money in the bank. Why was I even standing there getting my pants in a twist over some weird attraction to an owner's rep?

"Just messing with you. It'll be fine."

I caught a flash of pink out of the corner of my eyes and glanced over to see Quinn walking up to the main gate. Thankfully, I'd noticed him well before Micah, which gave me time to get myself the hell out of the way. I headed directly to Blake, with Sky right on my heels. I was the paid trainer, and Micah was the boss, so I wasn't feeling too bad about abandoning him. I took up a position in the barn right next to Blake, where I could see through a crack in the door to keep an eye on them.

Who was I kidding? I wanted to stare at Quinn; to understand him or lust after him, I wasn't sure.

He was deep in conversation with Micah, gesticulating toward the stable, dressed in his new stuff, still with the pink hair falling in soft waves to his collar, and not contained very well by the hat. I bet the boots were stiff, surely not broken in, and as for the light denim jacket, it suited him fine, but it was snugger than it should have been, and there wouldn't be much space for layering when winter hit. As if he'd heard my thoughts, he slipped off the jacket, and rolled his shoulders, glancing up at the blue sky and smiling. I had this absurd regret that I wished I'd stayed out with Micah so that I got to see him up close.

This attraction was a burr under my saddle, exasperating me in a ton of ways ever since he'd sat on my cock and wriggled his ass, then fluttered his eyelashes at me and called me cowboy in that soft, sexy tone of his.

He was chatting about something that made Micah laugh, and I narrowed my eyes as Quinn patted Micah's arm, the man was an out and out flirt with anyone in jeans, that much I could see. *I'm not special.* Then I stiffened when Micah gestured to the barn and Quinn stalked my way, out of the sunshine and into the shadows.

"Levi? Are you here?" He stopped inside the barn door, and I was out of sight at this angle, hidden behind a huffy Blake with Sky tangled around my legs. I could've stayed right there and pretended that small and sexy hadn't walked in to mess with my life.

But I was an adult, and grown-ups didn't do that kind of crap.

"Mr. Rhodes." I stepped out of Blake's stall and tipped my hat, and the smile that lit up Quinn's face was blinding. I'd noticed earlier that his hair really wasn't so pink—at least not vibrant, a warm rose in this light, and his smile sent my blood south as quickly as you could say *oh fuck*.

"I said you should call me Quinn," he corrected me, glancing past me at Blake and his eyes widening as Blake snorted and tossed his head.

"Go slow," I warned. Blake was a grouchy asshole who'd eat small and cute for breakfast.

But no, Mr. Rep decided to make friends with my horse and slipped past me so fast I didn't have a chance to stop him.

"Oh, you're beautiful," Quinn crooned, leaning over the gate, and extending his hand to reach Blake. My entire life flashed before me. *Client gets bitten on day one of hiring local trainers.*

"Careful," I warned, and went to his side, ready to pull him away, but *what the hell?*

Blake was letting Quinn pet him, nosing back, all bashful and loveable, and then nudging his visitor, causing Quinn to laugh. Blake's ears pricked forward, but it wasn't in warning, it was as if he was curious about the laugh, and he nudged Quinn again as Quinn petted him to the extreme. I knew Blake well enough to see he was relaxed—he wasn't going to toss his head in that superior way he had, he wasn't going to bite, or stomp, or get himself all riled up. He was loving every bit of the attention.

"What's his name?" Quinn asked, and I joined in by scratching between Blake's eyes.

"Blake's Billy, Blake for short."

"Can you trace his line?"

"Loosely, but no, he's not the caliber of your horses."

"He's definitely special, look at his face," Quinn crooned and leaned farther over to press a kiss to Blake's nose. "What's on a piece of paper means nothing. Who your parents are doesn't make the pers—horse what they are today."

That was a heartfelt statement, and I got the sense it held more than what was on the surface. He was wrong though, because my parents had made me exactly who I was, when they'd dumped me with my aunt and uncle. Not that I was going to argue with Quinn, because doing that would've opened wounds far deeper than anything this casual chatting warranted. There was a reason it was just me, my horse, and my dog, because otherwise it meant I had to talk to people about serious things like feelings.

"So." He finally clambered down, and laughed again when Blake stepped forward to get more love, traitor. "Micah says you'll be working with Glimmer and Sunny."

"Yep."

"Where do you start? Micah said you'd be able to explain?"

I could've knocked Micah into Sunday for throwing me on the fence for this because I wasn't known for talking to the owners about the process. I was all about the horses, and I was damn good at my job, but explaining the intricacies of what I did wasn't in my wheelhouse. Neither me nor Micah were the sparkling cowboys who ended up on YouTube as freaking horse whisperers. We just did our job, and we did it well.

"Laying groundwork to develop trust." That much I could tell him because generally that was what I'd be doing.

"Spending a lot of time with them, stroking them, talking to them so you bond?"

I thought back to the intensity in Sunny's eyes, at the way his gaze bored into mine—I couldn't see much stroking and rubbing in the near future.

"With Glimmer maybe, Sunny not so much."

"Because?"

"Different horses, different techniques."

"Okay, makes sense."

Sky asked to be let out, and sat at my side, staring up at Quinn with her ears back. He went into a crouch and petted her, and she offered her paw, clearly recalling the previous belly rubs.

When he stood, Quinn was smiling so hard I thought his face might break. He had a very open expression, all smiles, and bright eyes, as if nothing in this world could hurt him. Maybe Blake and Sky were responding to Quinn's wide-eyed innocence and were drawn to him for that reason.

Not me. I could ignore all that shit, and there was no way I was rolling onto my back and exposing my belly any time soon.

"And you've met Sky," I said on a sigh.

"So, she's yours?"

Sky and I exchanged glances. "I'm hers," I offered after a pause, which made Quinn laugh.

Stop with the sexy laughing.

He brushed the knees of his new jeans, even though there was nothing there, and Sky took advantage, jumping at him for more love. He flailed awkwardly, and I caught him and tugged him close, so he didn't face-plant on the ground. He gripped me hard, yelped, and then relaxed into my hold. I didn't let him go. I didn't want to let him go. I wanted him right there in my arms, all safe and secure and smelling so good.

"Oops," he muttered against my chest, and then eased himself away before meeting my gaze. His hat was awry, and he moved it to settle properly, I saw him mouthing the two inches rule, and waited until he was all organized and back to normal. "My bad," he finally offered, his plump kissable lips curved into a smile.

"Like I said, I'm used to it."

He stepped past me, his hand brushing mine. I didn't think it was deliberate, but just that innocent touch burned me with a need to grab him and haul him in for a kiss.

"So, when do we start?"

"Start what?" I asked, still in post-Quinn-against-my-chest confused mode and wondering how I could get my cock to settle down. I hadn't been this horny and confused since I'd left home at sixteen and ended up losing the big V to a cowboy twice my age. Henry had been nothing but attentive all that summer, had offered me a job when I'd had nothing, and I'd fallen for his gruffness and his take-no-shit attitude. Of course, finding out he was married had put a damper on things —little had I known that his wife had been away visiting a sick aunt. He'd said it was okay, that she knew what he needed, and as long as I kept my mouth shut, I could stay.

I left then, the same as I'd left home, upset, determined, focused on never falling for that kind of crap again, and then I kept leaving. Every summer there was a new ranch, and each fall I'd head south and work somewhere with warmer winters. I honed my skills, I didn't make friends, and most of all I kept to myself. I'd gotten so used to it that this thing that I had flaring inside me for Quinn was a shock to my quietly hidden system.

"... working with the horses," Quinn petted I realized I'd lost track of what he was saying. Oh yeah, he'd said when do *we* start, and I wasn't following that line at all.

"There is no 'we,' Mr. Rhodes," I said. "You're here representing the owners, who pay us to work with their horses, until they decide what they want to do with them. Talking of which—"

He interrupted me with a shake of his head. "No, they pay *you* to work with their horses, but I'm here to oversee the entire process, so it only makes sense I get to be involved from the start. I want to watch, learn how you work with them," he supplied helpfully after a short pause. "So I can report back."

"I'm not a show you pay cable prices to watch."

"They're my responsibility, and as Mr. Ebben-Loner's representative here, he respects my opinion. I can always explain to him that I need to take them somewhere else if you don't feel you can work with me."

I rolled my eyes at that gentle threat, then checked his expression. I got the sense he didn't mean the words, and I could call him on it, but also that it was important to him that he was part of the process. I didn't need an audience of one; particularly when said audience was so distracting. But what if he was being serious and I'd fucked everything up for Micah?

He must have seen my dramatic reaction because he crossed his arms over his chest, tipped his chin and set a stubborn line to his lips. "I'll watch."

Jeez, he was as immovable as Blake.

But why did I get the feeling he was twice as dangerous?

Chapter Thirteen

QUINN

I WILL NOT CRUSH ON THE COWBOY. I'M NOT HERE TO GET what's left of my heart broken. I'm here to see Laurie, and then I need to leave. No inappropriate attraction to Levi.

By telling him I was watching, it gave me a heap of reasons to be at the ranch. I wanted to become a fixture of sorts, someone people expected to see there, and then I could strike up a conversation, *accidentally* get to know Rachel better, and then I could meet Laurie and I would be able to see if he was Max's son.

But first, with no sign of Rachel or Laurie anywhere obvious, I wanted to visit with my horses, and Micah had said that it was Levi who would be working with them, so it was Levi I needed to connect with. As much as I could connect with someone who had rolled their eyes at me, run me over with a truck, and ambushed me in a store full of Stetsons.

"Can we start by looking at my horses?" I attempted to hide my excitement, but I wanted to see Glimmer and

Sunny again, having only met them for a very brief time at the stables where I'd paid over the best part of a hundred thousand for them. Molly's dad had said they were the best, and I trusted him. The rest had been up to the stable I'd bought them from to connect with the Lennox Ranch for transfer but to see them here where I needed them to be, was perfect.

"This way," Levi murmured after a moment's hesitation where I imagined he was going to tell me to go away. He strode past the house and to the fenced-off corrals beyond. I saw sweet Glimmer first.

"She's so beautiful," I breathed, and leaned on the fence, peace trickling through my veins. I was on Lennox land, checking out my horse, and if I was lucky then today I might meet Rachel again, and maybe even get my first glimpse of Laurie. "You think she's good?" I didn't mean to sound unsure, but while I'd spent many summers at Molly's childhood home, I wasn't super confident in what I knew.

"Definitely. Sunny will be more of a challenge."

He gestured for me to continue up the hill, and we came to Sunny in all his bad-tempered glory. I leaned on the fence and stared at the horse who was pawing the ground and then stomping his way around the far side of the corral. Molly's dad had assured me he was the perfect buy, but I couldn't see how a horse as worked-up as Sunny would ever be able to be ridden, and part of me didn't want him to lose that spirit. Maybe I should say that to Levi? Or would he think I was an idiot? The whole point of having the horses there was to get them ready to be ridden, right? Increase their value, make them the best

there. What he suggested was way too long to wait when I was right down the road and ready to start my investigations. What was I going to do with my time? I guessed I could read or something, but how long did that take? Micah joined us before I could come up with anything reasonable which wasn't me walking up to the house and asking to see Rachel again.

"Everything okay here?" he asked.

I bit my tongue even as I saw the careful way Levi was looking at me. I got the feeling he was challenging me to speak to Micah about how he wasn't going to be starting fast enough. Instead, I went a very different route.

"I'd like to ride out and see the ranch, then maybe spend some time up here and relax. You know, city life is hard," I blurted, and Micah's eyes widened, not so much at the request as I'm sure that is what owners did, but more at my tone which was one-hundred-percent clutching-at-straws panicked.

"I expected you'd want a tour," Micah lied after a short pause. I got the feeling that the last thing he expected was me wanting to stay up at the ranch for seemingly no reason. "Levi here will show you around."

Levi cleared his throat. "A word?" he said to Micah, then gripped his arm. "Excuse me, Mr. Rhodes," he said to me, unfailingly polite, and then dragged Micah out of the barn.

"Call me Quinn," I reminded his back, but he didn't answer.

They were going to be talking about me, and I could stand there and wait for them to come back, or I could do something proactive like listen in. Sneak around. I was good at that. It was sneaking around that had given me the heads up that my parents were going to send me back to the facility when I was fourteen. Sneaking meant I'd gotten a head start on running to the city and hiding out in a hotel. Sneaking was a skill I owned, and I went close to a tiny gap in the barn wall. I couldn't see the two cowboys from here, but I could listen.

"… and that's typically the ranch boss's responsibility, *Mikey*."

"It's Micah, ass, and I can't spare the time, I'm at a critical point with—"

"He clearly knows very little about horses, I haven't got time to—"

"Levi, his boss is paying way more than he should do for the work here, enough for me to pay for you plus some. Hell, he's indirectly paying your salary."

"But it's not Quinn paying."

"Quinn is his representative."

"I don't need reminding, but what do you want me to do?"

"It's not hard, you'll be working closely with Quinn's horses, I'd like you to take this, work with him, keep him sweet. I wouldn't ordinarily ask this, and I know you don't owe me a thing, but please?" I heard a heavy sigh but didn't know either man well enough to know who the sigh belonged to. "If that's okay with you?"

I heard some low words, and thought I caught a soft curse.

"There's something off with him, he's edgy and all over the fucking place. He'll end up scaring the horses," Levi muttered, but the voice sounded nearer, and I scrambled back to where they'd left me, idly staring at the roof as if I hadn't moved at all. It hurt that Levi wanted to say no. Even though being classified as being all over the place wasn't a new accusation. I couldn't help it if I was overexcited by everything happening there, hell, I was vibrating inside with excitement at being next to him, and so close to the house and Rachel. But I kept my cool, because if I got snippy then I'd mess everything up. I needed to weigh up coming over as a demanding asshole against staying with Levi.

"Everything okay?" I asked with a ton of innocence plastered over the words.

What could Levi say? He was stuck, and when Micah made his excuses I was alone again with a resigned and frustrated Levi.

"Can you ride a horse, *Quinn*?" The exasperation that dripped from my name as he spoke didn't escape me.

Well, duh. "Of course."

He stopped himself before he rolled his eyes, but I could see he was having his own moment of irritation. "There's no 'of course' about it."

"I wouldn't have invested in horses if I didn't know…" I stopped stricken when I realized what I'd said, "I mean yes, I can ride."

"And you *can* saddle a horse?"

I went on the defensive, I may not have looked like a cowboy, but I had the spirit of a cowboy. Well, not *exactly* a cowboy, but I wasn't an idiot. "Yes."

"You take Beans." He pointed at a horse in the opposite stall, who twitched her ears at her name. I petted her, and thanked Levi when he dumped what I needed next to me.

"Hey, Beans," I crooned, and scratched her nose, laughing as the mare snuffled at my pockets in the hope of treats. "You're beautiful, aren't you. Let's get you fixed up and you can show me where you live." I knew it was stupid, talking to her as if she could talk back, but the only part of the vast Dawson property I'd felt happy in was around the stables that were nothing more than a status symbol to my parents. Neither of them went anywhere near them, and they were about as far from the main house as they could be, but there were horses and a ton of groomsmen and the odd cowboy type that I'd loved to follow around like a puppy. Not a single man or woman there had been unkind to me, and it had become my safe space.

I'd even had my own horse, Daisy, a beautiful mare that loved me as much as I loved her. Until she'd disappeared from the stables.

She'd made me gay. Apparently.

Forced on a troubled teen program to see if exposure to the elements and shock therapy cured the gay part of me that shouldn't have existed, according to my parents, I'd come home, and Daisy had gone. I'd been thirteen, Max had hugged me when I cried, but even with Daisy absent, I'd never stopped talking to the horses. I'd just never called one mine again. Glimmer reminded me of Daisy, not in looks, but in the way she was timid, shy, but curious as well.

I missed Daisy.

"You want me to get the tack done?" Levi sounded grumpy.

I wondered if I wasn't doing it fast enough for him, but I felt as if he was waiting for me to fall. I ran a hand down the mare's back and then picked up the saddle blanket. "I'm communing with the horse," I said and waited for him to laugh. He didn't, but he did leave me to saddle his own horse. "It's what a proper rider does."

Levi muttered a curse under his breath. Hell, could this cowboy have gotten any more lonesome-cliché-grumpy?

"I could have sworn I was paying *you* to be nice to me," I muttered, used to defending myself when people had issues with me. I used a combination of sass which escalated to feigned boredom if I needed it. Levi stopped dead in the process of walking over to where his horse was, and then turned to face me. I didn't know whether to laugh at his pained expression, be turned on at the way he stood there all stoic, or be scared that he was big enough to flatten me if he took me by surprise.

"My apologies, *Mr. Rhodes*," he said, as if he hadn't just that moment cursed at me.

I tucked my falling bangs behind my ear, knowing I'd messed up. My sarcastic mouth had gotten me in a lot of trouble because Levi had gone straight back to being annoyed with me, only this time with a layer of ice. "No, I'm sorry. I know the last thing you want is to chaperone me around the ranch when you could be doing other things."

He didn't soften, but he did incline his head to

acknowledge my apology, or maybe it was to agree with my self-assessment.

We saddled up then led our respective horses out to the yard front, and he tested his mount before checking Beans. He stooped to offer me a hand up, but years of gym and ballet had paid off in me having strong legs, and a ton of flexibility. In the blink of an eye, I had a foot in the stirrup and had swung my body up and over, landing as light as a feather on Beans' back, then stroking her mane and whispering sweet nothings. Levi didn't seem impressed with my agility, in fact he seemed pissed, but then maybe that was the default setting for him, pissed with a side helping of sexy. He mounted Blake as easily as I did, and I didn't watch his muscles bunch as his thick legs did their thing.

Well, I did, because he was ticking all my boxes—all apart from one of them. Or maybe two. Or three. Fuck. One, he looked at me as though he wanted to do something to me, but he might have wanted to hit me, two, was he even remotely interested, and be willing to let me try calling the shots at least once, and three… shit I couldn't even remember what three was. It fled from my thoughts when he clucked for Blake to move, and his flexed ass was right in front of my face. That and imagining me in control of all that sensual, hot… *I need to stop*. He petted Blake, who tossed his mane as if he wanted to get rid of the things holding him in place, but at Levi's murmured reassurance Blake settled for scraping his hoof on the ground and snorting.

Beans knew her thing, following Blake out of the yard and heading up the hill past Glimmer, and then up even farther. We were at the same level as the roof of the house, and I couldn't help noticing that the roof needed some work done.

I peered into the rear yard, fenced-off and safe, but couldn't see a sign of Laurie, or Rachel, and had to ignore the pang of disappointment and instead did my best to focus on the tour. I was struck with the beauty of the place; the scenery was stunning, the purple-blue of mountains as a backdrop, the tree lines swooping down to the farthest part of the ranch. Some fences were strong, others leaned back, and I didn't need to be an expert to see the work that needed doing there. I'd never fixed a fence.

I tightened my legs, encouraging Beans to catch up with Blake, and falling into a rhythm next to him.

"So have you been working at the ranch a long time?" I asked, not staring at him but back down at the fields where I'd seen the children playing yesterday. I was making conversation because I hated silences, but what I *really* wanted to do was guide this tour around every bit of the ranch in case we happened upon my nephew.

Maybe nephew.

"Not long," he murmured, and then edged ahead of me again, heading through a stand of trees. It seemed like this was going to be a silent tour if that was all I was getting.

"So, you're new then." What the hell did I just say? *So, you're new then?*

"You could say that."

"And you don't know much about the ranch?"

"I know enough," he pulled Blake to a halt, and I didn't even have to tell Beans to stop. "Does your momma know you're up there?" I thought he was talking to me, and I was about to deadpan deliver a monolog about my vapid excuse for a mother when I realized he was talking to a tree. Then I heard laughter.

"Yes, sir," a boy's voice came from the branches of the smallest tree, and I peered up through the leaves. Two faces stared back down, and my chest tightened. It could have been my brother staring at me, and my chest hurt from shock, grief, and a small amount of hope. I didn't need to be up close to know that he was my nephew. My heart stopped, and I knew.

I *knew*.

"So, boys, if I was to go down and ask Rachel where you were, she'd know you were in a tree that is full of broken branches?"

The first boy, tall and lanky with ginger hair and a broad grin, swung out on his branch, which cracked ominously. He ignored Levi standing in the saddle to catch him, and clambered down, followed by the other boy.

Max. He looks so much like Max that my heart can't stand it.

"I'm Archie," the red-haired boy said. "An' he's Laurie. Who are you?"

"You can't ask like that," Laurie whispered loudly.

"Think you'd better stay away from the trees now," Levi said.

Archie shook his head. "We're finding a place for a tree house." He crossed his thin arms over his chest. "Like a big one, with a ladder, where I can live when my momma is tired."

That story didn't make sense, but I could see the softening in Levi's expression, and knew there was something behind that throwaway line from young Archie.

"A tree house, yeah." Laurie nodded.

"Don't you realize how dangerous it is messing about in trees? Laurie, you'd best be talking to your Uncle Micah before you do sh—stuff like that," Levi settled back into the saddle.

"Yes, sir," Laurie said, and I waited for Levi to add some more, but it seemed he'd done his bit.

"And, Archie, I'm responsible for you when I see you messing about up here, okay?"

Archie blinked up at Levi, as if he couldn't believe his ears. "I don't need no one being responsible for me," he murmured.

"Yep, you do," Levi pointed out.

I got the feeling both boys were about to run, and I wanted to grab Laurie to get a proper look at him. I dismounted, and held out a hand, first to Archie so as not to make it obvious, and then to Laurie. Both boys shook hands in the politest fashion, but it was Laurie's eyes, and the way he smiled that pierced my heart. I didn't need a DNA test, this *was* Max's son, my nephew, I knew for sure. I wanted to cry. I wanted to grab him close and tell him who I was. I wanted Max right here next to me, proud and happy with his son.

I felt fierce with the passion of it all, my stomach in knots, my mouth dry, but I fought the urge to tell him. *I won't let anyone hurt you.* I knew with absolute certainty that I would do anything to protect Laurie from this world. Him and Rachel, and the baby. *Anything*. If I was never able to tell them the truth then I would live with that, because Laurie deserved a better life than his dad ever had.

Or me.

Laurie's smile was beautiful, and so many memories of Max flooded me. I had to stop staring and focus on making words that made sense, just casual hellos, nothing more.

"I could help you build a tree house," I offered, to the astonishment of myself, the kids, and Levi who growled.

"Kids, back down the hill," Levi ordered.

"Bye," Laurie called, and then the two of them ran toward the house, whooping like madmen.

I mounted Beans with ease, gripping the reins and waiting for the lecture. I was a total stranger offering to build a tree house for two kids, and the worst thing about that was that I wouldn't have known where to start building a tree house.

"Mr. Rhodes, I'm sure I don't have to tell you that the children are off-limits," Levi said.

"I was just—"

"You're here for the horses."

"I love building tree houses," I lied. *I love building tree houses. The fuck?*

He didn't listen to my weak explanation, instead, urging his horse up and out of the trees to flat pasture. He gave Blake his head, and Beans broke into a steady canter, as smooth as butter with a steady lope. I didn't have to work hard, which was a good job, because all I could think was that I'd met my nephew.

I should go straight to Rachel, tell her in no uncertain words who I was, that I knew Laurie was my nephew, and then I should leave.

But Laurie could be everything to me. He could be my sunshine, and a wide sky, and the future, and he was all wrapped up in my past. He was Max's son; I was his uncle for sure, and he wanted a tree house.

And I would've done anything for him.

Anything.

Chapter Fourteen

LEVI

Trees weren't safe if they weren't looked after, particularly those wild, tangled ones up there that had never seen any kind of maintenance. They needed cutting back before the winter storms, and I mentally added it to the fix list, knowing it would be going right to the top if I had my way. Along with the fencing in the top field, the track subsidence, the stream, the old barns, the house roof, maybe even more if I'd been staying longer than a summer.

Beans matched Blake stride for stride as I gave him his head, and only when we were nearing the easternmost point of the ranch, with the hill then the graveyard in view did I pull the reins to let Blake gather his composure. He was never happier than when he was speeding across open land, with or without me. We slowed to a trot, and then to a walk, Beans doing the same, and I side-eyed Quinn who was red-cheeked with pleasure and grinning from ear to ear. That had been the most unprofessional thing I'd ever done—what if Quinn had landed on his ass all because I was letting shit get inside my head?

"That was some tour." He laughed as he reached down to scratch and stroke Beans. I didn't think his grin could've gotten any wider, and there was excitement and happiness in his expression. "I forgot how good it is to ride."

I hadn't properly seen his form, given Beans was chasing Blake, but he knew horses, seemed comfortable on them, only I should have held back, given he was a client and there were a ton of health and safety implications with me racing off and letting him follow. I tugged Blake to a standstill by the creek that Micah had shown me on my welcome tour, explaining how a landslip had changed the course. We'd project-planned how we needed to clear the stones, build up structures, get the creek back on track, and for a moment I fixated on one of the largest stones we would need to shift. Half buried in mud, it clung stubbornly to the hillside, and the creek had formed a new offshoot that zigzagged through the softer earth. I expected it was faster-flowing during spring and summer rainstorms, but for now it was a slow-moving shallow channel of water.

"I shouldn't have let Blake have his head like that," I began, but Quinn glanced at me, and his grin didn't falter.

"I'm glad you did, because this place is amazing," he announced and released the reins, dismounting as though he was a trick rider, and then petting Beans who stood there leaning into the touch. "It needs some work though," Quinn observed, and crouched by the creek, "fencing, the house, and this creek needs stones moved. Not to mention the trees."

"If you're worried about how your boss's horses will be cared for, don't, the stables are some of the best I've seen, and the training facilities were created by Micah, and believe me he knows what he's doing."

"I didn't mean anything by it," Quinn apologized.

"Yeah, well," was about all I could manage in return. From the way Quinn was, it seemed like he had money—his boss probably paid him well—and the way he spoke implied he'd had more of an education than I'd had. I'd seen photos of the Ebben-Loner stables, and the people who owned them were some rich media couple and it showed. If someone wanted the movie-perfect image of a ranch, then it was Ebben-Loner they visited. On the other hand, the Lennox Ranch was grit and determination wrapped up in lack of money, which meant it needed fixing. The bones of it were good, not to mention Micah was one of the best horse trainers in the business, and now he had me for the summer. I felt defensive of the ranch, and that was an uneasy feeling to have because it either meant that the place was growing on me, or it meant that Quinn's opinion mattered.

Either way it was dangerous.

"Do Archie and Laurie play up in the woods a lot?" Quinn trailed his fingers in the water.

What that had to do with him I don't know, and instead of answering I leaned on the pommel and sighed. "We should get back." He stared at me and then stood, stretching up on his toes and then lithely jumping the stream and landing like a surefooted goat on one of the larger stones the other side.

"Just a while longer," he murmured and then pointed to the highest point of the rockfall. "I want to see from up there."

"It's not safe," I lied.

I didn't know when the rockfall had happened, and there was a ton of weeds and earth all mixed in, but what if the rocks were loose and he fell? He ignored me and clambered up more rocks that had slid and formed an outlook of sorts, then looking like a high diver on a board he stood at the top and tilted his head. "Stunning." It seemed as if he was communing with nature, soaking in the sun's rays same as I did, and when he took off his Stetson and then ran a hand through his hair, he made such an image that I couldn't tear my gaze away from him.

I slid out of the saddle and began to move. To do what I didn't know. Catch him if he fell? Hold back a landslide with my bare hands? "Get the hell down!" I ordered.

"Okay, I'm coming."

"Idiots who don't know better," I snapped, but after he took one final deep breath he slid down the nearest rock, tumbled sideways and then did this handstand thing that ended with him landing next to me as soft as if he'd taken a single step. "What the hell was that. You don't go climbing shit on a ranch when you don't even know if it's safe!" I was angry, to cover the embarrassment of being close to letting out a whistle at the sexy, confident man that was Quinn Rhodes. He shouldn't have been breaking unwritten rules as easy as he did, and I needed to pull up my big boy's pants and show him who was in charge.

"Sorry." With another athletic twist, Quinn was up in the saddle, and then with a twitch of the reins he turns Beans to head down the hill and back toward the house.

"Seriously, those rocks could have shifted."

"I didn't know," he called back at me.

I sped up a little to corral him, and grabbed Beans' reins. Eyes wide, Quinn sat back in shock. "Then you listen to the person who *does* know!" I was right up in his face, staring into his eyes, and all I wanted to do was yank him close and kiss him until he begged me to stop.

He bit his lip. "Okay."

Then he leaned toward me, and I was drawn to him, like a moth to a flame, a horse to water, a—

The kiss stole my thoughts, and it wasn't even a big kiss, just that small press of his lips to mine and then I could feel him smile against my mouth and I pulled back.

"What are you doing?"

He blinked at me and seemed confused. "I thought you wanted to kiss me."

I wiped my mouth with the back of my hand. "I didn't." I pretended as if I hadn't leaned in as well, and for a few seconds I could see he was deciding what to say, and I waited for him to call bullshit. He didn't say a single damn thing, only raised an eyebrow that was lost under his rose-colored bangs, and then he tugged the reins from my grip and headed down the hillside past the trail that led down to town through the graveyard Micah had told me about. I took a short moment to pull myself together then followed him down past my place, and the front fields that had been turned over to wildflower meadow. Who knew that riding a horse with a hard-on after a simple butterfly-weight kiss tinged with guilt was awkward and uncomfortable? Damn man shouldn't have been leaning in like that and stealing kisses when he wasn't entitled.

I shouldn't have leaned back. I let him kiss me.

"You didn't want me to kiss you?" he asked as we neared the trailer.

"It's not appropriate, no."

"I misread the signals," he murmured. "Sorry," he offered as we passed my home.

Signals? Had I been *that* obvious? "You didn't misread, it wasn't all you," I admitted after a pause. "It can't happen again. I'm here for the horses, not for kissing clients." I glanced back, but he was lost in thought, staring at the house, and I took a moment to *really* look at him. He was small but muscled, strong as well, after all he'd taken me down, and the way he'd done that backflip thing off the stones was enough to make me feel as if kissing was the least of what I wanted to do to him. He had muscles, and a flat stomach, and that damn hair… it was distracting me. He must have sensed me staring because he settled his gaze back on me, and I turned away as if I hadn't been checking him out. Awkward.

We finally reached the stables and I imagined he would hand me the reins to Beans as soon as we stopped but he was dismounting, had hitched his horse, and was already removing the saddle, undoing the cinch, and then fussing with Beans as if he was going to be the one to tend to her.

I didn't understand the way he was at all, and worse, I

didn't have a convenient label for him. He was so far outside my comfort zone that I felt all out of sorts. He messed with my mind and made me want things I couldn't have.

And that sucked.

We'd stabled the horses, done everything that could conceivably be done in and around the stables, and I could see that Quinn did not want to leave. It wasn't that he'd said he didn't want to go, but he was looking for things to do, tidying up, even taking a rake, and cleaning out Beans' already clean stall.

"So," he began, and glanced around him at the immaculate stall and then sighing. "I guess I'm done."

"Yep." *Man of few words strikes back.*

"Should I talk to Micah about the tree house?"

"If you have to."

Maybe he would get the hint and leave before I did something stupid. He was standing right in my space and making me itch with the need to drag him close and kiss his perfect lips. One taste was not enough, and I could imagine picking him up, his legs wrapped around me, and I could hold him, push him back against the wall, and we'd just take our fill of each other. *And then what, idiot?* We'd get off, and he would want me to be big and strong and call the shots, and I would want less of that and more equality, and then he'd stare at me as if I were stupid, he'd laugh, and then I'd feel like an idiot.

Wow. All that from the fact he isn't moving out of my space.

He seemed uncertain, then he nodded. "Okay then, maybe I'll do that. Thank you for the tour, I'll see you tomorrow."

It didn't sink in what he said for a few moments, but I caught on just as he was leaving the barn. "What do you mean, tomorrow?"

"I'm sure there are things you'll be doing with my—our horses." He seemed confused, as if he was shocked that he had to state the obvious.

"I said a week or more."

"Yeah, but I could stand with them and get them used to me."

"No. You're not fussing around me and randomly standing with the horses."

"I want to see everything."

"That's not how it works."

He put his hands on his hips. "It's what I—we paid for. Full involvement with the complete training experience."

"It's not an *experience* you can buy into." I refused to snap at him, but training didn't happen at set times in a day, and I had him there. "What if I walk out here at five a.m. just to get them familiar with me?"

"Call me, I can be up any time." He frowned. "I'm still at the hotel, but I can be here in fifteen minutes."

"I'm not calling you—"

"I'll give you my number."

He exasperated me, there was no other word for it. It wasn't just the absolute idiocy of what he was proposing, but my traitorous lizard brain was imagining him tumbling out of bed, all sleep-creased and warm, his hair all over the place, and stumbling up to the ranch.

"I don't want your number," I argued, but he wasn't listening. He came back to my side and bent his head thumbing through his details and then holding out a hand.

"Give me your phone, but remember, this isn't so we can hook up."

"We're not hooking up," I snapped.

"Which is what I said," he said with exaggerated patience as if I wasn't getting what he was saying, but I understood everything.

"And we're not doing that again."

"What?"

"Kissing. We can't do the kissing thing."

He appeared to consider me. "Would it help if I told you that you are the first person I've kissed in a very long time?"

"No it wouldn't."

"Ahh, you'd prefer it if I was the kind to kiss random men then?"

"No, I wouldn't. What I mean is…" I gave up because he lifted an eyebrow, and fuck, even his damn eyebrow was making me hot.

"Your phone?" he interrupted my soon-to-be-X-rated thoughts.

"I don't have a phone."

"Okay." He glanced around him, and I didn't know what he was searching for, because it wasn't as if there was a local cellphone shop in the barn. Then his eyes widened, and he headed for the chalkboard where the ranch kept chore lists and supply counts. With the tip of his tongue poking out, he wrote a long string of numbers at the bottom of the board, and then a dash, followed by his name. "That's me," he explained, and stepped backward, right into me as I peered at what he'd written. I caught him and some instinct had me dragging him close, the scent of him all around me. He spun to face me, and his wide smile didn't drop for a second.

"You're always catching me," he murmured.

For the longest time it seemed we were caught in each other's gaze, and all it would've taken was for either of us to move that final inch and we could've kissed again. We were lost in it, but before I did anything stupid, he tugged himself away from me and headed out of the barn.

Leaving me stunned, as if a tornado had passed over the ranch, lifted me up, shaken me to bits, and then dropped me ass-over-tail onto the ground.

I didn't kiss random strangers, even ones as pretty and sexy as Quinn. Kissing was for people who wanted connection and second dates. I didn't do either of those.

What was it about Quinn that had me in knots?

Chapter Fifteen

QUINN

I DON'T KNOW WHY THE KISS HAD HAPPENED. I'D BEEN SO happy to see Laurie, and when I'd seen my brother's features in him, I'd gone from excited to grieving, to confused and then excited again. Levi had been collateral damage to my happiness, but that kiss had been electric, and the way Levi had leaned into me, and offered me his lips, it was *everything* to my affection-starved soul and I'd taken it for much more than it was. I'd seen hearts and flowers and a rush of affection, and I'd *needed* that kiss. Only I'd misread the situation as usual, and crossed an invisible line, and I felt like shit.

I tried not to be a pain in the ass, but clearly, I was. I didn't even stop to ask Micah about the tree house, and I was all caught up in myself, too much to knock on the ranch door and maybe see Rachel. So, instead of asking, as soon as I left the ranch I headed into town and found the hardware store, which was tucked away in a side street and manned by a couple in their seventies who had forgotten more about tree house building than I'd ever known. They didn't seem to care who I was or why I was asking for supplies, they quarreled about what I should be doing.

"Keep weight and stability in mind," Ed warned.

Ed Lewiston and his wife June had been married fifty years this Christmas coming. I heard all of that in the first few minutes of arriving, and I felt immediately at home with the gently bickering couple.

"But it's vital that it looks good at the same time," June interjected.

"As long as it's stable," Ed repeated.

"Well Ed, now isn't it a given that it will be stable, the young man here won't be building a tree house that collapses on him, will he?"

Ed squinted at me, and appeared to agree that no, I wouldn't build a wobbly tree house.

"Hmmm," he said, "check the tree."

"He'll check the tree, Ed." June sighed. "Have you thought about diagonal bracing for the extra strength."

"Absolutely," I lied.

"It's easy to get carried away with ideas, but the load has to be on the base of the tree," June continued.

"To keep it stable," Ed added.

June side-eyed her husband, and I had to admit this was the funniest thing I'd seen all day.

"You'll need to cantilever the beams and support them from below." June scribbled that down on the page of a notebook, and then drew a simple design.

"I want something like they have in the Simpsons," I said as she sketched.

"Do we know them?" Ed peered at me over his glasses.

"Maybe he means the Sampson family over in Collier Springs," June said helpfully. "We know them, lovely couple, they have a dog called Cat, which is an odd name for a dog if you ask me."

Ed snapped his fingers. "I remember them, drive a Chevy."

"Yes, the blue one."

"Nice family," Ed stared back at me. "Friends of yours?"

"No, it's a show, a cartoon, with uhmmm…" Both stared at me as if I was talking gibberish, and they were right, I was. "Anyway, the tree house, sturdy, balanced, four walls, a window, a roof, cantilevered, balanced, and with uhm… diagonal bracing." They nodded and I'd clearly hit all the right notes. Then I blew it. "And a trap door with a rope."

June hissed her disapproval, and Ed sucked his teeth so dramatically I wondered if they would fall out.

"You need a properly constructed wooden staircase," June advised in a prim tone, and added a sketch of that to the page.

Hell, I hadn't even worked out how I was going to get the wood up to the trees to construct a house, *let alone* a staircase.

"Okay then, well I want to order all the wood, for a big tree house, six-feet-by-six-feet, tall, maybe eight feet? The lumber I mean, and nails, and a window thing, and a nail gun, or a hammer, and screwdrivers, and…" I turned to check out the shop with all its tiny containers of screws and nails, then back at them. "And whatever else you think I need."

"What is your budget?" June asked, her pen poised over the paper.

Jeez, how much was a tree house? I'd had closets built in the second bedroom of my Boston Bay apartment and that hadn't left me change from sixty thousand. Although that was special wood, or so they said, and it *was* Boston, so I scaled it down a bit in my head.

"Twenty thousand?" I said hopefully.

June hissed again, and hell, if Ed had sucked his teeth any harder then I'd have to have driven him to an emergency dentist for real.

"Is that not enough?" I asked, wondering if I'd insulted them. "Thirty? Forty? I'm not too worried about price." I pulled out my shiny new bank card and waited for them to tell me.

"A word, June-bug," Ed murmured, and tugged his wife through a door, which didn't hide their conversation at all. I caught most of it, including June getting very irate with Ed at the very idea of adding twenty percent because I was an out-of-towner, and something about Moira at the dry cleaners saying I had money. Guess they'd heard about me from that first bank meeting as the sheriff had said people would. When they returned June was smiling, and Ed seemed subdued as if he'd been on the end of a tongue-lashing.

"I'll cost it up for you, but I doubt you'll be looking at more than a thousand dollars," she said.

Ed whimpered a little.

"Is that with the extra twenty percent for out-of-towners?" I joked, and thank goodness, June got the joke because she huffed a laugh.

"No." She tilted her chin. "I don't hold with that nonsense however much money a man has, so that's our price."

I appreciated her honesty, and then decided to triple a lot of the stuff so that Laurie and his friend Archie could maybe help me. "Could you add in triple of the hammers and things, and an extra drill, wood for the stairs, and all that, and then call me when it's all ready. No wait, could you have the whole lot delivered to the Lennox Ranch."

"Lennox Ranch eh?" Ed nudged June who tried her hardest not to react, her face schooled into an innocent expression.

"Is the tree house for the boys?" she asked, and I wondered at that moment if I was walking into a well laid trap.

"Yes, ma'am." I'd removed my Stetson when I walked into the store, but I tipped an imaginary hat anyway.

I could see the gleam in her eye, and I knew that bit by bit she'd get to know enough to pass around Whisper Ridge. I hoped she didn't have Insta or Twitter, or knew how to stitch, then I'd be fucked. I forged ahead nevertheless because the tree house was my thing; my one shiny project that would leave a part of me with Laurie.

"How about I pay the thousand now, and you can let me know if you need more," I suggested, just to get her off the subject of where the supplies were going.

She peered at the list. "That's fine, but you understand it could be one or two weeks before we have everything in."

"That's fine, deliver it all in one go, and refer it to Micah Lennox."

"He's a good man," Ed said with feeling. "I don't hold with judging a man for his past just because he spent time in prison."

Prison? Huh? Molly's dad had never once said anything about Micah Lennox having spent time in prison. And he was around my nephew?

"Poor Isaac, though," June sounded sad.

That name rang a bell, Isaac, it was the name on the bridge, and it reminded me that I never did check into the name or the reason for the plaque. Only, if it connected to Rachel and Laurie, I wanted to know everything. Maybe I should ask Connor—he'd root everything out that I needed to know.

"They were young," Ed added.

June nodded. "So young. Anyway, let me take payment."

I was gutted that they spent ages talking about the Sampson family from Collier Springs but were all coy about Micah Lennox. Typical. Once I'd paid, I headed straight out into the warm afternoon with a thank you, and then I walked to the hotel to call Connor before I forgot again.

He answered on the first ring, as he always did—I really think he was taking working for me way too serious.

"Quinn," he acknowledged. At least he wasn't calling me sir, which was a step in the right direction.

"Hello to you too, how are you?"

"What's wrong?" he demanded, and I imagined him grabbing his keys ready to race here to save me from imaginary ninjas, the media, or worse, my father.

"Nothing's wrong."

"Then why are you calling?"

"I could ask why you're answering."

"Because you pay my wages."

"Good point, but nothing's wrong. I was being polite and asking you how you were, is all."

"So, what's wrong, do you need me to come to you?" That was Connor's impatient tone, the one that said he didn't have time for my shit, or indeed anyone else's shit.

"No, I need you to stay with Molly and run interference and keep an eye on my father and the media." I heard him curse, but he'd clearly covered the phone, so it was muffled. He hated this inaction, and I know he wanted to be by my side, but I was safe out here when everyone thought I was somewhere else. "I have a question about the background you ran on Micah."

"You explicitly told me *not* to run backgrounds," he reminded me.

Of course, I'd told him that, but I knew he'd run them, because he was Connor, and he was one hundred and ten percent behind keeping me safe. "So, you don't know anything about someone called Isaac?"

"No."

I could just tell he was lying.

"I *know* you ran backgrounds on everyone at the ranch, it's what you do. So, tell me what you know about Isaac, and what Micah has to do with this person, and do I have to worry about Laurie in connection with any of it?"

"Hang on," he said, and I heard the clatter of him collecting whatever he needed to be able to tell me what I needed to know.

"Okay, Micah Lennox, Isaac Jennings, and Christopher Sheridan. Car accident. Micah driving. Christopher lost a leg, both he and Micah suffered burns, seems as if Micah got his from dragging Christopher from the car. Isaac didn't make it. Micah spent a year in prison, but consensus is that the accident was a one-off. Christopher was being fast-tracked to a pro-ball contract, he's currently a high school teacher. Christopher is the brother of Daniel Sheridan who is now Micah's husband. Micah left Whisper Ridge after he got out of prison, but returned later with his pregnant sister, Rachel, plus of course, Laurie her son. Which is where I came into the story after being hired by your father to search for Max, when he heard I was looking for my cousin."

He delivered the entire story in monotone, but I detected pain when he got to the part about his cousin. He never spoke about Natalie, but I knew it must've killed him that she'd died, as much as Max dying affected me. I worked my way through the information, but there was nothing in there that I thought might put Laurie in harm's way.

"And your opinion?"

Connor huffed. "I met Micah, he was protective of his family, I didn't see anything that made me feel as if he needed to be watched."

"Did you run a check on Levi as well?"

"I might have," he hedged. "Do you need it?"

"No, jeez, I don't like that you even thought you had to do that."

"You hired me as security, I just took over from what

my predecessor was doing, which I'm telling you now was far worse."

Walking away from the family was freeing from all things Dawson, the media interest, the scandals, the things I'd seen and done, but I had to accept that walking away didn't give me real freedom. Connor had skills, and in all fairness to him he'd tracked down Rachel, he'd kept the knowledge of her and Laurie to himself and me, and he'd trusted me with that secret. I owed him everything. I hated he had to step over the edges, but it was the life handed to me, and I needed him.

With the call ended, and my worries about Micah eased, I immediately went into guilt mode as if I wasn't allowing myself any time to feel things were going okay. What right did I have to worry about Micah's past when it was nothing compared to what kind of things my dad had done? What if he ended up part of Laurie's life and Laurie came to his grandpa and said he was gay, or bi, or any one of the many things that colored outside Alexander Dawson's lines? The consequences of that were too horrible to contemplate.

After all, look what he'd done to Max.

Then me.

When I arrived at the ranch I didn't get out of the Lexus for the longest time as I tried my hardest to get my thoughts straight. Once I'd worked my way through my fears I focused on the positives, on Laurie first, because I was an uncle, and that made my heart lighter. I couldn't stay around him, but I could pay his way through college, I could help the ranch, I could do something *positive* for everyone here. My throat tightened with unshed tears, because all I wanted to do was hug Laurie and tell him all about his dad, all the good things that Max was, and all the things he could have been.

I miss you, brother.

From here I couldn't see the house, but the stables were right there, and I considered heading over first to see Levi, because maybe I wasn't in the right frame of mind to talk to anyone about freaking tree houses. Levi was creating space in my head for things that weren't life-shattering. There was no family angst, or grief, or pain when I let thoughts of Levi take up real estate. Our kiss hadn't been long, and he'd kissed me back, without a doubt. That was acting on attraction stage one, and I desperately needed to move to stage two, which in my mind was more kissing, for a much longer time. The sexy cowboy was a distraction that I should've ignored but didn't want to while I was on Lennox Ranch.

The path of my thoughts from pain to desire was unusual but it served to settle my panic, and I headed to the house, knocking on the door before my nerves got the better of me. I even had my practiced smile ready to go for if Rachel talked to me, then I could think rationally. Only, it wasn't Rachel who answered the door, but an older woman who eyed me with suspicion. She checked me out from head to toe and I felt the weight of her gaze as if she was judging me and found me wanting.

"Can I help you?" she asked as she wiped her hands on a dishcloth.

"I was looking for Rachel, ma'am." I removed my hat quickly, and her eyes widened at my hair, although she blushed after she realized she was staring.

"She's out with the boys and Scott," she answered.

Disappointment gripped me. I'd had this image of telling Rachel what I planned about the tree house and her smiling and being happy, and then Laurie hugging me maybe.

Never let it be said I don't dream up a million happy endings for my fucked-up days.

"How about Micah?"

"Up in the top field with the new horses."

"They're my horses," I said, with pride. She didn't seem impressed at all, if her pursed lips was anything to go by. "I'll go find him," I announced and stepped back, and then realized that she didn't know who I was. "I'm Quinn Rhodes, call me Quinn."

I extended a hand, and after a while she took it. "Don't know much about the *new* horses," she said with a curl of that thin lip. Maybe she was the only Lennox who didn't subscribe to the training as a way of getting Lennox Ranch stable. At last, she relented with the silent treatment. "Amy Lennox, aunt to Micah and Rachel. You can call me Mrs. Lennox."

I nodded and suspected that *Mrs. Lennox* was a hard nut to crack.

"I'll go on up then, ma'am." I backed away, waiting for her to tell me I couldn't, because she had *that* kind of face. She didn't say a word, and if I ever wondered what scurrying was, then I was doing it up the hill.

Only I didn't find Micah, I found something a whole lot better.

Levi. He was in a corral, with a crop and attached to it was a small flag, and he was waving it every so often at the horse's rump, the flag gently touching, just to get the beautiful animal to move in a smooth circle around him. I didn't approach, hid myself half behind a tree and watched. It wasn't one of my horses, but I was fascinated.

"I wonder if he'll get Lucifer to join up?" Micah asked right next to me, and I jumped a mile in the air.

"Holy…" I hoped I hadn't yelped that as loud as it was in my head.

"Sorry." He gave me a smile that was a little sheepish.

"No, it's fine, it's me, I was…"

"Hiding?"

"Observing," I corrected him. "I hope that's okay?" I glanced at him, and he didn't appear any different now I knew he'd been in prison, than he had before. Transgressions made at such a young age should be forgiven, that was the one thing I'd learned from being Max's little brother. He had a ready smile, and a confidence about him that made me feel as if Laurie would always have at least one strong uncle in his life.

Micah let out a soft huff of a laugh. "I reckon Levi will hate it, so feel free to go ahead and watch." He grew more serious. "Just avoid getting too close when he's working unless he says it's okay."

"I will. But, in general, you're okay with me spending time up here?"

"We have a lot of land, and the horses always need exercise."

"I'd like that, to help I mean. Also, the boys, I mean Laurie and Archie, were talking about a tree house, and I wondered if it was okay to build them one, give me a project in my down time?"

He eyed me with curiosity, as if he couldn't quite make me out. If he said no then I'd have to cancel the order, or donate everything to a charity, but I'd cross that bridge if I came to it.

"For real? A tree house?"

"Yeah, I mean, I'll cover all the costs and so on, but it could be a good thing for me to focus on, to find my center and my inner Zen. You know it's all about connecting with the earth."

His eyes glassed over then, and I think I'd bamboozled him with peace and love enough so that in the end he gave me another smile.

"Sure," he said, "ask Levi if you need help, or me, because we'll need to ensure it's safe."

"Of course."

He nodded, then headed down to the stables, and I watched Levi from my nice safe distance. I didn't know how long I stood there, but I observed every moment of what he was doing, every muscle that flexed, every calm, steady motion, the way he was strong in the center of the ring, the way he grinned when the horse, who was a quiet thing and didn't seem much like a Lucifer to me, decided to come to Levi and nuzzle him. I watched as he led the horse to a field beyond, petting and releasing him. And then he returned to the corral, to tidy up I guess, only he didn't open the gate. He did this climbing, leaping action, landing, sorting out what was in the ring, dumping it over the fence and then vaulting again, and I swear every molecule of blood collected in my groin.

All my worries, fears, everything, all disappeared in a second because this was innocence, this wasn't the mess in my head, this was just simple lust and it stopped me from second-guessing everything else.

Hell, I might as well make all the mistakes I wanted with Levi, then I could keep my head in the game with all the chaos I was trying to cage.

Because, in all my entire gay life, clubs, porn, my few and far between hookups, I had *never* seen anything as sexy as Levi vaulting a fence. I stepped out from where I was hiding, startling the shit out of him, to the point he clutched his chest, which in my lighter, playful, fuck-normal life focus, I found so ridiculously funny that I snorted a laugh. He stalked over, then stopped about two feet from me. We were hidden from the house and stables, and I wondered if this was the moment I'd pushed it too far. Laughing at a cowboy wasn't the way it should go.

"What are you doing here?" He glanced around him as if he expected me to be up to something nefarious.

"Watching you," I managed, but words were hard when I was faced with the sexy cowboy.

"I thought I said—"

"That was very sexy," I stumbled over my words, "the way you did the thing, and then the horse did the thing, and then you jumped the thing, the fence I mean." I was scarlet, I could feel the heat in my face. I needed to kiss him again, I needed to get my hands on him, I wanted to touch him so bad that I shoved him, and he stumbled back toward the tree I'd been hiding behind.

"The fuck?" he asked as he steadied himself, but I was too far gone into this safe space of not giving a shit about anything and just *enjoying* Levi, and I shoved him again.

"I want to kiss you again," I warned him briefly, and

then with one final shove, we were hidden from anyone who might casually pass by.

"Nope," he murmured, although he wasn't pushing me back, and his tongue darted out to wet his lips. Shit. That was so damn hot. I stepped back to give him a chance to stalk off, but I wanted a chance to show him that he didn't have to leave. "If I have a choice then it's a big no." He stared at me. What did he mean, *if I have a choice*? He always had a choice. Only there was something in his expression that made me think he didn't want to have a choice.

"Come on, cowboy, let's have some summer fun." I wanted to dive at him, but if he said no, I wasn't going to shove him again. I liked to have my time in charge, taking what I needed, giving the exact same back, I craved it, but he was a cowboy with attitude and confidence, and I was seeing this all wrong.

"You're a client and I—"

"Don't say another word that implies any kind of client relationship."

"I shouldn't kiss you. It's the rules," he muttered, his tone harsh, as if he had to force himself to say the words. It sounded to me that he was having doubts and maybe actually he did want to kiss me. Perhaps he didn't want to take the first step. Maybe he wanted *me* to make the choice for him.

"Then how about I kiss you first so it's not your choice, but mine?" I untangled his words, so it came from a different perspective.

He looked baffled but then determined. "I don't know that this is right." There was heat in his expression, and he pressed the heel of a hand to his cock, and I knew then that he wanted this as much as I did.

"What if I make that choice? Huh? Do you want *me* to kiss *you*?"

He removed his hat and dropped it, then lowered his gaze a little. "Fuck, I want it."

Shit. Was he really asking me to start this? Was he waiting for me? Seriously? I was expecting him to top the fuck out of me, but instead he was there, vulnerable, and so desperate for me to kiss him first. He was within my reach, so I didn't waste a single second.

I tackled him to the soft, mossy ground as gently but firmly as I could, protecting his head, and captured his lips with mine. It wasn't so much a kiss as him huffing a breath when he hit the grass and me stealing in to taste him when his mouth was open. He grappled for a moment, and then his lips moved against mine, his tongue tangling, and in a few seconds, he'd flipped me to push me down in the dirt.

"What if I'd said I want you to make me do everything," he muttered, but he was hard as iron against me. I was desperate to touch him, but he gripped my hands and held them flat to the ground, and I was pinned. "What if I said I *needed* you to push me?" All I heard was a chorus of freaking angels singing in my head. A big guy wanting me to be the one to push *him* around? Hell, that was every single one of my fantasies rolled into one. Some might've said it was me craving control when I'd had nothing like that power growing up. I just called it hot as the sun and twice as sexy when a man asked me to be in charge.

Not that it happened often outside of my fevered imagination, and I was momentarily lost in his amber gaze. My mouth was dry, my heart beating out of my chest, and he was watching me with vulnerability in his gaze.

"I can do that," I blurted. "I want that."

He loosened his hold, and in an instant, he was on his back, and I was the one on top, grabbing his hands and holding them above his head, shifting the grip until he was the one under my control. His eyes widened, and I wondered if I'd pushed him too far.

We stared at each other, and he was either going to push me off, and I'd let him up if that was what he wanted, or we were going to get off right there and then in the middle of a stand of trees. The pause was too long, and a million questions passed over his expression, but then he leaned up, and I leaned down, and with his hands still captured in mine, he kissed me. He didn't make a move to get me to let go, he arched into me, tasted me as if he was never going to be able to kiss me again. He tasted, and sucked, our tongues tangling, and I pushed harder on his hands, making sure that he knew I was in charge, hoping to hell I was doing it right. He groaned into the kiss, ground against me, and I shifted enough so that we were perfectly aligned, his belt buckle digging into me, his breath harsh, his cock as hard as mine.

The kisses lasted forever, desperate and uncoordinated, and then softer and deeper, and then just as quickly back to desperate.

I opened my eyes and pulled back a little. "You like me holding you down?" I didn't have to ask.

For a moment he fought the hold, but then he relaxed. "Fuck you." He didn't fight back.

I swallowed the words until the kisses grew messy again, and the grinding was getting dangerously close to us both coming in our pants. He widened his legs, moaning into the kiss, and I tightened my hold on his hands, staring into his face, wishing he'd open his eyes so that I could see the amber gaze that would tell me how close he was.

"I think I'm going to get rope," I whispered in his ear, "tie your hands so you can't get away, fuck you so hard and you're begging me to hold you down..."

He opened his eyes briefly, long enough for me to see the need there, and I pressed harder on his hands mimicking how I could hold him still. He chased me with a kiss, whining low in his throat.

"I can't do this," he groaned, shoving himself up and grinding against me, his fingers curling around mine.

"I'll take care of you." I was so close to coming, but I wanted him finished first. I didn't want to let go of his hands. I shifted a little so he could press against my thigh, and his breathing changed, enough so I knew he was close as he offered me his throat and I bit into his neck.

"Fuuuuck," he gasped, and then he opened his mouth in a silent shout.

I stole a sloppy, hot kiss as he stiffened in orgasm. It was enough to send me tumbling over the edge, and I relaxed on top of him, but after he pushed his hands up against my hold, I released him and rolled half off. We lay there breathing hard for a moment, and then he shoved me away from him, until I tumbled on my back to the ground.

"That can never happen again." He stood, brushed himself down, then wiped his mouth and collected his hat.

I waited until he was a few steps away before I delivered my answer.

"You're perfect," I said as I propped myself up on one elbow.

He threw me a glance of complete confusion. I wanted to call him back to explain what I meant, to get him to understand that for the first time ever in sex I'd felt right in my own skin. How did I even go about explaining that to him? He hadn't given me the time to think of what to say. He turned and carried on walking down to the stables. I could have joined him but right now everything was right in my world. Levi had begged me to push and control, and in doing so I could show him the parts of me I kept hidden from everyone.

And I wanted to care for him, hold him tight, and maybe never let him go.

I'd never felt so much peace.

Chapter Sixteen

LEVI

I HEADED STRAIGHT FOR MY TRAILER, AND MY embarrassment helped me all the way back without thinking one thought about Quinn and what had just happened. I bypassed my usual visit with Blake, ignored Sky who unrolled herself from her sleeping space under the trailer, and I stomped inside and locked the door behind me. Sky scratched at the metal, but I couldn't even face her. I slumped into my chair and buried my head in my hands.

"The fuck," I groaned, and felt as if I should've been kicking myself up and down this damn ranch for what I'd let happen. The most erotic sexual encounter of my entire life. How had he known I liked to be held down? How did he know that I was okay with my hands being pushed into the earth? It was only an illusion, I could have bucked him off easily enough, but I hadn't wanted to. Fuck, I'd begged him for it with kisses and groans, and rubbing up against him as if I hadn't had sex before.

I groaned. I was supposed to be professional, lording it

over Micah, training horses, not scrabbling around in the dirt with the elfin fae who was turning me upside down. Every single sexual encounter I'd ever had ended with me either on my knees or fucked up against a wall outside some nameless bar. If I loved it when a hook-up gripped my hair and fucked my face or shoved me and held me still, then that shit was staying in my head.

But he'd known. I'd asked him to kiss me. I'd asked him to make me feel.

It certainly wasn't spilling all over my personal or professional life. Guys got off using my mouth or my ass, under cover of darkness, they didn't have to know I craved the extra roughness. Some cowboys had been so far in the closet that they fucked with anger, and that was close enough to what I needed, if I didn't think about their self-hatred too much. Another man pushing me to my knees, telling me what was happening, that was at the core of my sexual self, at least that is what the Internet said. I always thought it would be a bigger man who could take me down, but one whisper of what Quinn wanted to do to me, and I'd been lost.

I envied Quinn his conviction. He didn't hate himself. Quinn had known what I wanted, and fuck, I'd felt safe asking. In a flurry of motion, I pushed off my boots, stripped and went into my small shower which was barely big enough for a Quinn-sized man, let alone me. I stood for a while under the warm water with my fingers twisted in my hair, tugging hard enough to chill the fuck down, and then I wrapped myself in a towel and sat back on my chair. I wasn't done for the day, I had to get back out there and maybe deal with seeing Quinn again. What the fuck would Micah think if he thought I was doing *that* with the client who could make a difference to the ranch?

He'd talked about ropes, he'd said he wanted to hold me down, make me feel, and that was everything I wanted. I'd never told another person in my entire life that I was desperate for that.

Thinking his name had me getting hard at remembering what he'd done—*what we'd done*—and that was dangerous. I dressed quickly, balling up my wet underwear, and shoving it in with my laundry, and then stepped outside to pet Sky who was giving me her best sulky expression. I fed her which she demolished in a few minutes, then I went to a crouch, offered her a treat, and after a bit more sulking she deigned to take the treat, and even allowed me to pet her.

"Sorry." I scratched under her neck, and she loved me again. I wished life was that simple.

"Can you help me up in the creek field?" Micah striding toward me with a serious expression was enough to snap me out of thinking about Quinn.

"Yep, what's up?"

"Damn fence," was all Micah said, but it was enough to explain everything. Fences were as much a part of cowboy life as horses were, although he seemed off somehow as we walked up there, quiet, his expression dark.

I could handle fences, whether I could put up with angsty-Micah was another matter altogether. He bristled with stress and every so often he would glance at me with an expression I couldn't read. Was he angry at something? Had he found out what Quinn and I had done? I got that it was overstepping, and maybe I was putting the training contract in jeopardy.

"Sorry," I blurted before he got to the point when he exploded, which was his every right, after all I *was* there on a contract.

He side-eyed me. "What did you do?"

"What do you think I did?" I hedged.

"Did you mess up something I don't know about?" His eyes narrowed.

"No." Because kissing Quinn, and then getting off with him behind the trees wasn't wrong, unless Quinn pulled his contract, and then it was very wrong. But he'd been the one in charge of that, instigated it. *Only because you begged him.*

Micah frowned at me, but we didn't stop walking, and we didn't talk anymore when we picked up stragglers, Archie and Laurie bundling out of the car, leaving Rachel, Scott, and the baby behind, and running after us.

"Kids! Don't forget your chores!" Rachel called.

"We won't, Mom!" Laurie called back.

"We won't!" Archie said at the same time.

The two of them were more interested in whatever we were up to though, because I guessed fence-fixing was more interesting than feeding the chickens, or mowing the back yard, or whatever was on their chore list.

"Watcha doing?" Archie asked, jamming his baseball hat down onto his head, and bouncing alongside us.

"Can we help, Uncle Micah?" Laurie asked.

"Sure thing," Micah replied, as we arrived at the first of three broken fence posts in a row. These things happened, one post decayed enough to loosen and it could take a whole fence line down if it wasn't fixed. There was already a ton of supplies there, but by the time we'd gotten one upright in place, the kids were bored, and off climbing the same rockfall that Quinn had danced all over.

"Is it safe?" I nodded at the rocks, and at the water that was deeper after last night's summer storm.

Micah glanced over and then nodded. "Been there since I was a kid. I used to scramble up there all the time, though Rachel was always the better climber."

I couldn't imagine Rachel climbing rocks, but then there was a lot I didn't know about Micah and his sister. Archie, on the other hand, seemed to have no fear at all. He was climbing and jumping and whooping and hollering as if he wanted everyone to see just what he was doing. Laurie followed him but was quieter; still, he was grinning like a Cheshire cat, and their laughter was a happy sound.

I held a post straight as Micah leveled the cross beam and began to nail it in place. We worked in silence, but it was *too* quiet.

"We're talking about… me and Daniel I mean…" I wasn't listening really, so Micah may have said more, but it seemed as if he couldn't get words together, and maybe this was what had him grumpy. Had he and Doctor Daniel had a falling-out?

He finished nailing, and I didn't push for more, but I knew Micah well enough to know he had things eating away at him, but he'd never shown an interest in talking with me about anything that wasn't horses. I felt something in my chest, a sadness that maybe he and his husband were having issues, because they'd seemed so perfect together. I couldn't think of what else he'd want to talk to me about, having established that it wasn't about me in any way.

"We've been discussing, Daniel and me I mean, about the ranch, and how we saw it going."

"You're in trouble and looking to sell?" I assumed.

"No." He blinked at me as if he couldn't believe it himself. "Far from it, I've had to turn away work, and that's good. I don't want to overbook us, because I want to give the best to the horses we have."

"Hence hiring me," I deadpanned.

He rolled his eyes at me then he paused for the longest time. "Wanted to offer you something more permanent."

My stomach fell. I hadn't been there long, and Micah wanted me to commit to more. How much more? Weeks, months, years? My fight-or-flight kicked in. "No but thank you for the offer."

"You're good, Levi, but when you left the Denver Triple-K, you missed out on what we did there, what we achieved."

"You didn't need me for that." I'd watched from afar to see the Triple-K become the most respected horse training facility in Denver, with Micah playing his part. They'd asked me to stay but settling meant putting down roots and making friends, and that could only go bad when they found out I wasn't worth the time. I didn't have to see a therapist to know that having been abandoned as a kid played into my psyche, and that I had trust issues, add that to hiding who I was, and I had a desperate need for solitude.

Until Quinn. I hadn't hidden who I was or what I wanted with him. I'd broken the rules, kissed him, asked him to hold me down, asked him with my body and with words. I'd opened myself up to hurt when he laughed in my face next time we saw each other. The regrets were like acid inside me. I wasn't interested in more of anything because it might've ended up coming with affection and connection, and I wasn't interested in those lies.

I knew that same mythical counselor would have a field day with the deceptions I kept close to my chest.

"You could choose to stop here? We could work together, you'd have permanence, I'd give you good land so you were a full partner, and you could build a place, make it *our* business. Sign contracts and everything."

Okay, so I hadn't been expecting *that* kind of offer. The chance of owning something that I'd build with Micah would leave me in a position where I'd have a ton of responsibilities that I didn't want. What if Micah and I disagreed and I wanted to leave? I couldn't simply get in the trailer, take my money, and run. Confusion turned to fear, which yanked out cynical and indifferent Levi, who came with a healthy self-protective cloak of sarcasm.

"Wow, Doctor Dan has done a number on you."

Micah went from sincere and uncertain, to confused and then defensive.

"It was my idea."

"And what makes you think I'm capable of something like staying in one place."

He pressed a hand to my chest. "I see what you hide," he announced.

I wanted to laugh, or cry, or shout, or *something.* No one *saw* the broken, needy, messed-up me. "Fuck you, *Mikey.*" I shoved his hand away and stumbled back. What the hell was I doing? He was going to throw me off the ranch if I carried on this way.

"See, I know you don't mean that." Micah lifted an eyebrow and stared at me, daring me to contradict him.

"I don't do staying in one place and you know that."

"Why?"

"New adventures, new people."

"But you don't have roots, you don't settle, and what kind of life is that? Even I stopped at the Triple-K, and I was running from demons so terrifying they were killing me."

"'Demons'? Like having your own ranch? Like having an ex you clearly pined for and who loved you right back? What was so bad about your fucking life that makes you the expert in anything I feel?"

I was deflecting by pushing him, and I knew that. Hell, I wanted him to blurt out what he was holding back—the same things that had poisoned him that year I'd worked with him. Instead of talking, he sat on the pile of fence posts and gestured for me to sit as well. I balked at being asked to sit and listen to whatever he wanted to explain, because I bet all of it would be an attempt to manipulate me into staying.

"This is weird even for you," I snapped.

"Just sit your ass down and give me five minutes," he pleaded more than ordered, and that was so totally not him.

After a long pause when I considered grabbing Blake,

Sky, and heading out—whatever was going on with Quinn and this overwhelming attraction I had to him—I sat on a log opposite him. I had every single one of my defenses in place. Anger, distrust, denial—they were all there ready to leap into action.

"See there's something you don't know. The other thing Daniel and I were discussing is that we'd like Archie to stay with us more permanently."

Wait. That was nothing to do with me, so where was this going and why did I need to know that? He glanced around, probably checking to see if Archie was close by, and spotted them down by the house.

"His mom came to the doctor's office, saw Daniel, got test results that she shared with me as well. She's not well, and she's looking for help."

I glanced at his grim expression, wondering if he realized this was me he was talking to, because we'd gone a full one-eighty from talking about anything connected to me staying, and abruptly he was sharing something so deep that I was confused.

He stared down at his hands. I bet it killed him that he was talking to me of all people, but he didn't seem pissed. In fact, this was the new Micah who had replaced the one I'd known, sitting there wanting to talk, but it hurt to sit and listen because I knew this would circle back to me. Maybe this was to do with Quinn and the way he'd stared me right in the eyes and knew what I needed.

Fuck. Stop thinking about Quinn.

Micah glanced to where Archie and Laurie were rolling down the hill, their laughter reaching us. Sky had joined in, seemingly convinced in the time that I'd been there that they were her pack, and trailing the boys. Independence personified—same as me.

"Archie knows his mom is ill, but he doesn't know she asked Daniel and me… well, not me, just Daniel… to take Archie on for real, so this part of the story I'm trusting you keep to yourself." He didn't wait for me to agree.

The trust he was offering was heavy in my chest. I never imagined for one minute that he'd ever look to me as a confidant, and the feelings his trust evoked were unsettling. I didn't like carrying the weight of other people's secrets. Archie was the brightest soul, feisty, adventurous, respectful but cheeky, and he was good with the horses. He wasn't a kid who'd done anything to deserve losing his mom. No child deserved a painful childhood and it was clear that Micah was smitten with Daniel—they'd be good dads.

What is Micah doing to me today? I can't handle this up-and-down, back-and-forth. Then it hit me that he'd said *just* Daniel, and Micah and I might not have been friends, but he was a solid guy now by all accounts, and I was defensive of him for some weird cowboy code reason.

"Why just ask Daniel, he's your husband, so it's both of you who'd be taking him on," I vocalized my defensiveness, and my tone had an edge which caused Micah to smile.

"I knew you liked me."

"Fuck you."

He snorted a laugh, and then grew serious again. "It can't be all on me, because…" he glanced at me. "I spent a year in prison."

That was one of the least shocking things Micah had

ever said, and maybe explained more about the kind of man he was. Images of Micah doing time for something fit well with the closed-off man I'd gotten to know.

"You steal a horse or something?" I joked to loosen the tension in Micah, but he shook his head, and didn't relax at all.

"Killed one of my best friends in a car accident. Isaac." He hunched forward. "Coming to terms with it, working with Daniel, I'm…" He frowned. "You recall Chris, right?"

That was a change of subject when the first part of the announcement sent ice down my spine. Micah sounded broken.

"Chris? Daniel's brother, the one I'm setting up for riding?" We were just waiting on a modified support to accommodate his prosthetic, the leather work was taking a while, but hopefully it would be there by the weekend. What did Chris have to do with Micah being in prison?

"Yeah, well, he was in the car and was hurt when I crashed it." He absently pressed fingers into his arm, then pushed up his sleeve, and I saw the scarring. He always wore long-sleeved T-shirts, but I'd seen the scars quite by accident, only he'd never explained how he had thick burn marks on his skin. I didn't have to be a genius to put two and two together with this extra information.

That was a lot to lay on me when I'd thought Micah had the emotional depth of a stone, but there was real pain in his eyes, and it hit me that he was no different to me in a lot of ways. Still trying to outrun the past, closing ourselves off to connection so we didn't get hurt.

Somehow he'd found a way to stop. He'd discovered

love. Maybe I needed that? Was someone like Quinn part of the solution to a problem I never imagined I had?

"Well, shit," I said after a pause as the enormity of his announcement, plus the glimpse into my own psyche rolled over me.

Micah placed his hand behind his neck, then stretched out the tension. "Turns out that a record is enough to fuck you up no matter how much regret and pain you carry."

"I'm sorry." I didn't know what else to say, and after a moment he handed me a wry smile, a glimpse of familiar snarky Micah back where it belonged.

"But, you know, we're husbands now, so we're a joint package. I just hope everything will be okay," he added.

I nodded. "Archie would be lucky to have you two take him in."

"Maybe I'm not the best person to take on a child?"

Was he asking me for my opinion? How could I offer my point of view when up until a few moments ago I'd thought Micah was an asshole who'd changed by hooking up with Daniel. Instinctively I knew that Micah would be a good dad, and I didn't know Daniel that well, but they were in love.

The silence was uncomfortable, and I felt as if I needed to share part of myself to balance the dynamic before it tipped too far one way. Once Micah knew the real me then maybe I could kill two birds with one stone—reassure him he was doing the right thing and explain why I kept moving.

"My parents didn't want me," I began, then shook my head. "Though they kept my two older brothers. Guess three was just too much, eh? Dad dumped me at his sister's place, and I got taken in by my aunt and uncle when I was this tall," I held out a hand to indicate a short kid and Micah gave a nod, his eyes wide, most likely in shock I was talking at all, let alone giving him a glimpse into my past. "They were good people, but cancer took my aunt when I was eight, then just before I was sixteen, Uncle Lucas passed after a horse threw him. My uncle had a record, spent five inside when he was twenty for a bar fight that got out of hand. Their land wasn't much, but it went to their *real* son, Robbie, who wasn't all that keen on having me around. I left, but I was happy for a lot of years with them. So, if it helps, it didn't matter he had a record, he was still a good dad while I had him. Whatever was in your past, you could make a family, a good one."

I don't think I'd ever said so many words to Micah before, certainly not ones filled with so much passion. He could probably tell there was more to this story, but he wasn't going to ask me to carry on, any more than I would push him about his past.

"Maybe you should stop here," he said after a long pause. "'Take a stand, make a new family."

"With you?" I snorted and then realized he was being serious. "We're not even friends," I added. He stared at me, but he didn't seem hurt or pissed, in fact I saw understanding in his expression, and that had ants crawling under my skin. No one understood me, and they never would.

"I like to think we're friends," Micah murmured.

"Yeah, well, whatever, I guess you're okay…" *Snappy comeback. Asshole.*

We finished the fence in silence and then walked down to the stables side by side.

"Will you stay here?" And there it was, the question he'd wanted to ask me, on repeat.

"No." I wanted to be honest with him. I wasn't as far down the path of finding myself as he was, and I had to stay true to my convictions to keep moving to keep my heart safe.

"Okay if I keep asking?"

I side-eyed him. "You can ask, don't mean I'll ever say yes."

He punched my arm gently. "I will then, *friend*."

"You're an asshole." I punched him back.

"Takes one to know one," he deadpanned.

It was a short conversation, but weirdness settled in my chest, and it felt a lot like a longing to have a friend. I quickly pushed it down because, fuck that shit.

We finished covering tomorrow's schedule and caught up on progress with Lucifer, and Quinn's horse Glimmer.

Everything was going well with Quinn's horses, and it would carry on going well if I could keep my head in the game and not spend my time thinking about their owner's pink-haired representative.

If only I could get Quinn out of my thoughts.

And stop thinking about what it might be like if I stopped leaving places.

Chapter Seventeen

QUINN

Two days passed before I saw Levi alone, and it was way too early in the morning for the caffeine to have kicked in yet, and I couldn't think. I genuinely thought we would talk about what had happened at some point, getting off under the tree, or the kiss, or his need to be able to hand over control.

Hell, at least look at each other.

But he was a wily asshole who used anyone passing as a human shield, preventing any kind of meaningful discussion, or indeed orgasms. Two freaking days of early morning starts to watch him work with the horses, and there wasn't one moment when we were truly alone. The kids were there, or he'd ask Micah to stand there, at one point he even dragged Rachel up to watch.

Which was a damn shame, because I swear my imagination of what we *could* have been doing if only we talked was sending me insane, and the spark of powerful attraction had nowhere to go.

I was failing in my plan to get to know Rachel. I'd

imagined I would check she was a good mom and then leave, but I kept telling myself I hadn't seen enough. I was supposed to head away from there that weekend, but I wasn't done. I was trying to be friendly without flat out telling her who I was, but every day I turned up I wanted to be honest, because she'd known Max, and I'd bet she could tell me what he'd been like. Had they been in love when she'd fallen pregnant with Laurie? When had he died? Why?

Me revealing I was Max's brother meant exposing this wonderful family to media, money, headaches they couldn't imagine, and Laurie wouldn't be innocent anymore, he'd be hounded for his wealth, he'd have his photos everywhere, and if my father thought he was worth something to the family then that would put him into the limelight.

My cell vibrated, and I saw it was Connor.

"I have to take this," I told an uninterested Levi, and walked some distance from him to answer.

"Connor, hey."

"When are you finishing this," he said without preamble. He did that a lot, all dedication and tightly wound strength, but I wished he'd take more time to tell me how he was instead of leaping in with field reports.

"I'm fine, thank you," I deadpanned. "How are you doing? Everything okay with you?"

"Huh?" Connor sounded confused. "Fuck off. As if I've time for social shit," he added after a moment then huffed a laugh. I loved making him laugh—he didn't do enough laughing.

"It's okay, you can cut to the chase now." Getting to the point was Connor's happy place.

"There was a visitor to the clinic, asking about you, said he was a friend who was concerned about you. Only I called bullshit, because this one was a journalist. So I tracked back, turns out there's some chatter about you and the shares in Dawson Pharma that you're owed and the gossip pages are looking for your input. It's nothing I couldn't shut down."

That was good news, but Connor's tone freaked me out. "You don't normally tell me these things, what's special about this one? Are you really worried but just not telling me?"

He cursed and then muttered something before clearing his throat. "No, but Christ, you're in Wyoming, and I'm on a farm with Molly's dad, who keeps trying to get me to ride, and you hired me to look out for you, and I can't do it from here."

The dread unknotted in my chest. "I'm okay here."

"Whatever," he sighed. "Just don't get hurt or do anything stupid that I can't get you out of. Are you ready to leave soon?"

The quick change in conversation threw me. "No."

"I knew this would happen," Connor groused. "You're getting involved in things you shouldn't, aren't you?"

"No, I'm not," I lied, and I wasn't going to tell him about the tree house or Levi. "It's just that Laurie is definitely Max's, I just know, and I haven't seen a lot of him."

"Officially he's your nephew?"

Unofficially, officially, none of that mattered. "He's Max's son," I insisted.

"So what next? Are you going to get a test done to—"

"No."

"You can't just go with your gut. There's an entire trust fund at stake here."

Max's trust fund. Everything that could end up destroying Laurie as sure as it had shattered Max, and every cent of it was in my charity's name now. I didn't want it, but what did I do? Laurie was so innocent, and look what had happened to his dad, and me. *Think about the consequences*. What did I do?

I turned back to watch Levi, who was leaning on the fence outside the corral, chatting with Laurie and Archie. Both were listening with rapt attention to whatever wisdom he was dispensing. "I know. Trust me, I know."

"What about the baby?"

I hadn't been able to meet Oliver for real, all I knew was that he was Rachel's, and that he was Laurie's brother, but the timings were wrong for the baby to be Max's. Not unless Max had died a lot later than the coroner thought. It didn't matter. I would match every single cent I handed to Laurie with the baby, and Rachel. To me, that little family was everything, but Max would've been horrified that I was anywhere near them. He wouldn't have wanted them to have his money. He would've wanted them to be left alone.

I'm so fucking selfish.

"I don't know yet."

"Okay, boss," Connor said. "Call me soon."

"Quinn. My name is Quinn," I said, but Connor had

cut the call and I was talking to a dead phone. I sauntered over to stand next to Levi and the boys, frustration burning inside me. Mostly at not talking to Rachel, and Connor fretting about me, but also that there was this *thing* with Levi that sparked and fizzed in my belly and made me swoopy with desire whenever I was within six feet of him.

I joked with the boys, learned that Laurie had an eye for drawing, and that Archie was one of the funniest kids I'd ever met. I made them laugh and every time they curled up in stitches I was like a superhero of cool. But I also stared at Levi. A lot. And I flirted at every opportunity I could get when it was obvious to him what I was doing but not to anyone else. I'd accidentally slipped and fallen three times this week already, and he'd caught me the first two times before setting me aside. Yesterday though, he'd deliberately let my ass hit the ground, and then he'd stared at me and let me know in that single moment that he could see right through me. I'd rolled to a stand even as I met Levi's stare head-on.

At last, he'd dropped his gaze, and I knew I'd won that round, even if my tailbone was bruised. So falling over today wasn't going to work, but I stared a hell of a lot more after that, because he had to crack at some point. Right? I climbed up on the fence to watch him work, and didn't move when he and Micah went off to do whatever they did because Laurie came to sit next to me.

"Do you want to see something?" Laurie asked, both of us staring at the mountain. Archie had been there with us, but he'd scrambled after Micah when he'd called Levi to work in the barn. I expected Laurie to go as well, but he had a sketchbook under his arm and told me in no uncertain terms that he'd rather draw.

"Always." He grinned up at me and then more than a little shy he opened his sketchbook and handed it to me.

"I did a picture," he summarized.

I took the book with great care, turning it so I could see what he'd done. It was a drawing of a barn, and I recognized it as the one I'd seen on my tour with Levi that first day. Laurie wasn't even ten yet but he'd caught something of the barn, the broken door that was still padlocked, the boarded up windows, the fact the whole structure was tilting. There were vines climbing one side, but somehow in this drawing my nearly nine-year-old nephew had captured beauty. Max hadn't been able to draw anything, his creativity was around his guitar, and the music he made, but I could sketch. My degree had been in art and design, and along with the dance, I'd imagined myself with a creative future, not a present so mired in grief and anxiety.

"This is so good," I said, and we knocked elbows.

"I can't get the lock right," he pressed his lips together in a small pout, "it's super shiny, but the rest of the barn is old. Mom loved it but she's supposed to like it, because she's my mom."

Happy thoughts consumed my body with an intensity that shocked me. I'd never had a mom who cared enough to look at my art, or my dancing, or in fact any element of life that made up me. My mother had never been interested in Max and his music either, so anyone who says a mom must love their child enough to care was wrong. Rachel loved her son, he loved her, it was as things should be, but sometimes weren't.

"I love it, I think it's wonderful."

"Thank you."

"I like to draw things too."

"You do?"

"Do you want me to show you how I draw shiny things?" I didn't want to push Laurie to accept help, but he seemed hopeful, and handed me the small tin from his pocket. Inside was a pencil and an eraser, along with a sharpener, and I helped myself and then turned to a fresh page in his book. Now, how to explain?

Inspiration hit me, and I removed the sunglasses I wore and held them out in front of him.

"What do you see?" I asked, and he glanced at me confused then focused hard on the glasses.

"Metal, and glass, and screws," he said with caution, as if he expected me to say he was wrong. The fact he was seeing past the object to the parts that formed it was the sign of an artist at work, and I felt a flush of pride that he'd maybe gotten something from me. It struck me that I should get him a guitar, and see if he could sing, then he'd have part of Max as well. *You'll be gone soon, no point in messing things up.*

"Exactly, and what else do you see?" Back to the matter in hand, I tilted the glasses until they reflected the fencing.

"A reflection," he said.

"Exactly. Shiny things have reflections, you can see the fence, and the whiter parts where the sun is." I handed him the glasses so he could tilt them this way and that, and then perched the sketchbook on my lap, wondering if maybe we should move this somewhere more comfortable for only as long as it took to lose myself in sketching. Then, where we sat wasn't as important as the fact I was next to Laurie, with our shared talent. I sketched the shape of the lenses.

"See how the light reflects into the lenses?" I asked.

He nodded. "I can see the fence in there too." He peered closer and I wanted to hug him

"So when you draw anything shiny it will have a reflection. Like this." I sketched the fence, in a curve, and then shaded one side so it had both light and dark.

"That's so cool." He sounded impressed.

Pride mixed with happiness. I'd never known what I was going to do with my degree, arts and dance weren't really the thing for boardrooms, but I wasn't good enough to dance professionally, and art was me connecting to the world around me.

Maybe I should be a teacher? Run some classes in town for the kids here, even adults, or go over to the college in Collier Springs and volunteer?

"Can I have a go?"

I stopped imagining things that weren't going to happen, then handed him the book.

"You have a go, see if you can copy what I did."

I held out the glasses, only this time I tilted them so they reflected the clouds. With the tip of his tongue sticking out, he drew what he could see, and then beamed with pride when he'd made something flat become a shiny surface.

"That is so good." I was blown away that he had such

control over his pencil, and wondered if one day he'd be an artist.

The things I could teach him, the places we could go to draw. Mountains, streams, horses—we could spend hours chatting about Max and drawing.

Grief overwhelmed me again. That wasn't going to happen. I couldn't let that steal my precious time with Laurie though and I pulled myself out of the spiral.

"How about drawing my phone? That has shiny parts, and duller bits."

I laughed when he added legs and arms to the phone.

"This is Phoney-the-phone," he announced. "He has adventures when he goes to the city, or to space. I could make a book and sell it." Then he frowned at me. "I mean, if that's okay, Phoney is your phone."

"But you created the character, so it's all yours," I said, and he grinned, and *fuck* he was so much a mini-Max.

"I'll sell loads and buy Mom a present."

"Sounds like a great idea."

"Laurie?"

We both startled at Rachel's voice.

I smiled in encouragement and hoped I hadn't contravened some rule by being a client talking art with her son. Her instinctive smile dropped, and she glanced from me to Laurie and then back, and Mom-Rachel came to the fore.

"Chores, Laurie," she reminded him, and he scooted down, carefully placing the pencil and eraser into his tin, and thrusting the sketch book at his mom.

"Look what we did, Mom."

She looked at the drawings, and listened to Laurie rambling about Phoney, and how he was going to buy her the biggest bunch of flowers, but I got the sense that she was distracted. Of course, she was commenting on the drawings, hugging Laurie, but she kept glancing at me, and I wondered if I'd overstepped. *That wouldn't be the first time.*

"Thank you, Quinn," she murmured, and then the two of them left to go back to the house.

I tilted my face to the sun, and wondered what to do next. I heard a neigh and headed out to visit with Glimmer and Sunny.

Glimmer appeared happier, less terrified of life—she reminded me of Daisy, and my heart hurt a little at memories. Sunny was nothing like any horse I'd ever met, but he fascinated me, and I would have watched him for hours if I'd been able. He was quiet for now, pacing the ground he'd been allowed, shaking his head, but he was less angry and more confident. I heard Micah and Levi returning, but I didn't move, listening to them chat about training, and realizing I was focusing in on Levi's voice.

One glimpse of him, or hearing him talk, and I was hard. He and Micah split up, him walking toward me and I was excited by him being there with me one-on-one but then Laurie came bounding out, along with Archie, and yet again I wasn't going to have alone time with Levi.

I had to face it, I was addicted to this place, to being with Laurie, to the horses, and to being near Levi. Objectively, he was a fascinating man with the charm of the romantic old west, all rough, tough, sexy cowboy working with horses, and thinking nothing of lifting rocks with his bare hands.

Or I assumed he'd be able to lift them, because I hadn't been treated to the sight of him hefting anything but a switch with a cloth tied to the end of it as he worked with Lucifer, He went out there now, running the beautiful horse around the edge of the corral, turning him to run the other way, all the time staying silent, and not once did he look over at me. It had been like this for a long-ass week now, and I was growing weary of the clipped and surly cowboy act.

Not when I'd had him under me, with his hands pinned, begging me with his body to get off, not when I swallowed his low growl when he was coming. I swear I was raw from jerking off at the thought of those soft sounds of pleasure. Why would he deny himself more of the good stuff when I was clearly into it?

Levi derived great satisfaction from contacting me as early as he could on the hotel phone, dragging me out of bed and up to the ranch. In his defense it was my own fault—I had asked to be told when he was training, whatever the time—still, I was becoming part of the scenery at the ranch.

"Can I ask you something else?" Laurie climbed up to perch on the fence next to me, and I turned to face him, aware that Archie was some distance away doing something with a bucket and a stick. I dreaded to think what he was up to.

"Of course."

Laurie pushed his hair back, and my heart stopped again the same as it did whenever I saw my brother in him.

"Why is your hair pink?"

Of all the questions I could've been asked, I'd gotten so used to my hair that I never expected anyone to notice now. I could've given him some long, complicated reason why I'd decided to go pink.

"I like it that color." I opted for the truth.

"I like it, too," Laurie said shyly, and then stared at his feet. "Uncle Micah says that Levi likes it too much."

I nearly choked on my water. "He does?"

"Something about mooning, or I don't know, but Uncle Micah says Levi likes your hair too."

"He does?" Wow, I was repeating myself big time.

"Yep. Mom said it looked nice, and Levi said it was like soft cotton candy and then Uncle Micah said to Levi that he thought Levi was the kind of man who liked eating cotton candy, and then Levi coughed so hard that Mom had to slap him on the back. Levi cursed and Mom slapped him again. I might make my hair blue," he added.

"When you're older it can be any color you want," I reassured him, knowing I'd fight anyone who said otherwise, because Laurie was right there in my heart next to Max and I would protect him as much as I could.

How can I do that when I won't even be here?

I suspected Rachel would be the kind of mom to let her kids be who they wanted to be, but I didn't know that for sure because too much money could blacken even the purest of hearts, not to mention the media attention and the paparazzi.

You'd know if you spoke to her with any kind of honesty.

"Do you buy a lot of horses?" He leaped from one question to the next, and it made me smile.

"I just have two."

"I'm going to have a horse soon, Uncle Micah is buying me one, because Beans is still too big for me. It's going to be for my birthday, which is August the twelfth, I'm going to be nine. Levi is twenty-nine..." he screwed up his face, "an' three quarters. What about you?" He looked at me expectantly and I had to do some quick math in my head.

"Twenty-three and seven-twelfths," I said.

Now Laurie frowned. "I don't know what that is. Math is hard. I mean Mom is helping me, and Scott is good, but I do know what nine-times-seven is and that is a really hard one."

"It is. I like the easy ones."

"Two-times-two, stuff like that?" he asked.

I wanted to hug him, my arms felt empty with the need to hug my nephew and tell him who I was. "Yep, and three-times-three."

"Laurie! You wanna help me?" Archie shouted up from the bucket-stick experiment.

"Gotta go, Archie's making a bucket to climb into," Laurie informed, and I nodded as if that made total sense because that was a small bucket. "I'm coming!" he yelled and scampered down the hill to his friend.

Several things hit me. One, I loved him already, because I just *knew*, I felt him in my heart. Two, he found math hard, and I hated math, so that was yet another link. Although I hadn't spoken directly to Rachel, I'd seen enough of her with her fiancé Scott to know she was happy, and Laurie was content. Rachel was a good mom, and I knew that Max would have been so happy to have had a family with her in the real world.

What should I do, Max? I glanced to the sky where I

imagined Max was—funny that, as I wasn't religious—but the concept remained that somehow my brother was part of the beautiful Wyoming sky for no other reason than it made me smile.

Leave.

Chapter Eighteen

LEVI

RIDING OUT WITH CHRIS ENDED UP BEING EASIER THAN I'D thought. Not only was he a teacher at the local school, so had a ton of stories, but he was happy and smiling. I needed that today after a lack of sleep in which I tossed and turned thinking about Quinn, and the offer from Micah, and the fact that I needed neither Quinn nor the offer in my life.

Chris had eyed Beans with trepidation at first, but when Micah accidentally happened to walk into the stable, Chris's trepidation vanished in a flurry of shit talk.

"What are you even doing here?" Was Chris' opening shot.

"I work here, asshole." Micah stuck to the friend-script, and even added a smile, but after what he'd told me about the accident and how he'd been the one driving, I knew he was there for different reasons.

"I can ride a damn horse," Chris insisted.

"I never said you couldn't." Micah tried for innocent but there was worry in his expression.

I took a step backward and then another, just to move out of the way of whatever was going to happen.

"Then stop checking up on me."

"Daniel said—"

"Your *husband* needs to keep his nose out of what I'm doing." Chris was exasperated, and Micah slunk out of the stable like a whipped dog. "I don't know what I have to say to get them to stop fussing," he muttered to Beans.

I gave him a moment of communing before getting closer. The saddle, bridle, and reins didn't need any adaptations because Chris was a leg amputee, but there were still ways to make this easier, and we had the grips there if he needed them.

"I have leather hand holds?" I interrupted his horse chat, and he sent me a rueful smile. My only concern was stability and balance, but I never assumed the level of riding skill, or the invisible impairments that a rider might have had.

"Maybe, let's see." Chris was pragmatic, not defensive and blustering about how he didn't need anything, and I respected that. "I have a suction socket, because any jarring can gradually work the socket loose, and the suspension belt stops any rubbing where the top of my residual limb might pinch between the artificial limb and the saddle. I've thought it all through."

Stirrups that could trap his leg if he fell were dangerous. We had safety stirrups, which came with a latch that released the stirrup in the event of a fall, but just as important Chris' foot needed to be secure, so it was a delicate balance. I assisted him up onto Beans' back, fiddled with fastenings, and he held the reins like an expert.

"How does that feel?"

"Good. It feels good." He wriggled in the saddle, getting his balance, and grinning down at me. "It's been a while since I've been on a horse, not since Micah left, and then with Daniel and everything." He shrugged.

Unusually for me, I wanted to hear more about Micah from someone who'd known him before, during, and now after whatever had happened in the accident. I wasn't prying, but he'd changed so much, and even though I'd enjoyed our snarky relationship, and the added blowjobs, I was curious to understand why he'd become such a different man. He and Daniel were in love, I could see that, but was it *really* possible that just the act of loving Daniel could be responsible for Micah changing so much? The two men had built a life in Whisper Ridge, surrounded by family, and I found myself envious, which was a brand-new feeling for me.

"Okay," Chris murmured, and wriggled again.

"Do you need me to side-walk?" I hated asking that because Chris was relaxed and secure, but it was part of my job to keep horse and rider safe.

Chris paused a moment, as if he was checking himself over. "Nah, I'm good to go."

"Ready?"

He nodded.

I mounted Blake, then there was only a brief flash of hesitation before Chris urged Beans to move and Blake followed, and drew level. He looked confident, centered, and didn't seem to need me too close by, urging Beans into a trot, with Blake copying until we were past the training rings and onto empty land. I held back, within reach, but just enough to give Chris the chance to decide what he was comfortable with, and he took it easy, relaxing into the saddle. I caught a glimpse of his happy smile as he inhaled the fresh mountain air, and communed with both horse and nature. We headed away from the ranch, to the top fence and then ended up by the creek, with the view of the mountains, and the ranch.

He reined Beans to a stop, leaning over her neck to pet her and then sitting back. "I miss this," he said with a sharp laugh as if he couldn't believe he was up there at all. "You know I was always up at the ranch riding. Sometimes, the three of us would go out and ride for hours." He caught himself, and I wonder if he was thinking about Isaac, and the accident, which wasn't the point of getting up here. Today was about freedom. "We'd find a place to stop and stare at the mountain, anything to get away from Micah's dad."

"They didn't get along?" That seemed as if it was a safe question.

"Micah's dad was a complicated man, and their relationship was… yeah." The rest was unspoken, and I imagined Chris realized maybe he shouldn't have been sharing anything, which I guess he shouldn't have been. But the answers he gave to any questions I had might've helped me with my own messed-up thoughts, so I changed direction to non-secret-past information.

"Micah and Daniel seem very happy."

Chris nodded as he stared into the distance contemplating the sky. "They were always meant to be together, written in the stars and all that." He glanced at me with a wry smile. "Look at me, I'm a poet and I didn't know it. I genuinely never thought I'd be waxing lyrical over my idiot brother and my asshole best friend." The smile turned warm. "I'm just glad Micah's home and they worked things out, because Daniel was miserable without him."

"I worked with Micah a few years ago, at this place out in Denver, he mentioned Daniel's name once." I didn't expand on that. "He stayed, I left, and seeing him now it's obvious he's changed a lot since back then."

"Falling back in love will do that to a man." Chris gestured for us to carry on.

We headed deeper into Lennox land, where it was tangled and abandoned. With work this place could be everything—new fences, agricultural progress, maybe a few head of cattle for the horses to work with, a school for teaching—it had so much potential that Micah could explore. The statements in my head, the income I'd saved, the investments I made, I could buy something like this, smaller though, probably even more run down, but it was possible.

Or I could stay here and buy into Lennox Ranch.

Only I'd have to stay in one place to make it work, and that was an alien concept. I'd miss out on so much if I didn't keep moving; opportunities to work with new horses, and stables with the best facilities, and with cowboys I didn't have history with, and in the opposite direction from wherever Quinn was headed to when this was over.

Chris and I covered a lot of ground in comfortable

silence, and when we returned to the stables, Micah was there. I got the feeling he'd waited for Chris to get back, to make sure he was okay, and I knew for sure Chris thought the same thing as his mood shifted.

"Micah, if you even start anything," Chris threatened.

"What? I was in here moving..." he glanced to his left, "... the wheelbarrow." He finished with a nod.

"You were here waiting to see if I made it back alive," Chris snarked.

I dismounted to assist him in climbing down, hands on his arms until he was steady on his feet.

"I wasn't—"

"Jee-zus, I'm surprised you didn't get on a horse and follow me with training ropes."

"I wouldn't do that." Micah was indignant, but when they stared at each other, a lifetime of memories flickering in their expressions, Chris was the first to crack, and grinned.

"It was awesome," he said, and the two men met in the middle of the stable in a close hug. Best friends, reunited, guilt, caring, it was a weight of feelings that made me feel uncomfortable to be around, so I tied Blake and began to groom him. Archie and Laurie appeared from nowhere, Sky on their heels.

"Uncle Micah, can you show us how to tie knots?

At least their arrival cut through the emotion, and when Micah and the kids left the stable it was easy to see that Chris was back to being happy.

"He worries too much, blames himself still, whatever I say." He gestured at his leg. "Whatever, I want to come back if that's okay."

"Any time."

"We should groom them," Chris said, but I could see the pull of his body to the left, and the brackets of pain around his mouth. He might've been happy, but if this was the first time he'd been back on a horse in a while, then I was glad to take care of Beans.

"I need to check some things, so I got this," I said in an even tone, and he took it at face value, nodding his thanks.

He shook my hand, and limped back to the house, only a little unsteady on his feet. I watched him go, but it wasn't because I was worried he would fall, but because Micah was waiting again, and this time he and Chris bro-hugged and then Chris punched his friend in the arm. They laughed, there was ribbing, and I stood in the shadows and watched.

Story of my life.

But I could change that, I could take Micah up on his offer and stay, work with Chris more, make friends that stuck, maybe even do something about this thing I had for Quinn.

All it would take was one step in the right direction.

Chapter Nineteen

QUINN

ANOTHER WEEK PASSED, BY WHICH TIME I REALLY SHOULD have left, or built the tree house or something.

According to Connor I was batshit crazy to be staying in one place if I hoped to keep things quiet, and that the media had taken a sudden interest in the clinic amid rumors I wasn't even there. Fuck.

How could I leave Laurie now?

I need to build the damn tree house, and leave.

Then there was the fact I was infatuated with Levi, and my heart, which had been so sad, now not only had Laurie, but it had shining moments of Levi. I'd never been in love before, and I didn't know if what we had between us was anything like love, but the lust between us was tinged with something perfect inside me. What I was feeling with Levi had an incredible honesty. I wanted to hold him down and fuck him so bad and kiss him until we couldn't breathe. He was confused, I wanted more, he was reluctant, but jeez... I could love someone like him, all sexy-vulnerable and hot enough to melt the sheets.

Laurie wasn't there, off on some adventure with Archie that involved cats, and I was at a loose end, and not ready to go back to the hotel. Levi was working with Glimmer who was by far the easier of my two horses to work with and I was fascinated to watch what he was doing. He had this quiet way about him, focused, intense, and I could've stared at him all day.

He hadn't gotten into the ring with Sunny yet, who switched between temper and defiance on a dime. The day he stepped in there I wanted to be front row and center—or hiding behind a tree, whichever worked best. Levi switched direction in attempting to lay a blanket on Glimmer's back, step one in getting her used to having something there, and when she stopped her running, I could see they were close to the next step. She clearly trusted Levi a small amount and respected that he was in charge, that he would look out for her and keep her safe.

I wasn't at that level quite yet—I hadn't worked my way out of imagining Levi naked and sprawled on a bed under me.

Inappropriate erection alert.

He glanced at me again, but this time he was slowing Glimmer to a walk, and then he stopped, facing me, and turning his back on Glimmer. After a few short moments, the big horse shook her mane and then moved slowly to Levi, resting her nose on his shoulder for a moment as she had that first time. The smile that crossed Levi's face was beautiful, and he petted Glimmer a little.

"Sunny next then?" I joked, and he rolled his eyes. I hated it when he did that at me, acting as if he knew it all and I was a nuisance to be ignored.

"This is just the start with Glimmer," he said with exasperation. "We have a ways to go yet, could take all summer with her and Sunny."

"Well, I know *that*." I sighed, which was my standard reply to his eyeroll.

"Then why say that when you know Sunny is a long way off joining up."

"Because I was making a joke," I huffed, and clambered down from the fence.

He petted Glimmer, then patted her and sauntered to the gate. "It wasn't a very funny joke."

"I know lots of funny jokes."

"I'm sure you do." He sent me a glance that told me I was being weird.

"Maybe I was trying to just get you to talk to me." I followed him into the stable, inhaling the scent of hay and horses, and he went straight to the roster board where he made notations. At this point of the morning, I always felt lost, but I wanted to stay longer today. I had woken up with determination that I wasn't going to be dismissed and that somehow I could stay around and see Laurie, albeit briefly.

"We're finished with that now," Levi murmured, and I realized he was staring at me—dismissing me.

"What are you doing now?"

He seemed startled. "In what way?"

"Are you working with Sunny or something?" He snorted a laugh, and my simmering idiocy spiked. "There's no need to laugh at me." I regretted the words as soon as they'd left my mouth. He was surprised and he frowned that Levi-frown which was high on my list of sexy things that Levi did.

"I wasn't laughing at you; I was just being..."

"What? An asshole?"

He glanced away and then right back at me. "No. I'm sorry."

"Oh." Abruptly flustered I stepped back and away from him, and tripped over fuck knows what, and just as I tumbled, he caught me, yanking me against his hard chest, his eyes wide. "Did you push me?" I murmured, lost in his amber eyes.

"You keep saying that, but I was nowhere near you." His voice was growling hot, and I was hard and pressed right next to him. Finally, he was holding me. "Did you do that on purpose?" Levi whispered.

"Huh?"

"Did you fall over on purpose?" he asked and then he released one hand, cradled my face, and sighed, the huff of breath warm on my face. "Why are you so... you?" He sounded as if he was attempting to blame me for whatever was going on in this gloomy stable block.

I wanted to defend myself but then it was too late to do anything. "I can't help it."

"You make me so mad, so messed up."

"I don't mean to."

"I want to kiss you so bad."

He leaned in, I leaned in, and the kiss was gentle exploration, no searching tongues and grinding teeth, or grabbing and pulling, this was the sweetest kiss I'd ever had. I locked my hands behind his neck and held on to him. He took control for a moment, and I was happy to go along for the ride, then he released me as quickly as he'd caught me, but I was still holding him, stopping myself from falling.

"Well," he began.

"Yeah."

"That happened again. Shit."

"Yeah." Words escaped me. What were words?

"But it's wrong." He looked adorably confused.

My touch drifted from his neck to his hair, reveling in the soft layers of silk that I smoothed and petted. Then I went on tiptoes and pressed another kiss to his lips, although this time I caught him as he was about to talk, and my tongue matched his with ease, and the kiss became deeper, harder, something *more.* I gripped his hands and he whimpered like he had done before, all need and passion. I could've pushed him back into the nearest stall, only before I could do anything he took my hand, tugged me out of the stable, and straight up to the same stand of trees where I'd gotten toppy on him, and as soon as we were hidden, he fell to his knees.

"Oh fuck, Levi," I murmured, as he unbuttoned my jeans and pushed my shorts down to get his hands on my cock, which had been hard since we'd kissed, and was even harder when he held me gently and then stopped. What was he waiting for? His mouth was right there, and he stared up at me, and a rush of lust consumed me like fire to dry grass. I didn't know what I was doing, I could fuck everything up, but he needed me to do *something.* I closed my eyes for a moment, thought of everything to stop myself coming apart at the thought of his mouth on me.

Then I knocked off his hat, twisted one hand in his hair, and I held him still.

"Open your mouth," I demanded, and fuck, that was what he did as I fed him my cock. "Suck me." Oh fuck, I sounded like a bad porno, but if he needed me to tell him, then that was what I was going to do. My cock had far more control of me than my rational brain. He took me deep, too deep, choked, but stayed in place, then shifted back a little to lick and suck me.

"Use your hands," I asked, *begged,* and only then did he cover the distance between the root of my cock and his mouth with his hand. I was engulfed in the warm wet cavern of his mouth, and I wasn't going to last. I gripped his head and he groaned with his mouth full of my cock. I tightened my hold and he sucked harder, then slowed and I didn't want that, but I couldn't even think. When he cupped my balls, teasing me, licking, I had to release one of my hands to brace myself against the tree.

"So good," I praised but I needed to warn him, this wasn't good, I was going to come. I yanked his head back as my orgasm boiled inside me, arching over, and coming into my hand, absolutely breathless and lightheaded, and he stayed on his knees.

"Levi, shit," was all I could manage. He looked destroyed, his lips puffy, and then he reached for my hand and paused, his tongue darting out to wet his lips only inches from my release. "Lick it," I ordered, and he fell on the task with eager focus, all the time staring up at me. When my hand was clean he tugged at my finger with his teeth, and then rocked back. "You want to come?" I asked him, and his eyes widened, a long, shining moment where he tilted his chin, and then reached for his cock. "Get yourself off."

A clatter of something in the distance broke us apart, and he scrambled to stand, his eyes wide, as if he didn't understand what he'd just done, palming his cock, and I knew he hadn't finished himself off. He hurried to the barn, and I followed, finding him staring at the chore board.

Micah was in there, cleaning off an empty wheelbarrow that clattered as he wheeled it, a wide grin on his face.

"Seems where I find Levi, I find Quinn," he observed.

Levi stepped away from me so fast that he smacked into a wall, but *hey, let's not make it super obvious, eh?*

"You recall he's working with my horses, right?" I kept my tone light.

"Obviously." Micah smirked as he left the stables.

"Well, that was awkward," I teased.

Levi was deadly quiet, then he cursed as he scrubbed at his eyes. "I can't get enough of you." The admission appeared to have been dragged from dark place, and he was spiraling.

"N'awww, cowboy, I bet you wish you could quit me," I drawled in my best cowboy, then patted his hard chest, scraping a nail over his nipple.

"Huh?"

I guess the pop reference went over his head and that deserved a kiss, which he leaned into before rearing back and glancing over to where Micah had been standing. I supposed when you were a gay cowboy you didn't have a desperate need to watch movies about gay cowboys. At least, not the same need as I did. When this was all done and I was back home, wherever I ended up, I'd be playing *Brokeback Mountain* on repeat.

"It was a joke."

He gripped my upper arms. "You think this is a joke?"

"No, of course not."

"How can you be so normal?"

"No one ever called me 'normal' before." I put my hands on my hips and pouted, and he frowned, but I caught the way he appraised me from my toes up, which sent shivers to my libido.

"Why are you doing this to me?" He ran his hands through his hair, gripped himself, appearing to be having a major existential crisis, and then in a smooth move he cradled my face, then tugged me deeper into the shadows, thumbing my cheekbones, his eyes half closed.

"You're not the only one who's confused," I admitted.

He shook his head as if he couldn't understand what I was saying. "I've never felt like this before." The admission was torn from him; I could see the effort it had taken.

"You're a dangerous man, Levi," I murmured. "Making me want things I can't have."

"Quinn—"

"We need to do that again, maybe I could get down on my knees for you," I whispered.

He ignored me. "It can't happen again."

I couldn't make out what he was trying to say. "Levi—"

"You need to stop staring at me and making me feel all churned up inside. Making me do things I shouldn't."

"So, you dragging me in the bushes was my fault? I think we're even now." I was feeling a little desperate because I didn't want to go, I wanted another kiss, and to talk about whatever was going through his head.

"You and your hair, and your beautiful fucking eyes, and your stupid jokes…" We kissed again and just when I knew he was going to pull away, I took a step back and twirled in a full circle.

"What do you call an ant who fights crime?" I changed the subject completely and pulled on my stockpile of stupid jokes that took up too much real estate in my head.

His amber eyes filled with confusion. "Huh?"

"I asked, what do you call an ant who fights crime?"

He blinked at me and shook his head.

"A vigilanty!" I announced with added jazz hands, and was so smug that I'd managed to get a real joke in, but all he did was raise a single eyebrow. I thought I saw a twitch of his lips, but that was probably my overactive imagination. Finally, he did that huffing sound again.

"You're an idiot," he murmured without heat, and instead there was definite touch of affection.

More clattering, but this time it was Archie and a pile of buckets that he lined up against the wall.

"Told you I do jokes," I said and stepped away.

"Do you do jokes?" Archie asked, peering up at me with an amused expression. "I have one." He wrinkled his nose and he looked so uncertain.

"I'd love to hear it," I encouraged him.

"What is brown, hairy, and wears sunglasses? A coconut on vacation!" The whole sentence came out in one breath, and then Archie went scarlet. "I know it's stupid."

"What's stupid?" Laurie stepped around me to stand

next to Archie, and shoulder to shoulder they stared at Levi and me. "Archie's not stupid." Laurie elbowed his friend.

"I never said Archie was..." I threw Levi a helpless glance, but he was smirking, and I knew I couldn't count on him. "He was telling a joke—"

"Archie's jokes are cool." Laurie crossed his arms over his chest. I couldn't force the words out because it *was* Max. Right there in front of me, was the image of the brother I'd lost, and I wanted to sink to the floor and sob. "What joke did you tell 'em?" Laurie was staring at me but asking Archie.

"The coconut one," Archie said.

"That's awesome, my favorite one, see the coconut is brown, and he's hairy—"

"I thought the joke was so funny," I interrupted, and after a moment, Laurie relaxed. "Tell me another one."

The floodgates opened on the jokes, and as Levi busied himself in the stable, I was caught between watching him, chatting to the boys about the strength of rope and buckets, and thinking about Max and horses and Levi. After a while, Laurie and Archie vanished to look for rope, and it was me and Levi alone in the barn again. I stepped closer and he didn't move away, so I took it as agreement that I could be close enough so we could maybe kiss again. At the last moment he stiffened and seemed confused.

"Maybe we should talk about what happened between us?" I asked, but I could tell the moment had passed a long time before.

"Sure, we can talk, but I'm not interested in messing

things up for Micah, so unless it's about your horses, then I have to be done with blowjobs in the stable." Levi was firm, intractable, and I just about stopped myself from begging for another kiss.

"Oh."

He walked past me, knocking my hat. "Later."

By the time I followed, Micah and he were standing by Sunny and chatting, and with their backs to me I wasn't going to interrupt, not even to suggest some more kissing, because he was everything I ever wanted in a man. All I could think was thank goodness for my shirt, which I untucked to cover my erection.

"Quinn?" Rachel called from the front door.

I sketched a wave and trotted over to talk to her. "Morning."

"You're still here?"

"I was helping Levi."

She caught my gaze and held it without trying. She was beautiful, not delicate but strong and focused, and although she wasn't smiling, she wasn't scowling either. "I think you *really* need to come for lunch and meet the family." After thinking she was avoiding me, this was an unexpected invitation, and I wasn't going to turn it down. I could talk to Laurie again and meet Oliver for real.

"Thank you."

"Wash up, come in." She indicated a metal sink outside at the corner of the house, and I went over to wash my hands, lighter than I'd ever been that I'd scored an invite into the house. I went inside before she could change her mind and walked into a wide-open room that was a dining room and sitting room all mixed into one. The scent of tomato and cheese filled the air and there was a man standing with his back to me next to Rachel.

"Can I do anything?" Both turned to face me, and I recognized the man from the new house I'd walked past.

"Scott," he introduced himself and we shook hands.

"Quinn, we met—"

"At the house, yes, nice to see you again."

That was the pleasantries done, and I certainly didn't get anything from Rachel who'd turned back to cooking.

"Coffee?" Scott asked, already pouring me a mug, and then indicating the table where there was cream and sugar. I could talk to Rachel, get to know her, I could make it so that I was sitting next to Levi and maybe get to touch him again, in fact I couldn't see any downsides when coffee and food came as part of the package.

I was on tenterhooks waiting for my first up-close visit with Oliver. I could hear laughing from upstairs, an innocent happiness that I didn't think Max and me had ever really had as kids, followed by shouting and joking as Laurie, Archie, and Oliver came downstairs.

Archie was first with his red hair, freckles, and he was holding Oliver's hand as the toddler followed slowly, dressed in denim dungarees and a purple T-shirt, his butt fat with a diaper and cheeks so chubby I just wanted to kiss him. He giggled, and Archie grinned widely as he made slow work of getting down. This was the first time I'd had a good look at Oliver, and my dreams caught up with reality. Max would have been dead long before Oliver was conceived; the blackness hit me hard, and for a moment I couldn't breathe, and I wondered if my heart would start again.

"Faster," Laurie urged from behind and Archie turned and stuck his tongue out. I didn't have time to think anymore because I knew the absolute moment that Levi walked into the house. It wasn't that the air changed, or there was an electric charge, I *knew*.

As they came near my chair, Oliver caught sight of me, and headed to the table, using me as a ladder to get to his seat. I helped him up, and between us, Archie and I had Oliver strapped into his booster seat.

"Hey," I said to Oliver who was wriggling against the restraints. He stared up at me, and gave me a grin, and I was gone.

My heart was going to break into so many pieces from overwhelming grief and happiness fighting for space, that I might never be whole again.

I wanted to stay, and damn with the consequences.

But I'd already lost a brother, and I couldn't face losing anyone else.

Chapter Twenty

LEVI

QUINN HELPED OLIVER WITH HIS LUNCH AND GRINNED SO wide I thought his face may split. It seemed he was just one of those people who liked children, and the untidier the better.

"Bah!" Oliver announced, and slammed a chubby fist onto his plate, pizza and salad flying in all different directions. Most of it ended up on him, but Quinn got a healthy splash of pizza sauce all down the front of his lemon and white chambray shirt. He laughed, as if none of it mattered, and smoothly he wiped himself and Oliver down, and throughout all of it, Rachel didn't move a muscle.

"He's messy," Laurie explained, "Isn't he, Mom?"

She smooched a kiss on his head. "So messy."

I sipped coffee, watching mom and son chatting about normal things as they did every morning. I loved sitting here soaking up the happy as if I was starved for it, and this family was a five-course dinner.

I'd had a shit morning up until that kiss in the barn.

First, I hadn't been able to locate Sky anywhere, and had finally found her in an old decrepit locked up barn. I peered in through a broken board, but I couldn't see anything in there past shadows. Sky was slinking around a rotten siding, sniffing out something, and wouldn't come out even when I called, only leaving when a cat swerved past her and headed up the field with Sky sprinting after it. At least she was still on the ranch, so that was one thing, but as usual she was making herself queen of this new place, and we'd catch up when she needed feeding, and then some time in the evenings—I kinda missed her but loved how much time she was spending with the boys.

Then I'd had Quinn staring at me, kissing me, and getting up in my space, with that falling and me catching him, and it was all too much. Then the kiss—the softest of all kisses, and it had become a heat that threatened to consume me whole, and I'd fallen to my knees desperate for a taste of him.

"Where are we with Glimmer?" Micah interrupted my heated thought escalation.

I gave my full attention to him and the matter in hand, along with how the work with Sunny had gone. I chatted business, but I could feel the weight of Quinn's stare, and when lunch was done, he was on my heels, following me out to the barn.

"You need to leave me alone." I rounded on him, and he stumbled back from me, the only thing stopping him from face-planting was the wall behind him. "For someone who says they can dance, you're clumsy as shit," I huffed, because holding him sent my blood south and I wasn't going to let him know how he affected me, covering my attraction with gruffness.

He extricated himself from my hold, and then shimmied away from me before completing a complicated trio of dance moves, which were far too sexy, and which he really shouldn't have been doing in a barn, finishing by touching his toes and wiggling his ass like a five-dollar pole dancer.

But so much sexier. *Nope. Not looking.*

"You'll scare the horses," I muttered to hide my real feelings of holy-shit. I was getting good at ignoring him.

"The horses have never seen anything this sexy," Quinn teased, and then winked.

He winked, all sassy and cute and up in my face. I didn't know if it was the earlier kiss, my inability to work, self-denial, or the fact that I'd been witness to someone dying at the rough end of a cowboy's fists before. My fear and temper soared.

"You need to stop doing that shit. You can't be so… you… around ranches, what if…"

Quinn pivoted as gracefully as when he'd jumped from the rocks on that first tour. "What if what?" he asked in a flat tone.

"What if a man was to take offense?" Ouch. Was that the right way of explaining this? The last thing I wanted was for him to think it was cool to be so… himself… around men who weren't me or Micah. I'd seen some shit go down in my time, hell, I'd been in the middle of it and on the receiving end. I carried scars to this day from the time I'd lost Jamie. Fuck that wasn't a name I liked to think about, but seeing Quinn here just pulled back nightmares from where I'd shoved them. My scars itched with the sense memory of disgust and ire, and all the other poisonous words that filled my head.

My love for Jamie had been so innocent, we'd been so young, but I hadn't been able to protect him. What if I couldn't protect Quinn?

Why was I even thinking about this?

"I see your point," Quinn began, but then he removed his hat and tucked errant strands of pale rose-colored hair behind his ear. It had faded since that first day, but instead of lessening the impact he looked even more… beautiful. Like how the sunset painted the mountains with shades of blush. "But you see, this is me. Unapologetic, out, authentically me."

"What if they're not like me, what if they want *you* on your knees? Huh? How did you get this far without learning to hide yourself better?" I asked, taking in everything from his hair to his face where liner had smudged around his gorgeous clear gray eyes, right down to his slim hips, and the way he filled his jeans.

He cracked his neck. "The lessons I received in life made me a rebel," he joked, and the words were like a stab to my heart. Had other men hurt him? What kind of lessons did he mean?

I wanted to kill anyone who hurt him.

I am so fucked.

"You look so…" I waved at him, "small, and your hair is all… and your eyes. Look, fuck… whenever you go to your next ranch, with the horses, just be careful with cowboys." I worried about him, about the way he was so unapologetically him, when I'd spent my entire existence living in the shadows.

His lips thinned. "I apologize for teasing, and making you feel awkward. I promise you it wasn't my intention to overstep, I just got carried away after what we'd done." He leaned closer so he could whisper, "I thought we had a connection after the blowjob and when I held you down—"

"Stop."

He sighed in exasperation. "But it happened, and it's my nature to be flirty, so I'm sorry. I don't know what it is about *you* that brings out my sugar side, but it's wrong for me to make you feel uncomfortable and I promise you—*I promise you*—that I will keep myself to myself when you're training. Sincerely."

So many pretty words and I didn't know what to focus on first. "You didn't make *me* feel uncomfortable," I defended, because even though I didn't know what was happening, I wasn't the kind to judge a man. *Wait. Isn't that what you're doing right now?*

"Of course, I did, and I apologize." He wrinkled his nose, and he looked so damn… edible.

"Not all cowboys are like me and Micah…"

"Like you? Irritable and stubborn and sexy as fuck?"

I glanced around. What if someone was still here? What if Micah heard our client call me sexy? Why the hell was I even worried about that? I could leave anytime I wanted; Micah wouldn't hold me to a contract if I *really* needed to go. Right?

"No, like me being different."

"Different how?"

"Gay."

"Oh, *that.*"

"You go to another ranch, and wink at another cowboy, and they could make it their mission to hurt you, so be careful." I hated that I was suggesting putting a cage made of wariness around such a bright and beautiful bird, but Quinn didn't know this life the same as I did, and he needed to look after himself.

"Okay."

"I mean it."

He drew his shoulders back. "I can handle myself."

"So you say."

"I took you down, twice if I remember right?" He grinned at me, and somehow the smile made me feel all weird, because he wasn't taking this seriously.

"I was taken by surprise."

"As is anyone who tries to hurt me. Come on, let me show you," he flirted, and held out his hands, wiggling his fingers like a prize fighter.

Ignoring my decision not to get close to him in case I gave in to the lure of his lips and his body, I crowded him against the barn wall, my hands either side of his head. "What if a man comes up and traps you?"

"I can get out of this, easily," he replied. He didn't move though, instead he glanced up at me through his bangs and waited for me to say more of whatever was going on in my head. Why did he get me so tangled up?

"What if there's two of 'em, an' they get closer and back you in a corner." The thought of anyone hurting Quinn made my ire inflate exponentially. My voice was low and growling, drawling with the fear of what might happen to him, but even when I stepped a little closer, he didn't shift at all. There was nothing more than daylight separating us, and the scent of him made my head spin. All I wanted to do was go to my knees and bury my face in him, and then for him to take me out of myself, show me all the different ways that I could be around a man who cared about me. What in hell's name was I doing? He'd winked at me, and all I wanted to do was make him realize that another, more evil man, might take that as an invitation.

Not me, but another cowboy who wanted to hurt the man that I was with.

Am I with *him?* Neither of us were there for anything other than getting off. *So, what am I even thinking?*

"I have moves." Quinn pushed firmly against my chest, and he wasn't weak, but the press of his hand was more of a warning rather than a shove that was going to send me to the ground. "I showed you what I can do when you ran me over."

"You caught me by surprise," I repeated. "And it was just me on my own."

"And in the trees?"

"That was nothing," I dismissed, and saw the flash of pain in his eyes. I wished I hadn't said that, when it had been everything to me, and probably would be for a long time.

"I can run fast." The tip of his tongue darted out to wet his lips, and it was all I could do not to answer some unspoken invitation. I was so hard, and all I needed to do was step forward that extra inch and I could be up against all the warm, tempting goodness and honesty that was out and proud Quinn Rhodes. He could turn me around, hold my hands, make me keep them still, tell me what he wanted…

"What if there's more than one man?" I pulled myself back to warning him.

He blinked up at me. "I'm not inclined to be with more than one man at a time, Levi," he joked, and it was then I realized that yeah, he wasn't taking this seriously, or maybe I wasn't making my fears coherent enough for him to understand. There was something between us, even if it was over now, even if we never did anything again, I couldn't bear it if he was hurt.

I have *to get him to see that not every cowboy is like me.*

I took his hand, and he didn't pull away, even moved to lace his fingers with mine, but that wasn't what I wanted. I slid my hold to his slim wrist and then pinned his hand to the wall. "I could hold you here, then what would you do?"

"I don't get off on that as much as you do," he teased.

"Stop," I warned. "This isn't a game." I could imagine him rolling up to another ranch, thinking he could trust people, making himself vulnerable.

He held my gaze, and there was no fear, only confusion.

"I could just ask you to let me go."

"You need to think about keeping yourself safe," I restated. "You're asking to get yourself hurt." Why was I doing this? I was creating a fight, pushing this too far, just to take the attention off me and what I'd done. I'd gone to my knees and begged him to let me have his cock, and that was so far out of my comfort zone that my skin felt tight, and I was scared.

Scared for him? Scared for me? I didn't know which way was up. All I knew was that I wanted to kiss him then run in the opposite direction, hold him, and protect him with every part of me, then push him away. I didn't need someone like Quinn in my life, I didn't want it, because this was too much like a real connection and I didn't roll over like this for people. No one stayed around for me, no one wanted me, they wanted to hurt me, so why would it be any different from Quinn.

"We're done," I blurted, locked into asshole self-protection mode, scared about what could happen to Quinn, confused, overwhelmed. "I don't want this."

He was beautiful, and I wanted to kiss him, and I wanted him to show me what I needed, and he could get hurt, and I would be left with a broken heart for not being able to save him. Other men could've beaten me to the ground, and I could've taken it, but behind the strength in every line of Quinn, he was fragile, and I might not be there to help him.

His eyes looked glassy and for a second, I thought I'd made him cry, but it wasn't tears, it was a temper as sudden as a summer storm.

"Shit, Levi. You kissed me back, made me feel as if I could…" He yanked his hand out of my hold, and I let him go, and at the moment I thought we might've talked, he twisted, shoved, had his foot behind my knee, and abruptly I was on my knees in the dirt. "I'm sorry." He brushed off his hands, but I could see he was trembling, and it killed me that I'd done that to him because of my own confusion. I should tell him about Jamie, explain how things had gone so badly wrong, and how Jamie had died. Instead, I begged.

"Quinn—"

"Fuck you, Levi," he snapped. "Fuck you, and the horse you rode in on."

Chapter Twenty-One

QUINN

I was mortified. Completely and utterly humiliated and so damn angry at myself. What was I doing coming onto a ranch, pretending to be all business, then winking at Levi as if I was in a damn club? He was right—I shouldn't have been forcing my flirting on anyone, and I'd pushed it too damn far as usual, but he'd wanted me to do it. Hadn't he?

Had I misread everything? Had I taken advantage? A wave of guilt consumed me, and I bent at the waist to catch my breath, waiting for Levi to come out and tell me he was being stupid, that everything we'd done was because it was right, but there was no Levi tapping me on the back, no kind words to explain that I hadn't fucked up.

"Everything okay Mr. Rh—Quinn?"

I straightened and right in front of me, Micah smiled cautiously in a way which implied I needed to be asked.

"I just, I'm sorry, yes... everything is good." Jeez, I was

good at this lying. I glanced behind but there was no sign of Levi following me.

"It's just you looked… never mind. I had a call from Ed, about a delivery of lumber and tools and I'm guessing it's for the tree house."

"Great, I'll get started on that as soon as it arrives," I knew I'd be spending this evening in my hotel room boning up on tree house building for the hundredth time.

"I'll need to…" he paused and seemed uncomfortable about something. "You recall I want to check the work, you understand, right?"

"Of course."

"Maybe I could ask Levi to help out," he added.

Great. As if I needed to face Levi again, ever. "If you think that's a good idea."

"Yep, I'll do that, he's good with his hands."

My thoughts went a hundred ways at that innocent statement.

Then everything became weird, because he was waiting for me to go, and I had no other reason to be there, at least none I could think of on the fly. I nodded my goodbye, then headed to my truck and with the itch of humiliation and shame scratching under my skin, I left.

Levi said we were done.

That sent me on a misery spiral because I had no control and I'd humiliated myself with someone who didn't want me. It was the story of my life to want what I couldn't have and I was so desperate to connect on a human level that I'd evidently seen things that weren't there. I'd skimmed my time at the ranch, playing a role, and knowing I'd leave, and then I'd fallen in love with the ranch, and the family, and then there was Levi.

I drove straight through town and out the other side, following an old tourist sign that pointed to Whisper Ridge Outlook, and climbing the mountain on an old road that had seen better days. I parked up and clambered down from the cab, staring at the view. I wished I could've appreciated the beauty of what I was looking at, but all I could think of was sharing time with the family, knowing that Oliver wasn't Max's son, and then the shit with Levi in the barn. I'd gone from high to low and back again in the space of an hour, and my heart hurt from it all.

Standing here alone with my thoughts, I made a list. I couldn't do anything about what had happened with Levi. I had to push that to one side, he hadn't communicated what he'd meant to, I'd knocked him to the ground, he'd tried to tell me that I was wrong. I had to forget all of that and chalk Levi up to mistakes I'd made.

So that left Rachel, and by extension Laurie and Oliver, not to mention Micah, and Scott.

"I need to get my head straight," I said to the mountain.

I wanted to know Rachel's children, I wanted to capture that small part of Max that I craved. *She might think I want to take Laurie. Or fight for him.* I had to leave. No more horse training shit, or pretense, or any of the crap that I was doing to silently work my way into their lives. *I should own who I am. No more Levi.* Then I had to do what Max would do. Leave them alone so they could create perfect family lives without the taint of the Dawson name.

I'd desperately wanted Laurie to be my nephew. But I didn't want him to suffer the same life I had, exposed to greed and media and pain. Sighing I focused back on the view, trying to center myself.

From there I could see down into the town and to the back of Lennox Ranch, and there was even a monument with words chiseled into stone. For the longest time I wallowed in my stupid misery and uncertainty about everything, and then I stretched tall before crossing to the information board next to the stone.

"Whisper Ridge," I read as best as I could as half the words were worn away. Warm gusts of wind took my voice and threw it down the mountain, and the sun was hot on my back as I read any of the sentences I could still make out.

The board told the legend of a woman whose lover hadn't returned from war. Apparently, she'd shouted his name and the mountain told her that he was coming home and where he'd been all this time. It was fanciful, but I wondered for a second if I called out my brother's name, would the mountain tell me he was at peace? Would the echoes tell me what I needed to do next? I slumped to the ground, and crossed my legs, then shouted Max's name and it startled both me and the birds in the tree that was giving me shade. Even though I'd yelled my hardest, I didn't get a reply.

I gave up after half an hour.

Mountains knew nothing at all.

Chapter Twenty-Two

LEVI

Was it normal to change everything that shaped my life just because of one man? As soon as I'd done my days work I showered then headed for the hotel, because whatever I felt about myself, it wasn't fair to dump everything on Quinn. Guilt was acid in my gut, and I owed Quinn an explanation. The facts were clear; he made me feel as if I could one day have something with another man, one who might see me the way Quinn seemed to, and that had scared me to the point I'd pushed him away. Sex was confusing everything, and I had to focus on the fact that I was leaving, he was a client and leaving, and most of all, we were worlds apart.

First though, an apology, because what I'd said to him, what I'd implied, was acid inside me and I wasn't a person to hurt people intentionally. I wasn't cruel.

I wasn't.

I hovered for the longest time outside Quinn's door before I even thought of knocking. I felt guilt at what I'd said about how he had to be different, and then protective that he'd told me he'd do what he wanted.

I could hear music, something classical I think, with sweeping violins, and I imagined Quinn inside dancing to it. Because that was how I imagined Quinn doing anything—always moving. I knocked, loud enough to be heard over the swell of sound inside, and it stopped.

"I'm sorry, I turned it down," Quinn called.

"It's me," I called. "Levi."

"I don't need to talk," he sounded as if he was right on the other side of that piece of wood.

"I'm not here to talk," I lied.

There was a pause, and then the door opened, and Quinn peered out, his beautiful soft hair pulled up in a knot, his eyes narrowed.

"Can I come in?" I asked.

"Is something wrong with the horses?" He glanced around me into the corridor beyond as if he expected a horse to be standing there.

"Nope, not visiting about horses."

"Is there a fire?"

"No—"

"Then what do you want?"

I was getting tired of talking through a gap in the door, but I didn't want to make a big show of things in the hallway. I leaned right into the gap.

"I didn't like how things went," I murmured.

"When?" He blinked at me as if I hadn't spent ten minutes insulting him in the barn.

"When I said… look, let me in, so I can apologize face-to-face."

Finally, he stepped back and away to let me in. I moved inside before he changed his mind, shut the door. I pretended not to notice the way he was bare-chested, and that his sweats hung so low from his hipbones there was no doubt I would be interested in kissing my way down into his pants. So much for holding back. His treasure trail headed south, his feet were bare, and when I tracked back up I couldn't help but focus on his lightly furred chest and his cinnamon nipples.

"Eyes up here, cowboy," he said.

I snapped out of staring, heat rising in my face. "Sorry," I apologized before I realized I didn't want it to seem as if I was apologizing for staring. "I mean, sorry about what happened earlier. I never meant you to think I was judging you, or that any of what happened was your fault. But I know that was how it came across, and I don't know what to say."

"It was bullshit," Quinn said in an even tone.

I cringed. "It was mutual, what we did," I assured him.

He untied his hair and let it fall, probably giving himself time to think. "I know that, so you want to tell me why you freaked out?"

"I never meant to make you think that I… I know that you…" I stopped talking, realized I still had my hat on, and removed it quickly. Even messed up like I was right then I still had respect ingrained in me. It gave me a few moments to consider what to say next, but the words evaded me, and he needed to understand what was in my head.

I just had to understand it first. I sank to the sofa but

then I perched on the edge, ready to outrun my feelings if I needed to.

"When I was sixteen, I left home, took to using whatever skills I had, worked my way through South Dakota, then west, changing direction every summer. I knew I had a connection with horses, and I was valuable, earned a reputation as the kind of cowboy a ranch would hire. When I was seventeen, I met this boy, Jamie, a rootless kid like me, but he wanted to stay where we'd landed, and I could understand why. It was a good place, the owner was gay, so he didn't run a place that was full of hate, and Jamie," I glanced up at Quinn who was rapt with attention. "He planned on staying, and I fancied that I was in love, so I made plans in my head for a future where maybe Jamie and I would stay, make a new life. It didn't last, because the owner took on contracts he couldn't handle, and desperate for help he called on cowboys he didn't know, and they weren't good men. It wasn't his fault, I know that, but he didn't break up what happened next."

I didn't realize I'd stopped talking until Quinn pulled a chair over and set it in front of me, then touched my knee.

"What happened?"

I pressed a hand to my temple, where a faint scar reminded me of a day I didn't want to recall.

"They hurt Jamie, he was just this skinny kid with a big smile, and when they caught us kissing, which wasn't a big thing, it was just a fucking kiss, they got up in our faces." The memory of Jamie being carried to the ambulance, the cops there, the hurt and pain, and the sting of blood as it ran into my eyes, were things that I never wanted to share. "I buried Jamie, I stood up in court, I left the ranch, moved on. I'm okay, I have my horse, my dog, and I don't go around messing with men who can hurt me."

"I wouldn't hurt you." Quinn sounded confused, and he had every right to be.

"I know that. Not physically, although you have moves." I half smiled, but it didn't last long. "What we have isn't just kissing and blowjobs. Not when thinking about you makes my heart hurt, feeling as if we have something means you fill a space in here." I pressed a hand to my chest. "That hasn't happened since Jamie, and it scares the fuck out of me that I have feelings."

"Levi—"

"I've never felt the way I did when I was on my knees for you, when you stared down at me, and you made me think it was okay to let go. Then the kissing, and your jokes, and your smile."

Silence. He leaned forward, and for a moment I thought he might give me a speech where he'd make everything right, but then he closed his eyes and shook his head, and I knew this wasn't going to be good.

"Apology accepted," he whispered.

My heart sank, I don't know what I was expecting but it wasn't those gentle words.

"You're in my heart, Quinn."

He closed his eyes again and then buried his face in his hands, hiding behind the curtain of rose hair, and I leaned over and brushed his hair from his face.

"I'm so sorry I said all that shit, Quinn."

"It's okay." He pressed a kiss to the palm of my hand.

I pulled him toward me. I could no more ignore him being this close than I could walk out of there. I was addicted to Quinn, and I'd told him a secret that I'd locked in my heart, and he'd understood where I was coming from.

"Once more," Quinn murmured, and when I tugged he let me pull, and then I had a lap full of Quinn Rhodes with a body built only for me, and a lustful expression that made my cock so hard he must've felt it.

"What are we doing?" I had to know because I had boundaries, but he was an addiction, and he was staring at me with such intensity that it burned. I needed to taste him, and it had to be now, because if he didn't touch me in the next five-seconds, I might take myself in hand, right there in his room. His sweats were so low that the front rested on his cock which was hard and *right there* for me to touch.

"What you said about me being in your heart?"

"Yeah, I know it's stupid but—"

"You're in mine."

It was as if my body had been waiting to hear that, because I melted like ice in the sun and I cradled his face as we kissed, a clash of mouths that gentled immediately, licking and sucking, and I let him take control. He carded his hands through my hair, gripped my head, and then slowly lowered himself to kiss me. I couldn't move—I didn't *want* to move—and he captured my lips in heat and need, and with every lick and suck I was feeling looser, needier, and all I wanted was my hands on him. I walked my fingers from his hips to his loose sweats, and slid my thumbs inside, holding him, then when the kisses became more frantic I closed a hand around his cock, and I swore I moaned, or he did, I didn't know.

"You're wearing too much," he muttered, yanking at my official Lennox Ranch T-shirt, pulling it over my head, frustrated when it caught because there was no way I was letting go of him. He sat back from the kiss, then achingly slow, he explored each nipple, worrying them, then leaning down and sucking before biting hard enough for lightning to travel to my cock and have me bucking up under him. He didn't stop though, and I knew it was me who moaned, because I could hear it. He tugged at one nipple, twisted the nub, then licked around the delicious ache he'd caused. I had never been with someone who took the time to explore, but when he began to unbuckle my belt, I stopped one of his hands with mine.

"Do you have condoms?"

"Fuck. I don't know, I didn't pack my bags." He was confused, his lids heavy with passion, and I took my chance, running my nail across his nipple, twisting my hand on his cock where it was very happily sitting at home and wanting more to touch. "Fuck, cowboy—"

"Levi, my name is Levi," I ground out.

He kissed away the irritation, until I was loose under him again. "Levi?"

"Huh?"

"Stay here." He scrambled off, heading into the bathroom and there was smashing, and dropping noises, and I couldn't move from where I was, pinned by the weight of need that consumed me. He appeared at the door, holding up a box of condoms and lube in the other hand. "Bless Molls, she's one step ahead of me."

I didn't know who Molls was, I didn't care, as I finished unbuttoning my jeans and shoving them down my legs, getting them caught on my boots, but far enough so I could stand. "Fuck me."

"We need to have a conversation about—"

"I'm negative."

"Me too." His eyes darkened, and he shoved at his sweats, toeing them away, his erection bobbing, unrolling the condom, all while I twisted in a mess of jeans, and then leaned over the sofa and waited.

"You're beautiful," he muttered, and ran a hand down my back, squeezing me, "this ass is a thing of beauty," he added with a possessive growl, and I nearly died on the spot as I felt the cold lube when he slid a slick finger across my hole. "I can't believe you're giving it up like this."

I didn't want to think about that, I craved the burn and he needed to be inside me. "Stop talking and get the fuck inside me." Even if it was the only time. I wanted it more than breathing.

"I'm looking," he explained, and smoothed his hands all over me, my ass, my hole, up to my cock, pressing and sliding, until I was a mess of begging or defiance as I demanded he fuck me. I couldn't tell anymore. He worked a finger inside, and it had been a while, but I was desperate, my cock shiny with pre-cum as I reached down to relieve the pressure building inside me. With a curse he slapped my hand away.

"Hands off," he ordered.

I bowed my head and surrendered to the sensation of him pressing inside me, one finger, two, I didn't know, but he stilled and kissed my back, his long silky hair trailing down my spine, and I could feel it all. He twisted a hand in my hair, gripped it hard, then he moved his fingers and found the spot that made me close my eyes and bow up under him. He played with me, rubbing his finger there, pushed inside, pulled, and I was like putty in his hands as he held me still. I'd never found a man who knew what I needed, had never given myself the chance to find someone who could push me this far. He released my hair then reached around, but it wasn't to get his hand on my cock, but to pinch my nipples. I cursed him, and pressed back on his fingers, and *begged* him with my body for more. I wanted his fingers holding my hair, I wanted him biting and tugging at my nipples, I needed him to fuck me hard over the back of this sofa, until I didn't even know my own name.

I was frustrated but I wanted to wait. I had to have him inside me, but I *craved* the waiting.

"Please," I begged.

He pressed the head of his cock to me and pushed in enough for me to know he was there, hesitating as my body accepted him, and then he held still, stretching me, tugging and rolling my nipples, until I was incoherent with mumbled begging.

He fucked me so leisurely I never ever registered there was movement at all and I reached for my cock.

"Wait."

I wouldn't try to get myself off, because he'd told me not to, and he gripped my hips, pressed forward, and *relentlessly* kept going until he was balls-deep.

"Jeez, fuck…" he muttered, and bent over me, resting

his weight on me, pushing me down onto the back of the sofa, trapping my hands, and it was everything I craved and more. "Don't move," he groaned, and it was less of an order and more of a plea, but there was no way I was going to move, not when he was right there inside me. He began to rock, finding the angle, until finally he brushed over the nerve endings that sent me soaring again, and I gasped and groaned, and I writhed on his cock, and it was glorious. He rocked forward, I tried to meet the pressure back, but he held me, and I knew I was going to lose it any second and I needed something else.

"I'm close," I told him—tried to tell him—but he knew.

This time when he reached around, he gripped my neglected cock, and thumbed the head, sliding his fingers through the wet there, and biting down on my neck just as he pushed deeper. My orgasm consumed me, a whiteout of sheer sensation as I collapsed, and he fucked me down, shoved at me, sucked on my shoulder, and then cursed as he stiffened and emptied himself into the condom. I wished he was bare; I wished his come was inside me, I wanted it hot and slippery, evidence he'd been there, because I was lost and I wanted to remember it all.

"Are you okay?" he asked as he smoothed his hands over my skin. It felt like a goodbye, as if this was the last time, unless I could ease the fear that was the last part of me locked away.

"Stay inside me," I replied and closed my eyes, burying my face into the cotton of the sofa and feeling so peaceful.

Only when he was soft enough did he pull out, heading for the bathroom, coming back with a cloth, wiping me, then I felt the coolness of cream, and he helped me dress, until I was able to collapse, sated, on the sofa. I thought he would move away then, but instead he climbed onto my lap again, naked, and tucked himself into my neck. I didn't expect post-sex cuddles, and I thought I didn't want it.

It seemed Quinn had other ideas, and I couldn't do anything but cradle him, caring for him in a way that meant more than just a fuck. This was special, because I *wanted* to hold him close, and inhale the scent of his rose-tinted hair, and feel his breath on my skin.

"Damn it, Levi, what you do to me."

If I could've spoken, I'd have repeated the same thing, but I was boneless.

VOICES PULLED me out of my doze, and I found myself flat on the sofa, my feet on the floor, and covered in a thin sheet. Taking care of the men he fucked was clearly Quinn's thing.

"I don't want to leave." Quinn's voice echoed from the bedroom, and he sounded frustrated.

"I get that, but if you truly want them to stay off the radar then you're pushing this." A man's voice, and he was warning Quinn about something. Somehow, he'd extricated himself from my hold and had left me sleeping, and regrets began to burn in my belly. I'd cuddled him as if we were real lovers, held onto him and if I hadn't fallen asleep would I have spent time whispering sweet nothings? Fucking was one thing, but thoughts of it being more was another thing all together. Quinn had taken the call into his bedroom, but he was talking hands-free.

"What do you suggest?" Quinn sounded worried.

I was torn between staying to protect him against whatever was upsetting him or running as if the hounds of hell were nipping at my feet. Protect? Where had that thought come from? If the scene in the barn had shown me anything, it's Quinn didn't need my protection when he had control of his life.

"I'll fix it," the man said, echoing what I wished I could've said.

I stood and buckled my belt, feeling the twinge in my ass, and my cock already hardening behind my zip at the sensory memory of coming on the end of Quinn's cock. He'd pushed me to the edge so hard that I'd been out of my mind with the need to come. I'd never met anyone like him, but we didn't fit together in any way other than this insane fiery attraction, it was just sex.

But I cuddled him. I wanted to hold onto him. I wanted more.

He saw me move, watched me, still talking to whoever was on the phone and for a long moment he held my gaze. Then I let myself out before I could second guess what I was doing. I wasn't fighting feelings for him, I wasn't imagining more, I wasn't falling for him. This thing between me and Quinn was one and done, and I'd gotten what I'd come for. He was in my heart, but he didn't have to stay there.

That would have to be enough.

It *was* enough.

Liar.

Chapter Twenty-Three

QUINN

I WANTED TO END THE CALL, BUT CONNOR WAS WORRIED about me, Molly was joining in, and I didn't have the defensive capability to argue with them. Team!Quinn was breaking apart, because I'd gone off-script, and it needed my full attention.

I couldn't stop thinking about what had happened. When we'd finished, I'd gotten the impression Levi wanted to get up and leave, but he'd been so tired, slipping into sleep, and I'd broken my own rule about it *only* being sex. I'd climbed into his strong arms and pressed my lips to his throat, and I'd held on so tight it was as if I never wanted to let him go. This connection was heat but it was also a raw need that I had never felt before. I'd been searching my entire adult life for a man who would put up with my shit, who didn't care that I was a switch, who saw through the physical me and saw right into my head.

The yin to my yang.

Was Levi that to me?

I had things to do there; set the kids up with whatever they needed, build a tree house. Levi was too dangerous to put on that list, because I'd never met anyone like him, rough and tough, and the way he'd opened up about himself was precious and something I would never forget. He'd sat there and told me something so hard, yet I'd let him talk and I hadn't stopped him to give him my truth. I'd lied by omission, but I'd wanted so much to tell him. He messed with my equilibrium though, case in point I'd lost the thread of what I was supposed to be talking about with Molly and Connor. *Money. That's right.*

"So, when *are* you coming home?"

I wasn't sure I was ever going back to Boston. In the city I was Alexander Dawson's son, but here in Whisper Ridge I was just Quinn Rhodes. "How are the money transfers going?" I was an expert in changing the subject with the best of them.

Connor cursed. Molly sighed.

"The last transfers are going through today," Molly said. "The final amount to the shelter."

I took them off speaker and took my phone into the main room and stared out of the window, checking the sidewalk and hoping to get one last glimpse of Levi. I needed to get my head back in the game. The queer youth support house was a new project, one that I'd created to be a safe place for people like me who lived in hostile families and had been subjected to the kind of invasive therapy at some point as they grew up. I closed my eyes.

"Yeah, that's a good call."

"Okay, I'll email the paperwork over as soon as it's

ready, and we're done. But, Quinn, you need to come home soon."

I ignored the question. "How is it looking with the cover story, Connor?"

He cursed again, then sighed with added drama. "I don't like you staying there, not considering this is personal. The media is making up all these stories about what you're really doing, and where you might be. It's a matter of time until you're tracked down, because no one is truly ever off-grid—you get that, right?"

"I've been thinking about that." I stopped, because how did I articulate that my priorities had shifted, that somewhere between drawing with Laurie, and falling for the idea of having Levi in my life, I was considering staying here.

"And?" This was from Molly who was normally the person I would've confided in.

"What if I want to stay? What if this could be my life?"

Silence. Connor didn't launch into a rant about justice, and Molly didn't immediately freak out about me leaving Boston.

"It's your decision," Connor said after a while. "But—"

"But you haven't even told Rachel who you are, you're lying to everyone, and there's no way back from that," Molly interrupted and laid her honesty on me like a brick to the head. "What do you think they'll say when they find out who you are, and withholding millions of dollars from them, not to mention that if the media find out where you are then your life out there won't be private anymore?"

"But, Molly—"

"Think this through. You're changing everything. Come home and leave them alone."

"I don't know if I can."

"Do you think Max would want you in their lives?"

She had me there. Max wouldn't have wanted me anywhere near them, and the thought of him telling me no was ice water in my veins. He'd always said we were cursed, that there was never going to be a good way for things to end for him or me.

"Okay."

"Okay, you're coming home?"

"Okay I'm leaving here," I corrected her. Where I ended up who knew, but it wouldn't be Boston. "I need you to draw up a document changing ownership of the horses to the Lennox Ranch, in Micah and Rachel's names, and I'm considering buying a house and transferring it to Rachel's name."

Silence.

Molly was the first to break it. "I assume it's not a house in Boston?"

"No, here in Whisper Ridge."

I'd pulled my sweats on, but the AC was giving me goosebumps. I tugged a T-shirt on, and smoothed it down, catching myself in the mirror and seeing nothing had changed outwardly with me even if I felt as though like a seismic shift had happened in my heart. Being in Wyoming had changed me. I was supposed to be there just checking in, then taking myself and my toxic family away from them. But add Levi, and I was fighting a battle against walking away. I'd never known craving as intense to stay at the ranch, be an uncle, and give this thing with Levi more time.

"Do you remember what you said to us at the beginning?"

"That I'm there to make a meaningful connection to potential family, then leave before anyone gets hurt."

I was despairing of ever connecting with anyone like *real* family. People who knew me and could love me for who I was, but money was all I knew, and that was the most fucking sad thing in the entire fucking world that was Alexander Quinn Dawson.

"The house could be for me then, an investment—"

"You're supposed to have left by now—"

"It's better than an extended stay in a hotel." I talked straight over her in the vain hope we wouldn't return to the fact I was meant to have left the ranch by now.

"You've already bought horses..."

Only when Connor started talking about security of data, and Max, and my father, and how the clinic wasn't an unending safety net, I was on information overload.

"The choice is simple," Connor began to summarize. "Stay, be an uncle, tell Rachel about Max's trust fund. Leave and don't tell them, then disperse the money the same as you're doing yours. If you're buying a house, then you're making a conscious decision to expose Max's son to the media, and worse of all, your father."

I clutched the phone, the thought of Alexander Dawson being in Laurie's life wasn't worth thinking about, and abruptly I couldn't take anymore. "Meeting adjourned?" I interrupted Connor who was mid flow talking about tactical this or that.

"If you won't take my advice then I'm all done here," Connor said crisply.

I knew I'd annoyed him. I paid Connor for his advice, and I'd just cut him off. "I'm sorry, I didn't mean… I'm scattered is all. What did you say?"

"Your father *explicitly* stated when he hired me that he wanted Max back under his control, or he wanted him gone. If he finds out that he's a grandfather, he'll use every resource at his disposal and Rachel could end up fighting to keep her son. Do you want Laurie to end up in the same situation as you and Max?"

"We have all the insider information—he can't hurt anyone all the time I have that."

"And I'll release it the very minute you say you want me to," Connor reassured. "But right now it's a threat, and I know it's kept your father out of your life but—"

"I know! Okay. I know." A familiar despair crashed over me, and I slumped to the bed. "I know it's all built on lies, but I just want to know them. I need my brother's family to know me."

"Oh, Quinn," Molly said, her voice broken as if she was on the verge of crying. Then she cleared her throat. "Connor, let's give Quinn a few more days to get his head straight, and Quinn, just take care, okay. Think long and hard about buying a house, think about what you're doing."

Between them they'd saved my sanity, but for the first time since Max had vanished my life goals had shifted. I couldn't bear the thought of leaving, and then there was Laurie. He was safe at the ranch, he'd never know the chaos that dogged my steps, or the events in

Max's life that led him to drugs, and then the commune.

Don't forget Levi.

"You know where I am," Connor said.

"I know and thank you, Connor."

He mumbled something and then dropped the call, and it was just me and Molly, but we didn't delay our goodbyes, and I got the feeling that she was disappointed I was moving the goalposts. When we'd first created this simple plan, I was supposed to be in and out in a week, not planning an entire summer based around family, horses, and not one of the contingencies we'd imagined included me falling in love with a cowboy.

Call ended, I had no idea what to do next. Connor and Molly were right about the house, in that it was one more thing that would give me roots in Whisper Ridge. After all, I had the horses, and I wouldn't be taking those with me, and now a house? I should listen to them, but the idea of investing in something for Rachel and the boys, and by extension Scott, was a burning goal that wouldn't leave me alone. I would be buying it with cash, my own money, part of a trust from my grandmother, which was more money than a man needed in ten lifetimes, so financially it was separate from the Dawson family, but of course there were deeds, legal documents, admin, and that put me on the radar of anyone who really cared to look.

In the end it wasn't a decision for me to make but an impulse to act on. I dressed in smart jeans and a white shirt, plus dress shoes. For what I was doing next, I had to present better than the scuffed dusty jeans and boots, although my Louboutin loafers weren't nearly as comfortable as my cowboy boots. Then I headed out, hoping that a realtor's office wouldn't be that hard to find in such a small town.

Sheridan Realty was based in a small office not far from the hotel, but the sign in the window was turned to *back in five* and my initial plans to talk about the house up near the ranch were thwarted. So, I did what every sensible person would do with time to kill, and headed for the coffee shop, thinking on my feet, and concluding coffee might help cheer me up. Only, as I got there, Scott walked out, donut hole half in his mouth and balancing two coffees. He gave me a donut smile and moved to one side to let me pass but stopped when I didn't go past.

"Could you show me that house where we first met?" I asked him. He blinked at me then juggled the coffees and removed the donut, wiping his mouth with a napkin.

"Uhmm, of course, Mr. Rhodes, I'll just put these in the… if you want to follow me."

"Quinn," I reminded him as I took the coffees from him so he could open the door to his office.

"Did you want one of the coffees? I have two, but I don't always drink both, it's just when I'm doing paperwork, I need the caffeine… hell, I'm rambling. Cream, no sugar," he indicated the coffees in my hand, and I passed one back to him. It was a hot day, but I'd never knowingly turned down caffeine.

He picked up a folder, keys, and his coffee, leaving the half-eaten donut on the desk, and then he locked up.

"You want me to drive?" I nodded to the Lexus, which was on the road by the hotel.

He glanced from me to the car, then nodded.

"Laurie and I decided it was the best car in town right now." He shot me a nervous smile. He couldn't know that I wanted to hear more about what Laurie said, or that hearing the interest in his voice for a car I didn't even want made me smile. I couldn't help the twinge of jealousy that he had a relationship with Laurie at all, which was just stupid, because that was next on my list.

Buy a house.

Figure out how Levi fitted into all of this.

Tell Rachel who I was.

Love her and the boys.

Explain how nineteen million dollars was sitting in a fund that had come to me on Max's death. Get them to understand why I didn't tell them about it when they couldn't know the killing pressure that money caused.

They deserve to know, to make the choices themselves.

I released the locks, then held out the keys. "You take the wheel," I said.

He took the keys after a small hesitation, and climbed into the driver's seat, running a reverential hand over the leather, and his eyes widening at the dash.

"It's at times like this that I wish the houses I'm selling were a hundred miles from here and not just a few miles out of town," he deadpanned.

"Go the long way, then."

He didn't have to be told again, we passed the outlook twice and by the time we reached the house and parked in the wide driveway he was grinning and chatting about Laurie this and Oliver that. I even got a glimpse into how he'd proposed to Rachel at New Year, and they were marrying soon. I couldn't help but smile at his enthusiasm.

"So, back to business I guess." He cleared his throat and the mask of a salesman slipped into place. I didn't underestimate this nice guy driving a hard bargain, although I'd probably have paid any amount. "This is the last remaining plot, the biggest we have here, and over there is where Micah and Daniel have a place, the one with the windmills, which Laurie and Micah built when they first moved in."

"I know the house," and I loved it even more now I knew Laurie had a hand in the sea of color.

"The rest of the neighbors are quiet and respectful. It's a good place to live, somewhere I aspire to." We stepped into a wide hall, with doors off from it, dressed simply in deep red accents against the wood. It smelled new, and light flooded in from floor-to-ceiling windows either side of the door. The furniture was sparse, just enough to show the house I guessed, but I instantly felt at home.

"This is the bathroom," Scott opened the door with a flourish, exposing what was clearly a bathroom. "I think the bath gives it away though," he added with a rueful smile.

I couldn't fault his enthusiasm for selling, and the interior was as solid and beautiful as the exterior.

"Each place is individually designed, with views of either the mountain, Whisper Ridge, or the town below, either way, it's a stunning spot."

"A good investment."

"I wouldn't be doing my job if I didn't mention the

rental market here is slow. It could be sitting empty for a long time."

I ignore that because it was no more than ten minutes' walk to the ranch. It would be a good investment for Rachel, Scott, and the boys, something positive that they could keep, or sell—it was entirely up to them.

I dutifully leaned past Scott to look at the room, which had an enormous bath, a two-man shower with a rain head and other interesting attachments, and two sinks, not to mention a wall of glossy cabinets with mirrors.

"It's a lovely bathroom." I pulled myself together.

He seemed more relaxed with every comment I made. "Rachel chose the bathrooms here, and the kitchens, said it shouldn't be left up to me." He rolled his eyes, but then he wrinkled his nose. "I agree, anyway, through here, there's a dressing room which we constructed using..." He was talking about wood and craft, and handmade items, and I knew I should have been listening, but we were at the back of the house and the view from the window held me transfixed.

"It's stunning, isn't it?" he murmured at my side.

"Yeah, I lost myself for a moment."

"There's room for parking, plus the double garage with the workroom."

"Great."

"You'll have no trouble getting the Lexus in there," he added. "If it's you that's buying the house, I don't want to assume."

"No, it would be me, but as an investment," I said, and he nodded as if it was every day someone wanted to buy a house in Whisper Ridge to make money. "The house really is beautiful." I wasn't lying. It wasn't the kind of place that Alexander Quinn Dawson would've been expected to buy, but it was exactly the house that Quinn Rhodes would have been happy in, close to Lennox Ranch, and to Rachel and the boys.

The thought of leaving hollowed my chest, I wanted to be part of Laurie's life, but I wanted to explore more with Levi and…

No, I was being stupid.

Scott smiled, then pulled out a notepad. "Can I book you in for a second viewing? Of course, we're open to offers but the square footage is—"

I interrupted him and extended a hand, "No need, I want it." Scott's eyes widened and for a few moments he stared down at his pad. "I can transfer the full price today."

"Huh?"

I smiled at him in encouragement, feeling as if a weight had lifted the moment I opened my mouth. "Today."

Shocked into silence, he pocketed the notebook and pen. "Okay, I'll have the paperwork drawn up, provide you with bank information." I could see Scott's brain was lagging with processing everything that had just happened. I bet it wasn't every day that someone viewed and then paid for a house all in the space of an hour.

I stopped just before the door and turned back to look at my new purchase. Four beds, two baths, a beautiful wood and chrome kitchen, polished wood floors, and a stunning fire surround complete with open fire ready for cold winter nights. I couldn't quite picture what other furniture would fit in here but I'm sure Rachel would have ideas if she moved in.

"I have to ask for complete confidentiality, this is a business transaction."

Scott pulled his shoulders back. "Sheridan Realty prides itself on confidentiality."

"It's only that you have a connection with the ranch." *Way to make a big thing out of something, moron. What am I going to do? Get out one of my father's famous NDAs?*

"I appreciate that." Scott's cheeks pinked. "I can certainly hand you over to another realtor, but I want to assure you the entire process between the parties remains private."

That would change when he found out who I was buying it for. I wondered if he would remember this moment kindly, or he'd feel pissed.

"And I'm keen on getting ownership fixed," I reminded him.

"I'm on it." He closed the door behind me, and then we headed back into town with him driving again. I waited until he was back in his office then drove out of town to the outlook. I wanted a bit more time to process the transition from seeing a house to buying it in mere minutes, and I sat on the ground staring out at the view, and called Molly.

"Don't shout at me but I bought the house," I said before she could even say hello. "It has the most awesome bathroom and views from the master bedroom."

"Shit, Quinn."

I nibbled at a hang nail and paused. "I bought the house," I repeated the statement of disbelief at what I'd done. I never meant to buy the place, not really, but again, it was an investment in the same way the horses were I guess. All for Rachel, Laurie, and Oliver.

"Quinn, listen to me—"

"I just want Max's little family to have something of him, Molls, and what if this is my one and only chance? I want to know what happened to Max and I know I'd have to tell them who I am, and I know I can't. So, with that in balance, I need to move forward." I'd spent my entire life *trying* desperately to move forward, and this was my first real moment of choice in anything at all. I felt powerful, as if in a few moments of compelling idiocy, I'd taken hold of my destiny or something equally as profound. I wouldn't stay in Wyoming, but I would have done right by Max, and then maybe I could find Levi when the dust settled. I didn't know where that last thought had come from, because I didn't know if he felt the same way I did, as if desire pricked and poked at every atom of me until Levi was part of this adventure.

There was something between us, and it was a new feeling. Love. *I love him.* He made my heart speed up, my hands shake, and I wanted to touch him at every opportunity.

I should ask him to leave with me.

Simple. Right?

Chapter Twenty-Four

LEVI

SOMETHING HAD CHANGED FOR ME, SOMETHING PROFOUND, and it wasn't only that somehow Quinn had worked his way inside me, literally and figuratively, but I'd let him. In the time he'd been hanging around the ranch he'd gotten me to the point where I begged him to hold me and fuck me.

I was embarrassed, but strangely peaceful. Maybe I needed to find more of that—a man who could take over, and perhaps I'd been judging potential partners all wrong.

Take Micah for instance. It had always been me on my knees for him, but it wasn't as if he'd made me go to my knees, or had held me there, or twisted his hand in my hair to hold me still. That was what I craved. When I looked it up, I fit the definition of versatile, but like I knew I loved coffee, I knew exactly who I wanted in my bed. Someone confident who didn't let me give them any shit, and who took control, but then sometimes just let me be.

So, I'd found Quinn, or he found me, or whatever, and

my outlook had shifted. Telling me stupid jokes, trying to fall over so I'd catch him, a mess of nonsense that endeared him to me. *He's a rich guy, a suit who answers to the boss of a ranch in Massachusetts for fuck's sake.* He wasn't who I wanted at all. *Liar. I want him. I'm captivated. Smitten. Obsessed.* I wanted him in bed, out of bed, I wanted to talk to him, and catch him when he fell on his stupid ass, and I wanted to run my fingers through his hair and kiss him, and then I wanted my turn pushing all his buttons.

I headed out for a ride, Blake happy for the exercise, Sky trotting alongside. She'd been spending so much time at the house that I think she'd adopted the family as her own, but at least it kept her occupied, and she loved Laurie and Archie, following them around like a little shadow. I caught them pushing her about in the stable wheelbarrow yesterday, which was cute and all, but I was concerned that the sulking I got from her when we left the Lennox Ranch at the end of the summer would be the worse yet. How was it that she made herself at home at every single ranch? Why couldn't I find it as easy?

The sun was still warm even this late in the evening, when dusk was collecting shadows and hiding all that was familiar. Blake and I kept to the trail, then sped up for a short run, before slowing as we approached the creek and the rocks. The curious peace inside me made my fingers tingle, and my head felt empty of all the worries I carried on a permanent basis.

"What am I doing?"

Could I plant my feet solidly on Lennox land, and call part of it my own? The town was friendly, the air clean, and Micah wasn't as much of an asshole as I'd thought.

I petted Blake, lost in stroking him, and for a while he let me but eventually shook me off. That was Blake, as crabby as they came. Which reminded me of Quinn's horse, Sunny, who was job number one in the morning. Sunny had handled me being in his space today—not for long but it was a step in the right direction. Wheeling Blake around, I headed back toward the ranch and the paddocks, but stopped by the trees and dismounted to check on the large tree where the kids were playing, only yet again Quinn filled my thoughts with his tree house and his smile.

"I don't need the complication," I told the twilight. Moving from ranch to ranch, never quite settling, never quite thinking it would be the place I would stop, was my happy place. I wasn't hot on complications, and that was that.

If casual sex had turned to weird feelings of wanting more with Quinn, hell, even thinking about what had happened in the barn, and his room, then I had to figure out how I felt. I huffed my way down to the stable, dealt with Blake, until he neatly shoved at me, so I'd leave.

Then I headed back to my trailer, and called an end to my long, confusing day. Tomorrow would be better, and in the cramped shower I'd convinced myself that I could handle building a tree house without touching Quinn and making a fool of myself. Sky scratched at the door to go out and I scuffed her head as I opened the door, coming face-to-face with Micah.

"Hi," he began, as awkward as fuck, and stepped back from Sky who slunk close to his legs and let out a low growl. They still hadn't made friends.

"How the hell do you expect me to stay here when you can't even make friends with my dog?" I pulled two beers from the small refrigerator and handed him one, then joined him outside, slumping into one of the beat-up chairs that sat there. He took the other and then raised the bottle in salute.

"So, you're thinking about it then," he said.

"I said I would."

"Is there anything that would swing it, so you stayed?"

"I'm not going anywhere for now."

"You could choose the land you want, but I was thinking ten acres at the top of the ranch, there's access past the stables, but we could put in a track up there, build you something good."

"Right now, we need to get these Ebben-Loaner horses back out, not to mention the others you're working on, and get paid, right?"

Micah raised an eyebrow and made a big show of swallowing his beer. "That sure sounds as if you're considering my offer."

"I could just move the rig up there until…" I stopped talking, aware I'd said out loud that I was considering staying. The thought of being somewhere that I could put down roots was a powerful thing, but in my head, Quinn was still there with me.

Micah stood and stretched tall then in an instant he crouched next to Sky, with a foot between them, no more. He held out a hand, and she ignored him, so he inched closer, and this time she sniffed him.

"Come on, Sky, there's a lot riding on this," he said to her, and she butted her head against his fingers. He stroked her head, petted her, made cute noises, and she might not have rolled on her back for belly rubs, but she took that single step the same as Micah. "See, Levi, your dog loves me, so now you *have* to stay."

I huffed a laugh. "All that's left is you taking Blake out."

His eyes widened and then he snorted. "I don't have a death wish."

When he stood, he clapped a hand on my shoulder, and then with a soft goodnight he headed for the house. So much for me decisively stating I hadn't made up my mind. After all I *had* said I couldn't stay if he didn't make friends with Sky, and that was exactly what he'd tried to do.

"Traitor," I murmured to Sky who tilted her head and then climbed the steps into the trailer, happy with her life, and nose to tail, she closed her eyes.

I settled back in the chair, tilting my face to the stars and avoiding thinking about anything at all, when the sound of an approaching car cut through my peace. I knew it was Quinn, and I was already hard when I heard his footsteps.

"Checking on the horses?" I asked and gestured at the other chair.

"Of course, what other reason would I have for coming up here in the dark," he said, as he made himself comfortable, then tipping back to examine the sky with as much focus as I did.

"Stargazing," I pointed out. "Do you want a beer?"

"I'm good. I've been thinking," he said after a pause.

"Did it hurt?"

"Now who's the one with the jokes," Quinn deadpanned. "Can we talk?"

"Sure."

He stood then, seemed restless, paced over to the fence and then back to the rig, finally stopping in front of me and offering me a hand. "Inside?"

I had the feeling that taking his hand would mean something more than him just helping me up out of the chair. If I took it then he might not let it go.

I don't want him to let it go.

He grasped my hand hard, and tugged me to stand, and we went into the rig. Sky opened an eye, wagged her tail, and then turned her back on us. I shut the door and then we climbed onto the high bed, crawling until we lay on the pillows face-to-face.

"Where will you go next?" he asked in a soft tone, his expression guarded.

"Next?" I was lost in his eyes and the question didn't make sense at first.

"When you leave Lennox Ranch?"

That was a leading question, and this was the second time someone wanted an answer about my plans in one night.

"I don't know, yet."

He sketched a pattern on my chest, then crawled a little closer. "Will you tell me? Will you find me and tell me so I can follow you?"

My heart expanded a million times bigger, so filled with emotion that I didn't know how to handle it.

"You want that?"

"I'm falling for you," he whispered, his lips so close to

mine. "I was expecting so much this summer, but I never expected to fall so hard."

"Quinn—"

He pressed a finger to my lips to stop me talking, then moved carefully to straddle me, knocking his head on the roof and smiling down at me. "No talking," he kissed the words onto my skin.

I melted into the mattress. In a few frenzied moments we'd removed our clothes, and for a long moment I held him close, wanting to remember what he felt like in my arms. I got the feeling this was our last night together, as if he was saying goodbye, but we were building the tree house tomorrow, and I was in the ring with Sunny early, so he wouldn't be leaving yet.

I felt despairing of this stupid thing in my head that was waiting for him to leave.

"What do you need?" Quinn kissed a path to my ear and nibbled my neck. "Tell me what you need?"

I laced my fingers on the pillow above my head, and his eyes darkened as he placed his hand over mine.

"Okay," he crooned, "I've got you." He held me there, the kisses lazy, the press of our bodies slow as if we had all night, and he brought me to the edge and then backed off. "Lube?"

I inclined my head to the small unit in the wall by the bed, recalling at the last moment that along with lube were condoms and a toy.

"Spread your legs," he instructed, pulling everything out, "and don't move your hands."

He kissed and worried each nipple, biting then licking the small hurt, moving lower, his chin nudged my cock and I hissed at the contact, my hips lifting the smallest amount. He pushed them down, slicking his fingers, smoothing the coldness behind my balls, and the touch of him against my hole made me whine in need. He swallowed the head of my cock, sucking, and all the time he was fingering me, stretching me, and I forced my cock into his mouth and then down on him with a soft whimper of pain and lust. He crooked his finger, and I arched up so fast that I nearly choked him.

"Stay still or I'll stop." He kissed me as he said the words, his long hair sweeping over my face, and my orgasm was so close I was going to come from hearing his voice. "Are you staying still for me?"

Fuck.

"Yes."

He went back to sucking, then changed his mind, and this time instead of his fingers, he lubed the toy and pressed the tip of it inside me, crouched back so he could watch.

"You're so beautiful taking this," he murmured, closed his hands over my cock as he twisted the dildo inside me. "Do you love it when you're full and you get your hands on your cock."

"Yes."

He twisted the dildo once more and I saw stars as he tilted it and then switched the button. The vibrations in my ass, his hand and lips worshipping my cock, and I had to warn him.

"I'm coming," I said between breaths.

I expected him to suck me harder, but instead he circled the base of my cock and stopped me coming, leaving the dildo inside but turned off, playing with my balls, just this side of painful until the orgasm backed off. When he was certain I was ready to go again he crouched over me, his hand on my belly, and turned on the vibration, his feet hooked around my slightly bent knees, holding me still. He edged me again, seemed to know the moment to stop, kissed me so dirty, with muttered praise, until I was ready to explode. My cock was wet, my ass full, and he was pushing every single button.

"I need you to fuck me," I begged.

After a few moments of teasing, where he edged me again, with an intense look of concentration, he wiped his hand on his discarded T-shirt and rolled on a condom.

"I want to see your eyes," he ordered, then moved his knees to curl my legs into my chest, and finally he gripped my wrists and stared down at me. "Ready?"

"Please." I needed him, and I nodded. He pushed inside me, until balls-deep he leaned up to kiss me, then watched me as he thrust into me over and over. It didn't take me long, the orgasm so hard I yelled my release. He wasn't far after me, groaning into a kiss as he fucked me hard and then stiffened. His expression was beautiful.

"I love you," he said as he came down from the high. "I'm sorry."

I didn't have the capacity to ask him what he meant, exhaustion pulling me under. I felt him cleaning me, taking care of me, and I smiled into a final kiss, and with my hands still above my head, and Quinn cuddled into my side, I closed my eyes.

I love you too.

Chapter Twenty-Five

QUINN

THE WORDS ON THE PRINTED TREE HOUSE PLANS DIDN'T make much sense, lots of references to this, that, and all kinds of other things, but the pictures were clear, and it had only taken two calls to Ed and June at the hardware store for help to get the frame as solid as it should be. Laurie and Archie spent most of the day with me, but they were more interested in what they were going to do once the tree house was done, than getting it there.

That was until Micah and Levi joined us, and then it was five boys against the world, and I refused to be miffed that Micah and Levi didn't even have to look at the plans. There was much discussion between Laurie and Archie about electricity, and running water, but I put a stop to that by reminding everyone it had to be simple. I kept glancing at Levi, memories of what we'd done last night filled my thoughts; something I would remember forever. When he'd held his hands still, when he'd let me take care of him, I'd felt like the most powerful man in the world. We'd woken early this morning, swapped blowjobs, with laughter, and soft sighs, which was so different from the night before, but it had been just as hot—just as meaningful.

"Micah, take the other end?" Levi was supporting the center of the main beam that ran between three adjacent trees, and I had the end nearest to him. "We'll walk it back into place."

I'd measured with precision so that the wood didn't rest on the tree, but on the stable frame, while leaving room for the branches to grow. They'd need to keep an eye on the tree growth, cut back what was needed to be cut in a few years, because I wouldn't be there to do that, but this was going to be a king among tree houses.

I walked back the wood, taking more weight as Levi lowered it into place, the notches matching exactly. I was so happy I shimmied, and Micah laughed when I popped a move, but all Levi did was stare and blush.

I shimmied a bit more, and then demi-plié'd my way off the platform.

It didn't hurt when I hit the ground.

Well, it *did*, but I refused to admit it because there was no blood, and no broken bones, and I didn't smack my head, so no real harm done. Levi jumped down, crouching next to me, cradling my head, and urging me to tell him that I was okay. There was fear in his voice, and I know I was telling him I was okay, but he scooped me up and held me firm and demanded I tell him again.

"I'm fine, let me down," I demanded, but entwining my arms around his neck and then cuddling him wasn't exactly begging for release.

"Okay then," I heard Micah say, and I peered up to see him, Laurie, and Archie grinning down at me.

"Are you okay?" Levi asked again.

I stole a kiss and then wriggled free, and he let me down. "Let's get the next beam on." I began to climb but he yanked at my T-shirt.

"No. More. Dancing."

I lifted an eyebrow, then stole a kiss he wasn't expecting. I didn't deserve him to swat my ass when I was on the ladder, but it was nice.

It was quiet affection, and added to the concern, plus the way he'd scooped me up, all big bad protector, I thought there was more to this cowboy than I'd first imagined. I had so much to discover, but I didn't have the time to work anything out. Today *really* had to be my last day, and I needed to kiss Levi goodbye, tell Rachel who I was, promise I'd stay away, then leave. Simple. I'd leave my heart at Lennox Ranch. Losing it to all those things that had taken root, for Laurie, for the tree house, for Sunny and Glimmer, for little Oliver, and Rachel. But there was a massive part of my heart that was going to be aching for Levi. I was leaving the love behind unless he told me he loved me back. I couldn't hurt myself like that if he didn't return the feelings I'd shared last night with him.

And wasn't that a kick in the head.

Rachel dropped off lunch just as my belly started to tell me I needed food. I took Oliver, held him close as he hugged me like a capuchin monkey, grinning at me and smelling of oranges. Rachel took Micah's hand and clambered up to the platform hoisting up a bag of snacks, plus a cushion that she used to prop herself up. The rest of us sprawled around her, and I felt absolute peace; the hum of conversation, Oliver fast asleep on a blanket in the corner, the taste of homemade bread, fresh tomatoes, cut ham, chicken, chips, then apples that tasted better than I'd ever had. Not to mention I was leaning against Levi, and he didn't push me away. If anything, he wriggled so I'd slot comfortably between his legs, and that added to the contented feeling that I was right where I should have been. He played with my hair as he chatted about horses, and his big laugh whenever Archie told a joke rumbled through my body. I didn't want to leave this moment, let alone the ranch, and a familiar angsty grumpiness began to build inside me.

"And then I draw'd this one." Laurie opened his sketchbook at another view of the old barn, this time focusing on the door, and I could see the detail of the lock, and it looked shiny.

"Drew," Rachel corrected.

"Huh?"

"You drew that one."

"Yep, I did," Laurie said proudly, then rolled his eyes when Rachel ruffled his hair. "All shiny, and then I did this." He turned the page and this one hadn't been done in pencil but had been colored in using the entire rainbow spectrum. It was Phoney-the-phone decked out from red to violet with all the colors in between. "He's gay," Laurie announced, and then he turned the page and there were two Phoney-the-phones, only the second one was black and white still. "He's looking for another gay Phoney," Laurie explained.

"They're so good." Rachel took the book from him, and flicked from the beginning, and exchanged a glance with Micah who shrugged.

"Guess we have an artist in the family," he said with a grin. "We'll have to check out any art clubs in Whisper Ridge, or over in Collier Springs."

"He's really good at art," Archie announced. "He could sell it one day and get rich." The boys tussled for a moment, and it was good to see Laurie so happy.

"Was my dad good at art?" Laurie asked Rachel.

My heart stopped and my breath caught. My entire world slowed down at that innocent question.

"I don't know," Rachel murmured. "He used to talk about colors in nature, and was always singing, so I think he felt art," she added.

My heart restarted but I felt nauseous. I wanted to be free to tell them all about Max, the parts of his life that they didn't know, and I was sick to the stomach that I had to leave.

Laurie stared down at his art and began to doodle random shapes in the corner of the page. Micah seemed concerned, Rachel sad, and I was frozen in Levi's hold.

"Are you okay?" Levi asked being far too perceptive. I shook it off when Rachel glanced at me with a frown. I just wanted a couple more hours of normal before I worked through the rest of the list and I knew how selfish I was being, but fuck life and the hand I'd been dealt.

Build the tree house, kiss Levi goodbye, tell Rachel who I am, then leave.

"I'm good, let's get this tree house finished!" I pushed a ton of enthusiasm into my tone, and everyone got up, excited to finish what they were doing, bagging up the remains of the picnic and Micah helping Rachel down and passing her a sleepy Oliver.

All too soon the tree house was done, the stairs were sturdy and led up to a solid landing with the house and windows closed off with shutters. The boys vanished and came back with pillows and bedding, plus books, and bottles of water.

"You can go now," Archie said, "if you like," he added.

I knew we were being dismissed, and it was dinner time and I think I was done with today. That was item one off my list. Maybe talking to Rachel could wait until tomorrow? That would give me one more night with Levi. Maybe I didn't even need to talk to her, and I could stay.

I owe her as much truth as I can give her.

Micah headed to his truck, heading home to his husband, and abruptly it was only me and Levi listening to Rachel explain with exaggerated patience why Laurie and Archie couldn't stay in the tree house overnight. Their persistence made me chuckle, and I felt all warm inside when Levi took my hand and tugged me up the road toward his rig.

"Are you hungry?" he asked when he fed Sky, and then shut the door on the outside world.

"What do you have?"

"Ramen? Beans?" He opened the one small cupboard, but it was empty apart from those two emergency items and bags of dog food. "I normally eat at the house," he said.

"Should you be there now?"

"No, I told Rachel I was eating with you, thought we could go into town, get food, y'know." He finished with a shrug.

"Get takeout and go back to the hotel?" I tugged him closer then rested my hands on his hips. As we kissed, we were already hard. "It's too far to go," I whispered, and in a smooth move he hoisted me up on his bed, then followed me, crawling up to cage me.

"I'll make you a special bean surprise. Later," he added, and then kissed me with promise.

I slid out from under him, turned to straddle his lap, and he was already taking off his T-shirt, revealing all the wonders of his body, from the hair on his chest, to his treasure trail, and my favorite thing, his cinnamon nipples, hard as a cool breeze passed over them.

"What do you need?" I asked, the same as last night.

"You," he whispered.

My chest tightened. I wanted him, not only for this last night, but for all the nights, and all the days to follow. My entire life had changed in the past few weeks, I'd fallen in love with everything. My family that didn't know who I was, a ranch with the horses I was leaving behind, the house I would never live in, and most of all…

Levi.

I'd fallen in love with Levi, with his smile and his gentle way with the horses, and the way he lay beneath me and trusted me so completely.

"I love you."

"I love you, too," he said, reaching up to cradle my face, and tug me down for a kiss. "I never thought I could ever have this, or want this, but I need you in my life." He chuckled and kissed me again, threading his fingers into my hair and holding me still. I wanted to tell him I could even imagine a future where it was me and Levi against the world.

But the world wasn't a good place, it was full of people who wanted money, and could chew up and spit out someone like Levi, or Rachel, or little Laurie.

"Are you okay?" he asked as he played with my hair and stared up at me with concern.

"I'm fine," I lied, and lay flat across him, burying my face into his neck, tears forcing their way up from my heart, and collecting in my eyes. I couldn't let them fall, I couldn't let him see how much I loved this life, loved Max's little family, loved Levi, and wanted more with all of them.

I couldn't think, and then it was hard to breathe. I needed to talk to Rachel, be honest with her about everything, I couldn't leave Levi. I didn't want to leave Laurie. I had a million questions about Max. What if I went up to Rachel now and explained what I'd done, who I was, and why I was so scared for her and the kids? She could hate me for lying, or she could hug me and tell me it was all okay. She could tell me that she didn't care if the media got wind of who Laurie was, and that she could handle anything they threw at us.

I can't think.

I crawled away from Levi, then dropped off the bed and yanked open the door.

"I have to go."

Levi was thrown for a second, then he grabbed his T-shirt and tugged it over his head. "What's wrong? Quinn?"

"No, you see, it's Max, I have to talk to Rachel for Max."

"Who's Max? Quinn, you're not making any sense."

"Stay there!" I shouted.

He stopped long enough for me to get my feet into my boots, then I backed out of the rig, stumbling over my own feet, and sprawling onto the ground, standing before backing away a few steps and running from the rig to the house. I could hear him calling me, but I had a head start on him, and I reached the front door and beat my fist on it, calling Rachel's name.

Scott answered, a welcome smile on his face, which dropped when he saw me wild-eyed at the door. Levi skidded to a halt next to me, but before he could ask me what in hell I was doing, Rachel reached past Scott and widened the door, letting me in and Levi standing, uncertain whether to follow. I turned back to him, seeing the confusion in his expression, and the wariness.

"You need to hear this, too," I murmured, and offered him a hand, which he took then allowed me to tug him in.

"What's going on?" Scott asked as he shut the door.

"What's wrong, Quinn?" Levi spoke at the same time.

Rachel took the nearest chair and sighed heavily. "Alexander Dawson," she whispered.

My shoulders slumped. Had she known all this time? Had she thought I was here to take the boys? What had I done? I had so much I needed to tell her, about the money, and how Max was, and our father, and… so much. *Where do I start?*

"I go by Quinn, my middle name," I slumped into the seat opposite her. "I'm sorry, Rachel."

She pressed a hand to her heart, and a tear slid down her face. "You have Max's ghost in your eyes."

Emotion choked me at those simple words.

"What the hell is going on?" Scott was angry, taking the seat next to Rachel and putting his arm over her shoulders. "Why are you crying?"

"Today when I was telling Laurie about his dad, I could see Max in your eyes the same as in Laurie's."

Levi leaned against the counter, not joining us at the table, as if he didn't know what else to do but wanted to show me that he wasn't going anywhere.

"So many secrets," she added, and then turned to face Scott, cradling his face and kissing him gently. "I'm sorry, Scott."

"Sorry for what? Rachel?" Scott sounded so confused and Rachel glanced at me with a pleading expression. I could do this for her, I could explain.

"My brother Max was at the same commune as Rachel, and he's Laurie's dad."

"Is he coming to take Laurie?" Scott said immediately. "Shit, he can't take Laurie."

"Max is dead," I said even as Scott grew angry and defensive and glared at me. "He died at the commune."

I shot a look at Levi who stared back at me with an inscrutable expression. I would lose him with these secrets, I couldn't lose him, or this family, but there was a heavy feeling in my chest.

"I wanted to tell you, I came here to tell you, but then I couldn't for so many reasons."

"So you lied," Rachel murmured then lifted her chin and met my gaze head-on. "Why?"

I had never meant to be the cause of any pain but all I'd done is mess it up by falling for a family and a man I could never have.

"Are they even your horses?" Scott's eyes were flinty with accusation.

"They are, it was just my way of being near Rachel and the boys."

"You can't have the boys," Scott snapped, and pulled Rachel close to him. "Micah will kill you if you try to take them and I won't stop him."

I scrubbed at my face. "He has every right," I admitted, and I could see this going from bad to worse, because I had to face Micah as well, and I'd lied with this stupid horse idea, and everything had gotten so out of control. I'd been living in fantasy land where everything was sunshine and roses, I'd fallen in love with Levi, and now I'd stepped straight into a brick wall.

"I'm not taking the boys, not Laurie." I took out my wallet, pulling out a worn photo and holding it out, a photo of me and Max when we were kids, all that I really had left of him. Rachel took the photo and nodded when she saw Max.

"I know. Max is Laurie's dad."

"What's going on?" Laurie said from the stairs. I didn't know how long he'd been standing there, or how much he'd heard, but his expression was determined. "Did you make my mom cry?" Laurie tilted his chin in a stubborn pose that was so like Max that my words vanished.

Rachel held out a hand and Laurie came in for a hug. "Quinn had a secret he wants to share with you sweetheart, he's your uncle," she explained softly.

His eyes widened as she rocked her world and mine to acknowledge that. “Uncle Micah and Uncle Daniel are my only uncles.” Laurie’s tone was brittle, and I had to understand that as a child he might accept me more readily, but he was bound to feel betrayal as he unpicked what Rachel had to tell him just because I’d come here and messed everything up.

“Your dad was a man called Max, and Quinn is his brother.”

“No, he has the horses.”

“He’s here to meet you.”

“Then why didn’t he say so.”

“I’m sorry,” I interjected.

Scott held out an arm, and Laurie climbed onto his lap, burying his face in Scott’s neck, seeking a safety that my brother could never give him, and abruptly this was nothing about me and what I needed here, but about the love of a father for his little boy. I wanted to be free to scoop Laurie into a hug and tell him all about my wonderful brother, and his soft heart, and how he suffered the years of our family but that even when the demons held him, I could swear that he would never have lost his ability to love Laurie.

“Max was at the commune with us, and he loved you so much, sweetheart,” Rachel said, and I don’t know if she was lying, but I clung to the hope that this was true and that Max had known.

“But he’s dead, right?” Laurie was taking everything at face value, and the love that was between mom and son gave him a safe space to listen and accept. She hesitated a moment. How much pain could one child carry? How much before Rachel and Laurie were destroyed by it all?

"Yes."

Her expression was troubled, tears spilled from her eyes, and Scott glared at me when she hiccuped a sob and Laurie crawled from his lap to his mom's.

"Don't cry, Mom," he begged, and my heart shattered when she held her son and buried her face in his hair. What had I done?

Rachel smiled at me, but the smile was unsteady, "Max said that he loved you, Quinn."

"I loved him so much, he was my big brother, he was everything." I didn't think I was crying, but my face was wet.

"He always said you were sunshine and smiles, that you'd be a great uncle."

Tears caught in my throat. "I'm sorry for how I did this, please don't make me go. I have so many questions."

Levi interrupted with a bitter edge to his tone. "Why did you lie?"

"I didn't mean to. The horses are mine, I own them, I'm not a manager and I know I shouldn't have lied."

He inclined his head as if I'd answered all his questions, and then he went to the door and walked out, closing it behind him. He took my heart with him.

"I don't like you," Laurie said from his mom's arms. "You made Mom cry and you lied, and I hate you."

"I think you should go," Rachel murmured.

"Please—"

"Come back in the morning."

"And we can talk?"

She glanced at Scott, and he tightened his hold on her and Laurie. They were a family, and I wasn't part of this. Finally, she nodded, and I had to leave.

When the door shut behind me, I didn't know where to go. Left and I would be heading for Levi, maybe begging him to understand, right was my car and heading back to town.

"I thought I loved you," Levi said from the darkness, and I whirled to face him.

"Levi—"

"No." He left then, heading for his trailer, and the *no* had been so decisive, so real, that I felt he was done with me. I headed for my car, and somehow, I made it off the ranch and through town, not stopping until I reached the outlook when it wasn't possible for me to drive any farther. I don't recall even getting here. Now I'd given myself permission to cry it seemed as if I couldn't stop the tears, and my chest hurt with the raw pain of them.

I had never meant to upset Rachel, but I knew in my heart that even talking to her would shake her world. So, I knew what would happen. Why had I even gone to the house tonight? Why hadn't I just left?

The tears ran dry when I stopped feeling sorry for myself, the jagged mess of my selfishness left me shaky, and I was desperate to regroup. I had a ton of information I needed to tell Rachel, about Max, trust funds filled with enough money to change life at Lennox Ranch forever.

Then Molly and Connor were right.

I should leave.

Chapter Twenty-Six

LEVI

I MADE IT ALL THE WAY TO THE TRAILER AND STARED AT THE door, willing myself to open it and nurse my wounds. Fucking liar had lied for whatever the fuck reason he had, and he'd taken me in with it.

I love you.

The way he'd stared down at me when we'd made love, that wasn't pretending, surely that had been real? He'd laughed with me, smiled, told me he'd loved me, and I'd felt something in my heart that I couldn't explain. I'd seen a future so bright and filled with happiness that I'd believed every word he said. *What is wrong with me?* I'd been vulnerable in my submissive role in our sex, but what was worse was that I'd opened my heart and been honest about my feelings for the first time in my life. I consented, I wanted, I *needed,* and then I'd fallen in love so hard that it hurt to think about a place where I wouldn't be in love any more. I wanted more with him, I wanted to feel what it was like to unravel him as much as he'd done to me, I had to see him.

I couldn't just leave this, not when I'd seen the tears that had fallen unbidden, forced up from some inner pain that he'd never shared with me. He'd held part of himself back, and did that mean I'd fallen in love with a lie? What about the moment he'd danced in front of the truck, or when I'd tucked his hair behind his ears, and he'd blushed? Or the moment he'd teased me, shoved me into the trees, made me feel things I'd suppressed my entire life? I'd begun to fall in love with him when he had first kissed me.

And I'd walked away from him.

I deserved to know the full truth, and I knew if I looked him in the eyes then I'd know if he'd lied about us as well. I don't know how long I stood there, alternating between anger and love and all the feelings in between, but I couldn't do nothing. Finally, it wasn't a decision so much as an impulse that had me checking in on Sky before heading to the hotel. Only I was thwarted by the keypad I'd need to use to get in. I could buzz the desk, but I couldn't see Quinn's flashy Lexus and it was times like this that I wished I did carry a cell phone then I could call him. Had he decided to cut and run? He wouldn't have, right? Rachel had said he could go back in the morning and talk about his brother, about Laurie, so he wouldn't leave them.

I heard his car and slipped into the shadows, not wanting to give him the chance to avoid me, and I watched him as he parked, then for the longest time, he rested his head on the steering wheel. Silent and still. Finally, he stepped out, jumping down from the cab, then stumbling. I moved to catch him, but he caught himself, and then slammed the car door so hard I was surprised it didn't rock. He was angry at himself, not for falling over, but for everything, and as he walked his shoulders were slumped.

"Quinn?"

He jumped a mile and then clutching his chest, he peered into the shadows.

"Levi? What's wrong? Did something happen? Is it Laurie? Is Rachel—?"

"I wanted to talk."

From startled and loud he became subdued and nodded. "Come on then." He pressed the numbers into the keypad and then held the door open for me, and together we made our way to his room. This time he went in first and crossed to the sofa to dump his hat as I shut the door behind me then leaned against it, not entirely sure what I should've been saying.

He turned to face me, with a wary expression. "I'm sorry," he whispered. "I didn't mean to—"

"What else did you lie about?"

His eyes widened, and there was pain in them. "Nothing, I promise you. My real name isn't even mine anymore, that's not who I am, and yes, I own Sunny and Glimmer, but I didn't lie to you about us. If that is what you meant."

Hope pricked at my heart, and he pushed ahead.

"I fell in love with you even though I wasn't supposed to. I was here to see Laurie, put some things in place for him whether he was Max's or not, because Rachel went through what he did and she deserves something good, but not so much money that she's a target, because I know what that's like and it's vicious poison that steals everything from you." He took a frustrated breath, and then calmer, he caught my gaze and held me there. "Loving you was never a lie."

"I don't understand why you did it, maybe you can explain it to me, but I have to tell you something for real."

"Okay?"

"I need you to know that I love you, and that whatever you've done here, however it turns out, that is not going to change."

His mouth dropped open and then his eyes filled with tears, and he dashed them away. "I'm sick of crying," he was frustrated, and he glanced up at me. "But damn it, Levi, what you do to me in here." He pressed a hand to his chest. "You're the smile that comes from right down in my heart."

We both moved at the same time, meeting in the middle and kissing as if we'd never get the chance to kiss again.

"I love you, so much," he told me, and I tucked his hair behind his ears, and I held him close.

"I love you, right back."

Was this a love that could last forever? Was it born out of lies, or confusion, I didn't know. I just knew one thing, for *right then* he was my everything.

"READY?"

Quinn didn't seem ready; he hadn't slept, and I knew because I'd stayed awake with him, watching old movies, and hugging him close. We didn't talk about what was happening, I didn't think we needed to because whatever happened, I'd hold his hand and have his back, and I would love him.

Everything in my head seemed so easy, but now arriving at Lennox Ranch, Micah already there, I considered whether I was throwing everything away. Even though the jury was out on whether I was going to stay with Micah and take him up on his offer of a partnership, I was ninety percent there. I'd even conjured a scenario where Quinn stayed with me, and we built our own place, and we were forever.

What happened here today would make or break where I was heading in my life.

Micah met us at the door, and I knew him well enough to see that he was dangerously close to losing his cool.

"Laurie isn't here," he announced, then turned his back on us and headed inside. He took a seat at the large table, right next to his husband, Daniel, who at least threw a sympathetic glance at Quinn.

"Where is he?" I heard Quinn ask.

"Chris is up at the stables and has him and Archie."

"I thought—"

"What? You expected him to sit here and listen to this?" Micah stood, but I took Quinn's hand and Micah stopped. He narrowed his eyes at me, and I gave him a shrug because what else could I do? *There goes the offer of a partnership.*

Rachel was there with Scott, he looked pissed, she had schooled her features into showing nothing at all. Finally, we sat at the same table, or at least Quinn did, I stood behind his chair for a moment until he tugged me down to sit next to him.

"Where do you want me to start?" Quinn said, and folded his hands on the table, white knuckling the emotion that was close to the surface.

"Why you lied?"

Quinn took a moment. "Media who think they own the Dawson family, and nineteen million, give or take a hundred thousand." He paused and glanced at me, and I touched his leg in reassurance. "That's how much Max was worth when he died." Micah inhaled, and Scott cursed. "Mostly in a trust he was due to inherit when he turned twenty-five, but the rest of it was holdings in our family company, Dawson Pharma. From a stipulation in the trust, it all passed to me when he died, which sounds bad, but I swear I didn't know about Laurie, and because I didn't want it, I sold the shares, put the money into a charitable foundation. Then, Connor found me, he's a PI."

"Connor Mason? The one who came here looking for a cousin?" Rachel asked. She and Micah exchanged glances, but then she turned back to Quinn and waited for more.

"Yeah, he works for me now, no, not for me, with me, part of my team, keeps an eye on my security, alongside my best friend Molly, who administers the fund. I have it all set up so we can hand over the admin. I was never staying part of it. I don't want anything to do with the money."

Micah leaned forward, "So, what you're saying is that Laurie's inheritance is locked away in a trust, and he has nothing?"

"He could have it all, one word from you and everything will be released to him, but I want you to... that's the reason that I..." He took his hands off the table, and reached for mine, lacing our fingers, and holding tight.

"Max was so unhappy," Rachel murmured, "desperately unhappy, but a strong man. I didn't have a choice where I ended up, addiction and running away I was caught up in the Brothers' cult without even realizing it. He chose to stay. At first it was because he was hiding, searching for a something, but he never told me any of that, only that he regretted leaving his brother behind. He told me he loved you, that it was the worst pain, but he was an addict the same as me."

"I know." Quinn's voice was thick with tears. "Our family was toxic, so much money, the poison was in everything."

"He knew he was a dad, but we never said anything. They took him one day." She rubbed her eyes. "I have to go back a step to explain. Callum Prince ran the compound, he was my..." she stopped and seemed stricken, leaning against Scott for support. "Callum owned me," she finished. "Max was a comfort to me, we didn't love each other, but it was different in there, it was anything to have a connection, and at the center of it was drugs, and it messed with your mind. I was clean when I found out I was pregnant, Callum hated that, but he believed Laurie was his. Until he found out the truth. Max faced him; he'd tried so hard to get clean for Laurie, said he'd show us a new life, find a cabin somewhere, just the three of us. I never saw him after that night he said we were leaving, and I hoped he'd made it out, hoped he'd been strong enough to get free."

"He wouldn't have left you behind," Quinn said with fierce devotion.

I didn't want to point out that Max had left Quinn, and it didn't sound as if their family was any better than a commune. What kind of life had they lived to have Max so destroyed he'd ended up in a cult, and what about Rachel? What didn't I know?

"We were both there searching for something, him for peace, me to escape from Whisper Ridge, we were kids. Stupid kids. But no, I knew in my heart he wouldn't leave me. I knew he was dead, this man who'd given me Laurie, but I didn't even have a last name, just that he had a brother who would be missing him."

Quinn's leg shook, and I pressed down to try to calm him, but I could feel the tension in him and so I shuffled my chair close enough to put my arm across his shoulder.

"We had everything money could buy," Quinn began. "Private education, tutors, access to anything we ever wanted, we just didn't have a family that cared. Money was all my parents knew, and there was so much of it, all tied to Dawson Pharma, impossible amounts of disgusting money that bought and sold and let people lie. When Max was sixteen he disappeared for the summer, my father had sent him to a camp for wayward teens, when he came back he was never the same; when my father tried to do the same to me it was Max who stood in his way, threatened to do an interview about the family and what had happened to him at the camp. He saved me, but I could never save him back."

"Poor little rich boy," Micah huffed, and I stiffened, only for Quinn to stop me moving.

"I know. It's such a tired fucking cliché." I didn't think Micah expected that, and he sat back in his chair. "But it's real, okay, having money shaped our lives, having parents who didn't care was one thing, but the despair and weight of it killed Max, and I didn't want that for Laurie—"

"That's not your choice to make," Micah was back to anger. "You don't come here like a creep, stalking us, deciding what is best for us—"

"Micah, stop." Rachel held up a hand, and Micah did cease talking even if he grumbled under his breath.

"It's okay," she said after a short pause, and then she reached across the table, her palm up. "It's okay, Quinn."

Quinn took her hand and they sat like that for a moment.

"I miss him." The admission was torn from deep inside Quinn, and my heart broke for him. Everything he'd done had come from a place of pain and despair, with a desperate need to care for family. "We buried him last fall, and I miss him so much. Some days I felt like I'd never smile again, and then when I saw Laurie, or fell in love with Levi, then I would find myself smiling and those are the days I want to hold onto, because they're the most precious of all."

Micah huffed, although the anger had subsided and in its place was confusion. "Rachel?"

"I'm okay," she said. "I don't want that kind of pain for Laurie, or Oliver, I can't speak for Laurie, but the money isn't for us. A charitable foundation sounds wonderful, a fitting monument to a confused, unhappy, but strong man."

"I've drawn up papers to make you and Micah trustees, the horses are for Laurie, and I bought a house."

"He did," Scott murmured. "He bought the last house in the development."

"It's for you and the boys, it's enough so you have somewhere that's yours, and of course, I'll set up college funds… I don't know what else I can say."

He'd laid out what he'd done, and why, and none of it made me love him any less, if anything I loved him more. My pink-haired fae was perfectly flawed, and I couldn't imagine a day without him in my life.

"You don't have to say anything," Rachel smiled. "Uncle Quinn—"

The door flew open, Archie there, his eyes wide. "Help! You have to help!" He left the doorway as quickly as he'd arrived, Sky barking and dancing around his feet, and with us being closest to the door Quinn and I were out first, running up the hill following Archie and Sky, heading for the old barn, the padlocked door swinging wide.

"We were faster than Chris! We were just looking! We didn't mean it!" Archie was panicking, and I took in the scene as Micah slid to a stop next to me. The cover was off the old well-head, Chris leaning over, gripping something, and yelling for help. He was scrambling to find purchase, but he couldn't stay like that for much longer.

Chapter Twenty-Seven

QUINN

Micah grabbed Chris, Levi leaned in to grab on to whatever Chris had been holding and I peered over the edge. About five feet below, a large stick was wedged, a bucket at angles, rope dangling from it. Below that was absolute darkness, and in the bucket, half in and half wedged, was a terrified Laurie.

"Help!" he yelled up at us, and when he did the bucket shifted.

"Don't move!" Levi shouted back, and Laurie whimpered.

"We were just exploring!" Archie said, "Just exploring."

"Call 911," Micah ordered, as Chris tumbled back, his prosthetic loose and his hands bleeding and raw.

Rachel reached us, Oliver in her arms. "What's wrong!"

Scott hid the scene from her, holding out a hand. "Laurie's stuck; we're getting him out." He had a phone to his ear, calling emergency services.

The way Laurie was sobbing rocked the bucket, and he could crash to the abyss below, and I had to do something.

I spotted loose rope, grabbed it, and put it around my middle, under my arms, guessing at the length, wondering if I could even reach Laurie.

"Someone tie this," I demanded because I knew fuck-all about knots.

"What are you doing?" Levi said, but Scott shoved him out of the way and began to tie knots.

"I'm small enough to go down." I wasn't asking for permission; this was my nephew in danger. I put my feet over the edge of the well and sat upright, uncertain how I was going to do this but knowing I had to.

"I've got you," Levi said close to me, wrapping the rope around himself and then searching for something to anchor the rest to. Scott took another part of the rope, taking the strain, and before I even knew I was safe, knowing I could trust Levi not to let me go, I eased off the side, and gripping bricks I climbed down enough so that I could pass where Laurie was wedged. My only thought was getting under him, so that if we fell it might be that he'd have me to land on. Nothing was going to happen to Laurie on my watch.

"Hey, Laurie," I shifted enough to wedge myself across the space, the bucket rested on me, but if it slid sideways then we'd both go.

"I'm scared," Laurie whimpered, gripping the stick hard. From the creaking sounds, I didn't think it was going to hold him much longer.

"I've got you," I repeated the words Levi had just said to me.

"I don't want to fall."

"I won't let you fall."

"They're twenty minutes out," Scott called down. "What can you see?"

"Tie off more rope," I called up. "Make a loop, throw it down." I took a moment to work this out. "Okay, Laurie, here's what we're going to do." I wriggled closer; the bucket had split, the metal digging into my thigh, but I had a firm wedge with my legs and I was stronger than I looked. Rope slithered down next to me, and I caught the loop that someone had made. "I need you to let go of the stick here."

"I can't," he whimpered, terror in his voice.

"You can. I need you to let go, I've got you."

"I'm scared."

"It's okay, I won't let you fall, try letting go of one hand, just one. Reach for my hand."

He refused to let go, he wasn't budging, but he sobbed harder and the bucket slid an inch. The pain in my thigh was impossible to ignore, I imagined the metal cutting into my skin, and hoped it didn't cut a freaking artery. Because falling in love, finding my nephew, and starting a new life was in my reach, and I wasn't losing it all now.

Max. help me.

"Did you know that your dad was a very brave person," I said and edged my hand a little closer to his, ready to prize his fingers from their grip if I needed to. It was so gloomy down there I couldn't tell if him letting go was even safe, but the stick's uneven surface was at a breaking point. "He once got a spider out of my room."

"A sp-sp-spider?" Laurie stuttered.

"A big spider. I don't like them, but he just picked it up and took it back to its family."

"I'm n-n-not scared of them," Laurie said, and whimpered when the bucket groaned and moved again. If he didn't loosen his hold soon then I was going to have to yank him to me and hope I could hold us both. I was strong but I didn't have the bulk of Levi or Micah, and what if…

Stop, little brother. Just stop and think.

Max would've known what to do, he'd have known *exactly* the right thing to say.

"Give me your hand, Laurie."

Finally, he released his fingers, held me tight, and I took the opportunity to slip the loop under his arm, then guided him to put his hand back. "Okay, I'm going to put this under you, and up to your arms, okay?"

He cried in fear, and I thought I could hear him saying the word *spiders* over and over. I didn't know, because I was lightheaded, my vision blurring.

"Okay." I managed to get the loop under him and the bucket, and I don't know how, but at last I had it under his arms. "There you go. We've got you." I felt such relief, tilting my head back, seeing Levi and Micah staring down. "Pull him up, gently."

They did as they were told, and I watched the scramble as he was pulled over the side. The bucket had shifted, but the pain in my thigh hadn't stopped, and as the adrenaline dimmed so did my vision. I felt the pull of the rope, and the tug at my skin, but I was stuck.

"Let go," I heard Levi say. "Come on, Quinn, let go of the side. We've got you."

I didn't realize I was holding on, and one finger at a time I pulled my hand from the brick, water running down my arm. Not water, blood. *Okay, I've done something* really *stupid here.* I let go, and in an instant, I felt the tightening of rope, and then hands were grabbing at me pulling me out, and I was on solid ground, cradled in Levi's arms, and there was a paramedic, cursing and slapping at me. Why was he hurting me?

"Levi?"

But it wasn't his voice I could hear. It was Laurie, and he was telling me over and over that I needed to stay awake.

So, I did.

I DIDN'T WANT to go to the hospital, because Laurie was hugging me and calling me Uncle Quinn, and Rachel was thanking me, and Micah shook my hand, and it was as though every single hero thing was happening to me. I grumbled when they insisted, moaned when they poked at me, was restless as I slept, only settling when Levi told me to calm the fuck down.

And when I woke to a light-filled hospital room, I was surrounded by people. Micah and Scott were leaning against the wall talking quietly, Archie between them leaning on Micah who was hugging him close. Chris was there, in a wheelchair, his hands bandaged, his eyes closed, Rachel asleep in a chair with a dozing Oliver in her lap and lying next to me Laurie was hugged into my side.

"Hey," I croaked, and coughed to clear my throat. I couldn't see Levi at first, but everyone else sparked to life in an instant, and then I saw him from where he'd been sitting right by me, too close for me to focus on.

"I'll get Daniel," Micah left in a flurry of motion.

Scott helped Rachel up, and took Oliver from her so she could see me.

"How are you feeling?" she pressed a hand to my chest.

"Ouch," I deadpanned. "What happened?"

"The bucket sliced into your leg, you lost blood, and you scraped your hand raw on the well bricks, then you hit your head when you fell out of our hold."

I lifted my hand, the one that I knew had been bleeding, and saw it was just as bandaged as Chris's. "Well, shit."

Scott pressed a hand to my foot, nodded, and in that male way of communicating with nothing more than nods and hand gestures with an added grunt, I knew I'd made things right with him. He left the room with Oliver.

Chris added his own nod, and then left the room too, but he didn't add a smile, if anything he seemed dazed and lost. Archie scuffed his feet and then approached the bed.

"We were exploring, it's all my fault."

"No, it wasn't," Laurie said as he stirred. "It was my idea to go in the bucket."

"It was me that followed the cat."

"It was me that said the stick would work."

They stopped attempting to outdo each other as to whose fault it was, and then Laurie sat up and hugged me.

"Thank you, Uncle Quinn."

"You're welcome, Laurie."

"If you ever have a spider, and you can't get rid of it, then I'll do it for you."

I reached up and ruffled his hair, then he kissed my forehead. "That's good to know."

The boys left to join Scott who hovered outside the door, and then it was Rachel and me, and Levi hovering. He hadn't said anything yet, leaving the space for Rachel to fill with words. All she did was press a kiss to my forehead the same as Laurie had done.

"We're going to talk," she said and I nodded.

"I know."

"But, welcome to the family, *Uncle* Quinn." Then she left, and still Levi didn't say anything, just gripped my unhurt hand and buried his face in my side. He moved a little when Daniel came in to check on me along with a hospital doctor. Micah shook my hand again, all stoic and manly, and then slapped me on the arm.

He didn't know his own strength.

Finally it was Levi and me alone, and he shuffled closer so we could talk.

"Are you feeling okay?" he asked, tracing the bandages on my hand.

"I'm good, I promise."

"We should talk."

Please don't tell me that this is all over. Please don't tell me things have changed.

"I love you," I said with urgency. He *had* to remember that.

"I know," he murmured. "I love you too. But I have things to decide, this is a huge crossroads that I never thought I'd get to."

"I'll do anything to be with you." I knew I sounded desperate. "Please don't say this is done. I have money, but

I'll get rid of it all, move to the next ranch with you, make a statement if you need me to, marry you."

Levi blinked at my verbal diarrhea. "Did you just propose to me?" he asked.

"No. Yes, no… what did you want to say." *Shit. I've probably freaked him out now.*

"Well, Micah offered me a partnership, and some land, not much but I thought I could build a house, with an office for you, so you can run this charity of yours, and we could stay here and fit into this family for real." His expression was calm and focused, but he was laying everything on the line just the same as I had.

I wanted to say yes with every part of me, but he had to know the bad things as well.

"It won't be easy," I began. "The media will still have an interest and I don't know how long that will last—"

"I get it won't be easy, nothing good ever is, but Connor explained that he was working on the media angle. Something about a pack of information he's ready to release if he needs to? He's a good guy, I'm glad he's here."

"Wait, Connor is here?"

"In the waiting room, said he wasn't coming in, but also he's standing guard."

"He is?"

"He says to tell you that the clinic released a blurry photo that included you, so you're good for another month, whatever that means."

I huffed a laugh, but it hurt my head.

"That's perfect."

"So this family thing? You want to give it a try? Stay with me, work this out, be Uncle Quinn?"

I was scared of every single day to come, because right now all I could think was that everything would change for the Lennox family if I stay. Only I couldn't imagine anything I wanted more than to stay. "It's a deal, cowboy."

And a kiss was all it took to seal the bargain.

My only wish was that Connor coming in when he wanted to check out the window security hadn't interrupted the kissing, because I've never had a blowjob in a hospital before, and we were close.

So close.

Epilogue

QUINN

Three months later

MOLLY TOOK A SODA FROM THE BARREL FILLED WITH ICE and sat in the chair opposite me, smiling like an idiot and tugging Greg close so they could snuggle. It was good to see her here in my new world, far away from the city and media and the money that corrupted the best of men. Connor was here as well, in fact he'd never left Whisper Ridge and had moved into town, renting a room in the Ridge Hotel. Between the two of us we'd dealt with the paparazzi who'd finally tracked me down a few weeks after word was leaked I'd been spotted in Wyoming.

We leaked the news, because I didn't want the axe there waiting to fall. Connor and Molly had become proficient at playing the media to our advantage.

Three intrepid reporters had wanted photos of me being a fish out of water, or doing something stupid. I gave one interview when I'd said I had no money left, and no inclination to return to the city, with added hints about my father and his lack of ethics, had sent them back. Add in my verbal dissertation about horse care and they decided I was too boring to sell anything.

I was living a life that didn't sell papers, or subscriptions. I wasn't the family disappointment, I was just Uncle Quinn to Laurie, and lover to Levi. Not that we mentioned my connection to Laurie or Rachel in the interview, and it wasn't a secret I would ever share willingly. Molly did some clever accounting with funds for the family, without leaving any audit trail back to me, Connor rubberstamped it, and I'd become yesterday's news without even trying.

Connor disappeared after the barbecue, as soon as it was dark, talking night maneuvers with a besotted Laurie, and telling my nephew all kinds of stories about his time as a SEAL. I wondered if he made a lot of them up, but it didn't matter, Laurie was happy, Archie was talking horses with Micah, and I was on my third beer and pleasantly buzzed.

I hadn't heard a word from my family. All that time I'd worried, and it was as if I hadn't needed to. Of course, we all waited for the other ball to drop, with my father still in the picture, but it seemed for once that I had the upper hand and that he was terrified of me releasing what I might know. Connor was doing a good job of keeping me off people's radars, and the town closed around me, holding me tight, and I felt as if I'd come home. Laurie called me Uncle Quinn, but I wasn't scared anymore, and it was a relief beyond anything else.

Turns out that being privy to years of insider information on Dawson Pharma would protect me and mine forever.

I'd spent hours talking to Rachel about Max, and how he'd died at the hands of the leader of the cult for trying to get Rachel to leave. He'd stayed for her, even though he could have left, he'd protected her, and had been so excited to be a dad. He'd never gotten to see Laurie, but I like to think his spirit lived on in his son.

I saluted the sky with my beer, sent up a heartfelt wish that would forever be tinged with sorrow. *Love you, big brother.*

Today had been a good one—spending the day watching Levi work with Sunny, who wasn't exactly compliant, but who deigned to carry a rider, as long as that rider was Levi or Micah. Then there was barbecue, beers, love, and family. Tomorrow was the big wedding, Scott and Rachel were getting married.

"Uncle Quinn! Look!" Laurie slid to a halt next to me, his face covered in mud in camouflage. "Connor says no bad guys can see me if I do this." A smirking Connor arrived just after, but didn't get to sit down as Laurie tugged him away and the two of them headed off to do more recon.

"Hey." Levi replaced my now empty beer, and settled next to me on the bench, his arm over my shoulder and his eyes sparkling with humor. "I won again!" he announced with glee.

"Won?"

"Yep, and Micah lost like the loser he is."

"Do I even want to know at what?" Micah and Levi

had a professional relationship tinged with behaving like big kids who'd grown closer after we'd become this huge blended family on a ranch in Wyoming. They messed with each other on a daily basis but they'd settled into working new contracts they had as equal partners, and I'd watch Levi grow more settled into this space every day.

"Idiot said I couldn't vault the tall gates." He brushed his knuckles on his shirt. "One go," he finished. "But best of all, Micah tried, caught his foot, and fell on his ass."

"Pretty boys are always falling at your feet, eh?"

His smile softened at the memory and he kissed me. I'd never imagined I'd find anything like this pure love I had for my cowboy, but never a day passed when I wasn't reminded how lucky I was. It wasn't in money, or in objects, it wasn't what I owned or what was owed to me; it was in finding a family, and have them embrace me as their own.

Me and Levi both.

"I have something to show you." Levi took my beer off me and tugged me to stand, leading me away from the group and into the growing dusk as night stole in, and then leading me up the hill to the stream and the rocks. The mountains were looming shadows from here, and the ranch was a blur of soft light, but I could still hear laughter and talking from below.

"What am I looking at?" I glanced around confused. My eyes adjusted to the gloom, but other than the things I could hear, the water, the laughing, the soft whisper of wind around me, there was nothing to see.

"This," Levi said, and uncurled his hand. I glanced down and then took a second look. In the center of his palm sat two rings, one chunky and large, the other thinner, smaller. "Will you marry me, Quinn Rhodes?"

I was lost for words, completely overwhelmed.

Say yes, the mountains whispered to me.

Love isn't easy to find, I felt Max add.

I didn't have to listen to the mountains, or Max's voice in my thoughts.

"Yes."

"Yes?" He sounded surprised, but I didn't give him a chance to ask me to repeat myself. I slid my hands up his arms, gently touched his neck, then cradled his face completely.

"A hundred times yes."

Then my cowboy kissed me. The breeze from Whisper Ridge curled around us, and I knew I'd found a love for all time.

Finally.

THE END

My other cowboy & rancher books:

Montana (Cowboys, Ranchers, Mystery)

Crooked Tree Ranch | The Rancher's Son | A Cowboy's Home | Snow In Montana | Second Chance Ranch | Montana Sky

Texas (Cowboy, Rancher, Millionaire, Family)

The Heart of Texas | Texas Winter | Texas Heat | Texas Family | Texas Christmas | Texas Fall | Texas Wedding | Texas Gift | Home For Christmas

Legacy (spin-off from Texas series)

Kyle | Gabriel | Daniel

Also by RJ Scott

For an up to date list of all books please visit www.rjscott.co.uk

Single Dads

Single | Today | Promise | Always | *Listen / Pride*

Lancaster Falls (Romantic Suspense)

What Lies Beneath | Without a Trace | All That Remains

Heroes

A Reason To Stay | Last Marine Standing | Deacon's Law

Harrisburg Railers (Hockey Romance)

Changing Lines | First Season | Deep Edge | Poke Check | Last Defense | Goal Line | Neutral Zone | Hat Trick | Save The Date | Baby Makes Three

Railers Volume 1 / Railers Volume 2 / Railers Volume 3

Owatonna U Hockey (Hockey Romance)

Ryker | Scott | Benoit | Christmas Lights | Valentine's Hearts

Arizona Raptors (Hockey Romance)

Coast To Coast | Across the Pond | Shadow and Light | Sugar and Ice | School and Rock

Boston Rebels (Hockey Romance)

Top Shelf | Back Check

Bodyguards Inc

Bodyguard to a Sex God | The Ex-Factor | Max and the Prince | Undercover Lovers | Love's Design | Kissing Alex

Sanctuary (Bodyguards, Secret Foundation)

Guarding Morgan | The Only Easy Day | Face Value | Still Waters | Full Circle | The Journal of Sanctuary 1 | World's Collide | Accidental Hero | Ghost | By The Numbers

Sanctuary Box Set (including Books 1-5 in the Sanctuary Series

Ellery Mountain (Small Town, First Responders, Military)

The Fireman & the Cop | The Teacher & the Soldier| The Carpenter & the Actor | The Doctor & the Bad Boy | The Paramedic & the Writer | The Barman & the SEAL | The Agent & the Model | The Sinner & the Saint

Boyfriends for Hire (with Meredith Russell)

Darcy | Kaden | Gideon | Jared | *Felix*

In the Shadow of the Wolf (Paranormal)

Shattered Secrets | Broken Memories | Splintered Lies

End Street Detective Agency (Paranormal)

End Street Volume 1 (Cupid Curse / Wicked Wolf) | End Street Volume 2 (Dragon's Dilemma / Sinful Santa) | End Street Volume 3 (Purple Pearl / Guilty Ghost)

Kingdom (Paranormal)

Kingdom Volume 1 (Vampire Contract, Guilty Werewolf, Warlock's Secret) | Kingdom Volume 2 (Demon's Blood, Incubus Agenda, Third Kingdom)

Whisper Ridge, Wyoming (Cowboys)

Winter Cowboy | Summer Drifter

Sapphire Cay (Tropical Island Romance)

Follow the Sun | Under the Sun | Chase The Sun | Christmas In The Sun | Capture The Sun | Forever In The Sun

Sapphire Cay Box Sets - Volume 1 | Volume 2

Salisbury

Heat | Ice

Standalone Christmas

Angel in a Book Shop | Christmas Prince | Jesse's Christmas | Love Happens Anyway | New York Christmas | The Christmas Throwaway | The Road to Frosty Hollow | Dallas Christmas | Cupcakes and Christmas

Standalone

Guarding Garrett | Alpha Delta | Seth & Casey | All The King's Men | The Gallows Tree | Spirit Bear | The Decisions We Make | Back Home | Boy Banned | Deefur Dog | For a Rainy Afternoon | Moments | One Night | Retrograde | Secrets | Seth & Casey | Snow & Secrets | The Art of Words | The Bucket List | The Fire Trilogy | The New Wolf | The Soldier's Tale | The Summer House | Three

Free Reads

Available here on my website

Never miss another release

To keep up to date with news and releases, free stories and sales, sign up here:

Newsletter - rjscott.co.uk/rjnews

FREE READS

You can also find free stories on my website

Meet RJ Scott

RJ is the author of the over one hundred published novels and discovered romance in books at a very young age. She realized that if there wasn't romance on the page, she could create it in her head, and is a lifelong writer.

She lives and works out of her home in the beautiful English countryside, spends her spare time reading, watching films, and enjoying time with her family.

The last time she had a week's break from writing she didn't like it one little bit and has yet to meet a bottle of wine she couldn't defeat.

www.rjscott.co.uk | rj@rjscott.co.uk

NEWSLETTER - rjscott.co.uk/rjnews

facebook.com/author.rjscott
twitter.com/Rjscott_author
instagram.com/rjscott_author
amazon.com/author/rj-scott
bookbub.com/authors/rj-scott
goodreads.com/rjscott
pinterest.com/rjscottauthor

Printed in Great Britain
by Amazon

41732714R00185